# Peach and Plum

*M Johnson*

*Dear Mom,*
*I finally got past page 50.*
*Miss you all the time.*
*xoxo*

Text Copyright © 2018 by M Johnson
Illustration copyright © 2019 Elum Johnson
Graphic Design copyright © 2020 Box-of-Wolves

All Rights Reserved. Published by 1072 Studio

This is a work of fiction. Names, characters, places, and incidents either are the product of the author's imagination or are used fictitiously. Any resemblance to actual persons, living or dead, events, or locales is entirely coincidental.

No part of this publication maybe reproduced, or stored in a retrieval system, or transmitted in any for or by any means, electronic, mechanical, photocopying, recording, or otherwise, without written permission of the publisher. For information regarding permission, write to: 1072 Studio - 6001 Main St, #1701 - Zachary, LA 70791

ISBN: 978-0-578-61389-5

Library of Congress-in-Publication Data

Johnson, M
Peach and Plum by M Johnson

First edition November 2019

Registration number: TXu 2-127-050
December 4th 2018

"Anybody with artistic ambitions is always trying to reconnect with the way they saw things as a child."
– Tim Burton

Mr. Ethan Glassman, Superintendent
City Wide Unified School District

RE: Neighborhood Curbside Block-Watch Program—
<u>Maverick Elementary</u>

Dear Ranunculus District Residents,

The new school year is just around the corner, and in keeping with our annual child safety watch program, we are currently seeking volunteers for our <u>Neighborhood Curbside Block-Watch Program</u>, which ensures the safety of the children who reside in the Ranunculus School District, who walk to and from school with a Curbside Volunteer to keep an eye out on them.

If you or someone in your household is home between the hours of 7 a.m. and 8:15 a.m., and/or from 3 p.m. to 4:30 p.m., we would surely need your help.

There will be a Volunteer Orientation on August 15th, 7 p.m. at Local High's gymnasium. All volunteers must bring:

1. A valid driver's license or photo I.D.
2. Your Social Security Number
3. Two proofs of residency
4. An electric/cable/water-garbabge bill stub

Background checks will be processed.

If there are any questions, comments, or concerns, please feel free to contact my office, with my secretary, Ms. Felicia Foster, at: f.foster@cw-usd.com.

We look forward to the new school year and seeing familiar and new Curbside Volunteers.

Sincerely,

*Ethan Glassman*

Ethan Glassman, M. Ed
Superintendent
Citywide Unified School District

# Chapter One

"Tuna fish, bumblebee, surfer boy Sue.
I like Dennis Dean and My Name Is Cool.
Helicopter, water park, letters O-P-and-Q.
I like Dennis Dean and so should you!"

– the theme song from *My Name Is Cool*

It was almost over, the season finale of the summer hit TV show *My Name Is Cool*, which came on Sunday nights at eight-thirty p.m., and Mayfair, like every other little girl between the ages of six and twelve, including the boys who watched the show but pretended that they didn't, was on the edge of her seat. She and everyone else knew something that Dennis Dean didn't know, but he was about to find out when he arrived at Julie Wang's house and rang the doorbell.

When Julie opened the door, looking pretty as ever, her smile deflated when she saw Dennis standing there. And just like the little snake that she was, she almost shut the door in his face.

"What's wrong?" Dennis asked.

"Um, nothing. Just that, I changed my mind." She said it like she had punched him in the gut.

"Changed your mind about what?"

"About *taking you*."

Julie forgot to tell him that she decided not to take him to her famous uncle's opening at The Five Pom Restaurant.

"But I thought we...why didn't you tell me before I came all the way over here?" Dennis asked.

"God, Dennis! I had a lot of things to do today, and it slipped my mind. Okay?!"

Dennis didn't know what to think. He just kind of stood there in disbelief while Julie gave him a smug look with some attitude sprinkled over it.

"Why did you even ask me to go with you in the first place? I mean, you could've let me know you changed your mind. Why didn't you tell me?" Dennis said.

But all he got from Julie was that ugly smirk on her face.

"You know what, Julie? You are so fake!"

Then, adding to Dennis's outrage, Keith Peters pulled up in the driveway with his mother. When Julie had overheard that Keith Peters, who was the exact opposite of Dennis in the looks department, came from a very wealthy family with connections to other wealthy families, Dennis was history.

"Keith? You're taking Keith Peters instead of me?!" Dennis desperately searched Julie's eyes for a glimmer of hope, something, anything, but the look on her face said it all. They were done. "She's fake, Keith! She's the fakest person on the planet!" Dennis yelled as Keith got out of the car.

Well, dang, Julie Wang! She didn't have to drop-kick Dennis like a pair of sweaty tube socks into the dirty-clothes hamper like that! Dennis was a good guy, and Kamen Wright, who played the lead character of Dennis Dean on *My Name Is Cool*, was a definite seventh-grade hottie. With his surfer-boy blonde hair, heart-stopping blue eyes, cushy dimples, and an infectious smile that made a girl squeal, he'd get hundreds of letters each week from girls who mailed in their staggering crushes to his TV show P.O. Box. But still, that was a cold-blooded move Julie did on Dennis, and the actress, Amanda Chen, who played Julie Wang, was definitely going to get a big truck load of brutal fan mail for what her character did.

With his heart crushed into a zillion pieces, and feeling like a complete fool in his dry-cleaned jeans and sports jacket, Dennis called his brother, who swung back around and picked him up a block away and took him to the movies. Overdressed and depressed, Dennis spotted Iesha Moore, who sat next to him in social studies, going into the restroom while he was in line for popcorn. And then it hit him. Iesha had been giving him adorable love signals the whole time, while he had both eyes on Julie Wang. How could he have been so stupid?

"Hey, Iesha, can I talk to you for a second?" Dennis said when she came out of the restroom. "I broke up with Julie today."

Iesha tried to hide a smile as she looked up at him with those big, soft brown eyes of hers.

"This whole time, I just realized..." And then he reached down and went in for an adorable kiss. Mayfair and the other *MNIC* fans went absolutely NUTS over it!

"Uh, hey, what's going on here?" It was Ben Carter, who was also in their social studies class. He walked up with a big bucket of popcorn and drinks.

"Hey, Ben," Dennis said.

"Weren't you supposed to be on a date at some restaurant with Julie Wang?" Ben asked as he gave Dennis a territorial glare. He took Iesha by the hand and led her down the corridor to their movie, leaving Dennis standing there, shocked.

When did Iesha start going out with Ben? What in the world was going on? Broke up with one girl, and just lost the other girl who actually meant something to him. What would Julie Wang think if she found out he had kissed her? Would she even care? Probably not.

After the TV commercial break, Dennis woke up the next morning to the sound of his mother knocking on his bedroom door.

"Dennis, I'm going to the store, and I want you to unload the dishwasher while I'm gone," his mother said.

"Okay, Mom."

"Oh, and you got a call from someone named Iesha. She wants you to call her. I left her number on the refrigerator."

As soon as his mother left, Dennis ran down to the kitchen and saw Iesha's number on a Post-it Note stuck on the refrigerator. First, he held it like a tiny, fragile baby bird, and then he stuck the note to the front of his shirt and pressed it to his heart.

"Hello, can I speak to Iesha? Hey. How's it going? I was surprised that you called. You got my number from Julie Wang? Uh-oh, yeah, I know...."

As the end credits started scrolling, the season finale was finally over, and the speculations of Dennis and Iesha would have to swish and swirl around until the start of the second season of *My Name Is Cool,* which would premiere next summer.

How could anybody get to sleep after that thrilling *MNIC* finale?

* * *

Well, Mayfair couldn't get to sleep when she crawled into bed around nine o'clock. She could hardly relax as her mind raced back over the episode, and couldn't wait to get to school and talk about it with her friends. But then she remembered that she wasn't going back to her old school. She totally forgot about the new school she was going to, and a mild panic attack curled up beside her. She tried to push it away, but the thing wouldn't budge, so she sang school yard songs to herself like "Tumble Weed on the Roll," "Prissy Miss Sissy," and the theme song to *My Name Is Cool* to pass the time, but none of it calmed her nerves. So then the mild panic attack got up and sat on Mayfair's chest like a warm, purring kitty cat, which turned into several purring kitty cats, curled up all over her body, and she was trapped underneath them. Luckily, though, her father had dozed off to sleep in the living room with the twenty-four-hour news channel, and the sound of his gargled snoring traveled down the hall and into Mayfair's bedroom and gently removed them.

As her stomach gurgled a bit, Mayfair turned over on her side, looked out her bedroom window, and saw how the warm, oven-baked Brother Moon lingered in the cool nighttime sky.

"Try to sleep tight. I'm here in plain sight, so no need to fight, the sleep that will get you through, the night," Brother Moon said, as a plump group of clouds in the shape of grazing sheep floated by and nibbled at the stars. "Tummy flies, go away! It's the children's sleep time. They are not yours. Tonight, they are mine," Brother Moon said in a deep and tender voice, as his soft beams of moonlight swept across the Ranunculus District neighborhoods.

There were other children with nervous tummies, as their bleary-eyed parents, who had just gone to bed with the late-night talk shows, found it hard to pull themselves out of bed and help their little ones to the bathroom, as sounds of bubbly flatulence and wretched gagging filled the quiet nighttime air. And after the children got tablets and spoonfuls of that chalky-tasting anti-acid medicine, they crawled back into their beds, as all were tucked in tight, with kissed foreheads and drowsy eyelids that quickly sent them off to sleep.

When Mayfair finally drifted off, she floated into the deepest realms of a soft slumber. Maybe getting a good night's sleep would ease her fears by the time she'd wake up in the morning as a new student on the first day of school.

While the children slept soundly under Brother Moon's powerful sway, they snuggled up with their dreams, as his beautifully arranged, tranquil lair in the sky quietly drifted from a blackened color of purple into a light, hazy blue that became the early-morning sky. The plump group of clouds that were shaped like grazing sheep quietly shifted into floating wisps of pale pink clouds, as the warm, oven-baked Brother Moon faded, and the glowing-spiritual Father Sun eased into the sky. With a hint of intimidation and a strict glare of authority, the Father Sun looked down onto everything with a raised eyebrow through dazzling rays of warm sunlight, as the birds began blinking their eyes open; and little fat, round-brown ones, pointy looking black ones, ones with faint red stripes, and ones with cantaloupe-colored beaks, all flew from the trees and balanced themselves on top of old telephone wires for an early morning of chitter-chat. There was a mockingbird who sat quietly atop one of the tallest trees in the Ranunculus District and twittered out a crooked little song at the top of his little lungs. The ancient eucalyptus tree that stood solid and firm underneath the mockingbird tried to sit still, but the hundred-year-old giant felt kind of silly with the little bird on top of its head, and its leaves began to tremble with the giggles.

Ladybug squadrons did nosedive flights off dew-covered Ranunculus flower petals; herds of snails hung upside down on wet blades of grass, like a packed yoga class; and a couple of midnight slugs tried not to fry like bacon against the warm sun on wet sidewalks that suddenly turned dry. There was hardly a breeze, and the air felt fresh and clean, like the sound of popping open an ice-cold can of lemon-lime soda on a hot day. Radio and TV weathermen were all giving the same forecast

of a nice and dry temperature of seventy-eight degre
day. It seemed like the first day of spring, but it was the tail end
of summer. Once the glowing-spiritual Father Sun was above
the horizon, his bright sunlight bounced off of the houses in
the Ranunculus District neighborhoods, making them look like
wild-colored Easter eggs. Pronounced Ruh-Nunk-U-Luh, it's the
lustrous multi-petal, herbaceous perennial type of flower that was
indigenous to the area and grew rampant in that part of the city.

There was the paper boy riding by, who was just finishing
up his early route on a street called Rodderdam Slope. A Native
Freshman over at Local High, the paper boy rode his bike hands-
free of the handlebars and threw newspapers at front doors, and
over parked cars in driveways, with such an athletic gift that
any college-football scout would've salivated at his mad skills.
Surprisingly, there were some people who still needed a morning
newspaper in the age of social media, like Mr. Murphy, who lived
at 2234 Rodderdam Slope, who always managed to catch his
paper with his bare hands before he'd leave for work.

Being that he was the younger brother of the legendary Flint
Swinns, a graduating Native Senior at Local High, there were all
kinds of hopes and dreams placed on the paper boy of following
his older brother's footsteps into football, but soccer was his game
of choice. Their father was a football junkie, and although it
would take some time, he would eventually give soccer a chance
when the paper boy would make the team in his sophomore year
in high school. His father would also wear T-shirts to his son's
games that said *Give soccer a chance*. Eventually, the paper boy
would play on a State University scholarship that would qualify
him for the city's Major League Soccer Team. But, for now, he
was content riding his bike in the morning, tossing newspapers.

The last house to get a newspaper was at 2236 Rodderdam
Slope—a soft orange and sophisticated brown home with windows
trimmed in off-white, that had pink Ranunculi that looked like

lollipops peeping through the dried grass against the side of the house. This was where Mayfair lived, and up in her bedroom she soundly slept as if she hadn't been bothered by a curled-up kitty-cat panic attack the night before. The glowing-spiritual Father Sun's soft, killer glare peered through the opening of her curtains and quietly moved across her face like a warm alarm clock, and Mayfair pulled the sheets over her head. But then she suddenly sat up with a jolt, remembered that it was the first day of school, and thought about clothes. *Yeah, clothes. I want to wear my denim dress, or maybe that slick jumpsuit my Aunt Raquel got me.* Mayfair jumped out of bed, started for her closet, and almost tripped over the lovely jumper ensemble that had a pair of quaint knee-high socks that were draped just so, over her desk-set chair. As she stood there looking at the garment, trying to figure out where it came from, the thing oozed and bubbled over with her mother's love, and she let out a light, terrifying gasp, and whispered, "Oh, no!"

There was a small knock at the door.

"Good morning, Mayfair."

Mayfair took one look at her little sisters, burst into tears, and flung herself on the bed with a round of dramatic sobbing.

Myla and Makayla were dressed in the same lovely jumper ensemble, standing there like a pair of honey-colored Kewpie dolls, looking like they belonged in a department-store catalog.

"What's wrong, Mayfair? Why you crying for?" Makayla asked as she climbed on the bed and put her pudgy little four-year-old hand on Mayfair's face.

Myla rested her soft, squishy cheek on Mayfair's forehead. "Don't cry. What's the matter?" Myla asked.

Through her sobbing, Mayfair could smell the low aroma of Miss Afua's Hair Oil on the twins' nicely plaited hair. "It's not fair! It's just not FAIR!" Mayfair shouted.

"What's not fair?" Myla asked.

Her eyes started to well up with tears, while a tear or two trickled down Makayla's face. They didn't like to see their big sister's feelings hurt, even if they didn't know what was wrong. But there was something that caught their attention and broke through Mayfair's little pity party.

"What is it?" Makayla asked.

Mayfair opened her window and spotted the mockingbird on top of a telephone pole across the street, just twittering his crooked little song at the top of his little lungs.

As the girls watched the mockingbird against the hazel blue sky that held the floating wisps of pale pink clouds, Mayfair thought that maybe wearing a lovely jumper ensemble with quaint knee-high socks that reeked of their mother's hugs and kisses wouldn't be so bad after all.

At least, that's what Mayfair tried to convince herself to believe, but it didn't work.

# Chapter Two

As Mayfair was putting on the quaint knee-high socks, her father entered her room. "Oh, you're up already. And dressed, too!" Richard Tootle said.

Mayfair's father was a tall, dark-haired, late-thirties, good-looking man that made you think of that actor in all of those romantic-action movies, who was like a thick slice of Black Forest chocolate cake, and made all the women swoon. Except Richard was more like a big, rich scoop of fat-free, lite mocha ice cream, and just as F-I-N-E as ever. He could've easily been on the cover of any men's magazine, or down the runway in some hot designer's NYC/Paris/Milan fashion show.

His heart swelled at the sight of his daughters. "Wait, let me get my camera!" he said, and came back with his 35mm digital camera and his cell phone. The twins readily smiled for photos while Mayfair frowned. "Come on, Mayfair, smile," her father said as her frown turned into tears. "Mayfair, what's wrong?"

"I don't want to wear this to school today." Mayfair couldn't bear the thought of anybody making silly jumper-ensemble jokes if she wore the stupid outfit to her new school.

"But you look beautiful, you and your sisters—just beautiful," Richard said, trying to understand, but not really.

"I don't want to look beautiful. I want to look...cool."

"And what you're wearing isn't cool?" Richard asked.

"No, Daddy, it isn't. I don't want to look like them. I want to look like...me."

On closer examination, Richard suddenly realized that his girls were dressed exactly alike.

"We're not triplets. They're the twins. I'm me."

Well, before he could think of something positive to say, Mayfair's mother, Roxanne Tootle, entered the room. Now, if Richard was just as F-I-N-E as ever, then his wife Roxanne was incredibly stunning. She was sleek, classy, and sophisticated, with little tolerance for nonsense. Roxanne took one look at Richard and the girls and ran to get her cell phone. When she came back, she could see that something was wrong.

"Go ahead, Mayfair, ask Mommy," Makayla said.

"Ask me what? What's wrong?"

Mayfair couldn't find the words to ask if she could wear something else to school, so she buried her head in her father's armpit.

"Mayfair doesn't want to wear the same thing we're wearing to school, Mama," Myla said as Richard and the twins watched for Roxanne's reaction.

"Mayfair, you don't like the jumper?" Roxanne could see the pain of embarrassment in Mayfair's eyes. "Well, you can wear something else if you'd like," she said, and went over to Mayfair's closet and started looking around.

"Wait, Mommy! Mayfair wants to pick out her own clothes, by herself," Makayla said.

Well, that never crossed Roxanne's mind, and she realized she was reaching for another jumper ensemble that wasn't as lovely. Richard and the girls watched for Roxanne's reaction again, because she always had the final word when it came to things like clothes, shoes, hair—everything—and the tight expression on her face said *You can make your own clothing decisions when you're eighteen, maybe*. But then she softened and said, "Well, all right. Let's allow Mayfair to pick something out, and give her some privacy."

When she quietly appeared in the kitchen, the twins gave her an adorable applause, and Richard took more pictures. Roxanne seemed pleased, as she carefully inspected the short-sleeved, dark-denim dress, with a cute jean jacket over it, that fit a few inches above Mayfair's waist, with black leggings, a pair of Barely There socks, and her pink button earrings that matched her cute pink high tops.

"Very nice. I like it. I think we need to go shopping," Roxanne said, and Mayfair's eyes lit up.

Her little girl was growing up, and Roxanne had to stop herself from fixing Mayfair's hair in the same style as the twins when she applied several dabs of Miss Afua's Hair Oil onto Mayfair's thick, light-auburn-colored hair. She was the only one in her family of dark-brown hair who glowed in an auburn hue, with a light smattering of freckles sprinkled across her nose, that she inherited from her grandmother's mother on Roxanne's side of the family.

"Your father will take you to school since I'm taking the twins," Roxanne said.

Mayfair thought about asking if she could walk to school, but she already knew the answer would be a big fat NO! So she decided to ask her father instead. If she was going to be told no, it was easier to hear it from him. Sometimes when Richard said no, it was negotiable, and Mayfair could cut a deal. When Roxanne said no, she had a way of making you feel like you no longer wanted what you asked for in the first place.

* * *

The twins waved good-bye, strapped down in their car seats in the back of Roxanne's SUV, as she backed out of the driveway. Mayfair and her father climbed in his old sports car that Richard maintained on the weekends, with a well-kept engine that had a nice, low-sounding hum when he started it up.

"So, Dad, I want to tell you something," Mayfair said.

"Uh-huh..." Richard said as he honked at Roxanne as she drove off.

"I wanted to walk to school...by myself."

"Oh, really?" Richard said with exaggerated, raised eyebrows.

"Yes, Daddy. I want to walk to school. Can I?"

"Mayfair, I don't know. Your mother would be very upset if I allowed you to do that." He remembered the thing they got in the mail about the Curbside Block-Watch Program, and he thought it was a great idea, but Roxanne was against it.

"I just don't trust the community enough to allow my baby to walk to school while being watched by a bunch of strangers," she had said.

They pulled out of the driveway, headed down the street, and saw a group of children turn the corner off of Rodderdam Slope and onto a very steep street called Yesterday Way.

"I bet those kids go to your school. Let's stop and ask them," Richard said.

But Mayfair was embarrassed at the idea, and said, almost in a panic, "No, Daddy! Please, don't!"

"Mayfair, there's no way I'm letting you walk to school by yourself," Richard said as he turned onto Yesterday Way and parked the car. "Well, on second thought, I have an idea that could work. This is what we'll do. I'll let you walk to school, *but*, I'll stay parked for every block you walk, until you get there. How about that?"

It wasn't such a bad idea, so Mayfair got out of the car and started up the steep street. She pushed against the gravitational pull of the hill and looked back at her father, who was reading his newspaper. Most of the homes on Yesterday Way were covered in white Ranunculi that spread across like twisted vine leaves, just like the little house that sat tucked away from the street, covered in white Ranunculi, with a long driveway.

The Birch sisters lived there, who were known as The Ladies of Yesterday Way, and they were also Curbside Volunteers. They sat on the front porch of their home and watched the children pass by on their way to school. Mayfair looked down the driveway and squinted at them as they waved hello. She waved back and continued up the street, but when she finally caught up to the children, that kitty-cat panic attack came back and curled itself around Mayfair's neck like a neck cushion. She was way too shy to say anything and decided to remain quiet.

"Well, the Shock Release isn't really a ride—well, it kinda is, but—it's pretty cool with the special effects and stuff. And you get to wear these digital 3D glasses," said the boy who sported a high-skin fade with a side part, strapped down in a solar-paneled backpack. Mayfair wondered if he had his own cell phone.

"Yeah, but it's only cool if you're not scared of the part where it drops into darkness," the other boy said, who sported a Mohawk burst fade and wore an unusual pair of sneakers that looked as if they were melded right onto his feet.

"But that was the best part. I mean, if you freak out while you're in the drop, then you have no business getting on the Shock Release in the first place," said the boy with the solar backpack.

The boys looked like a pair of Afro-Futuristic Blerds, and Mayfair wondered if they were brothers. But it was the girl who walked with them that was the star of the show, and Mayfair couldn't keep her eyes off of her. It was the girl's keen sense of fashion that had a sudden effect on Mayfair's self- esteem, and the confidence she had in her own little denim outfit melted into a pool of mush. Clearly, this girl had status and position, based on her understated junior pop-star glam, while she clutched a notebook that matched her brand-new Spitfire sneakers, and wore a T-shirt that simply said *I hate boys*. Mayfair wondered who she was in relation to the two Afro-Futuristic Blerds, because the girl was white.

As the boys rambled on, Pop Star Girl seemed uninterested in their conversation, giving off a tenth-grade attitude, and put her earbuds in and listened to music on her cell phone. Mayfair tried not to let the girl's style, and now her cell phone, intimidate her, so she thought it was a good time to say something.

"Hey, um, do you guys go to Maverick?" Mayfair stammered out.

She gave a nervous smile as the boys turned around, but when the fifth-grade Pop Star Girl turned around, in her earthy, grassroots beauty, with flowing light-brown hair, her light aquamarine eyes contradicted her prettiness, and it kind of threw everything off. They were ice cold, as they sized up Mayfair and took in every inch of her, every piece of clothing that Mayfair had on, from the side part in Mayfair's hair to the elastic that held up her Barely There socks around her ankles. Needless to say, she did not find Mayfair a fashion threat. Or at least, that's what Mayfair thought the girl was thinking about her.

But there was something going on with the boy with the weird sneakers. Unbeknownst to him, because at that age they don't really know what is going on, the very second he turned around and looked at Mayfair, he was smacked in the head with a school yard crush. From the way her hair was styled, to the book bag she carried, down to the cute pink high tops she wore, which made Mayfair even more appealing since he liked exotic footwear, the boy was hooked.

Pop Star Girl removed an earbud, and Mayfair became uncomfortable with the round of unreadable blank stares.

"Well, okay. Bye," she said, and quickly walked past them. She felt their eyes on her as she reached the top of the hill, and she wanted to look back at her father but didn't want everybody thinking she was looking back at them.

"Hey. Who's your teacher?" Weird Sneaker Boy asked, as the blank stares turned into curiosity.

"Mr. Marci is my teacher," Mayfair said, hoping for another question.

"Mr. Marci? What grade does he teach?"

"Second grade."

"Oh, okay," Weird Sneaker Boy said, a little bummed.

Mayfair hoped for another question, as their curiosity turned back into blank stares. She saw her father pull away from the curb at the bottom of the hill, so she continued on her way.

"You like her, don't you?" said the boy with the solar backpack.

Weird Sneaker Boy blushed at the accusation. "What does asking her what grade she's in have to do with liking her? I don't even know her, so stop asking stupid, idiotic questions!"

Pop Star Girl rolled her eyes and put the other earbud back in.

\* \* \*

Once Mayfair left Yesterday Way and crossed over onto Orchid Avenue, it was a straight shot to Maverick Elementary, or Maverick Elem, as the children called it.

"So, how'd it go? Were they friendly?" Richard asked when he pulled up.

"They were okay, I guess," Mayfair said.

"You still want to walk to school?"

"Yes, Daddy."

So, Richard parked again, and Mayfair continued down the block. Along the way, she passed up a few Maverick Elem alumni, who were now sixth graders over at Glick Mid(dle), and everyone was talking about the season finale of *My Name Is Cool*, mostly the girls because, you know, the boys watched but never talked about it. Mayfair wanted to join in on the discussions when some little obnoxious girl had the nerve to say that Dennis Dean wasn't all that.

"He ain't cute, and Iesha Moore could do way better than him. I hope she stays with Ben Carter. At least he took her to the movies."

There was one little boy who had no shame in his game about the show. "Man, Dennis Dean weak! If that was me, I wudda told Julie Wang to bounce! Ain't nobody gonna try to break with me. I do the droppin'! And I'ma be chillin' at the crib with my new girl."

Well, dang!

When Mayfair reached the corner at Ukulele Street, which crossed Orchid Avenue, and waited for her father, there was a little corner store across the street that the children were going inside of and coming out with little brown paper bags.

"Can I go in, Daddy?" Mayfair asked when Richard pulled up, and he gave her a few dollars.

Everyone pretty much knew Mr. Akrahm and his brother, Mr. Fariq, who both owned the S&K grocery store and looked every bit like wealthy Middle Eastern celebrities. The S&K was just a little neighborhood corner store, and during the school week it was a popular hotspot for Maverick Elem and Glick Mid students. Mr. Akrahm and Mr. Fariq regarded their young customers as if they were the sons and daughters of multi-millionaires, because the children had money to burn, gobs of it, and spent all of it on the endless supply of candy.

Chick-Checks, Shellbombs, Juber Jabs, and Zotties were always in demand, and candy fan-favorite classics like Lemonheads, Pop Rocks, Smarties, Whatchamacallits, Mike & Ike, and the all-time classic Now and Laters (which everyone pronounced NowLaters) never got old. The newest item to hit the scene was a white-chocolaty candy called Frebbies, and the children were buying them up like crazy. Mayfair couldn't resist the urge and got in line.

"What's it gonna be today, Chi-Chi?" Mr. Fariq said to a pretty fourth-grade girl who held a wad of one-dollar bills.

"All I want is Frebbies. Give me ten packs," she said.

Mr. Fariq put everything in a small brown paper bag, and the girl handed over the cash.

"What's up, Yo? Whatcha got for me?" Mr. Fariq said to a nerdy fifth-grade boy.

"Morning, Mr. Fariq. Let's see, gimme two Flatback bars, a couple of Yorties, a Big Beef Crunch stick, and three packs of Frebbies."

Mr. Fariq shoved the boy's candy in the bag, and the boy slapped down the cash.

It was Mayfair's turn, but she didn't know what she wanted.

"Whatcha say, La-La?" Mr. Fariq said.

Mayfair just stood there.

"Not sure what you want, girlie?"

"Um, I dunno. There's so much to choose from," Mayfair said as she looked at the wall of candy behind the counter.

"Well, let me help you," Mr. Fariq said in a thick Farsi accent. "First, you must try at least one pack of these." He put a pack of Frebbies on the counter. "Then, you'll need some of these." He put several Crunchies on the counter. "And the coup de grace to top it off, a pack of these." He handed Mayfair a pack of Digital flavored NowLaters for effect, as a couple of "Ooohs" and "Awws" came from some of the children in line behind her. When Mayfair's eyes didn't light up, Mr. Fariq took the pack of NowLaters and held it up with much respect. "Young lady, I'm guessing you have no idea what I just gave you, do you?"

Mayfair was clueless.

"This right here, in my hand, is a highly sought-after flavor in the Now and Later conglomerate. S&K Groceries, named for my father, Salim Kasood, is the only store on this side of town that has the Digital flavored Now and Later, and as I give you this pack, it will bring you luck. Enjoy it. Savor it. Because we're going to run out of it very soon."

Mayfair didn't know what to say, but Mr. Fariq finally saw the sparkle in her eyes.

"You know what I'm going to do? For you, just for today, everything, on the house. Didn't I just tell you that this pack of Now and Later will bring you luck? Well, luck has already been bestowed upon you." He put Mayfair's candy in the little brown bag and handed it to her. "Now go. And when I see you again, I want to know your thoughts, especially on the Now and Later. Be well."

Mayfair quietly thanked him and walked out of the store feeling honored.

"Get anything good?" Richard asked.

"Yeah, Daddy. He gave me all of this for free when I didn't know what I wanted."

The first thing Mayfair opened was the pack of Frebbies and shared them with her father. OMG! It was the most delicious taste of vanilla, with a hint of mint that was like a dream.

"Not bad. What are they?" Richard said.

"They're Frebbies, Daddy. Look what else I got. The man told me to try this one and tell him what I think about it." Mayfair held up the Digital flavored pack of NowLaters.

"It's kind of early for candy, Mayfair. Your mother would kill us if she saw us eating all of this."

What Roxanne would've done was thrown Richard a look so intense that it would've wiped out an entire insect species, and the thought of it made him look around to see if she had pulled up beside them.

"Just save it for later. Okay? I gotta get going, so I'll just drive you the rest of the way to school," Richard said as Pop Star Girl and the two Blerds walked by.

"Look, Daddy. There they go." Mayfair watched as the boys crossed the street and met up with some other boys in front of the S&K, while Pop Star Girl continued up the block.

"What up, Q-Tech? I know you got something weird going on," said a fourth-grade boy.

Apparently, the boy with the solar-panel backpack went by his street name of Q-Tech. He turned around and showed off his backpack.

"What is that?" the fourth grader asked.

"Well, overall it's just a backpack, but the solar panel supplies renewable energy to any of the electronic devices I have at home, like my mother's cell phone or my father's laptop—things like that."

The fourth grader looked at his friend and just shook his head. "Yup. I knew you had something strange."

"But how is this strange when it's something good for the planet?"

The fourth grader turned to Weird Sneaker Boy. "What up, Sneaks? Let me see your new kicks."

And as if on cue, as if he had practiced for this very moment, for the first question of the day about his shoes, Weird Sneaker Boy, who went by his street name of Sneaks, went right into the Heisman Trophy stance with a serious game face, and showed off his brand-new kicks. And at that very moment, his eye caught Mayfair's eye, looking him dead in his face as she and her father drove by. Sneaks became so discombobulated that he pretended like he heard someone call his name from inside the store, and ran in.

"Well, that was weird," said the fourth-grade boy.

"Dude, you just dropped like, fifty cool points for running in the store like that. I know you can hear me!" Q-Tech said as he pretended to scoop up the cool points. "Welp, they're mine now."

✳ ✳ ✳

When Mayfair and her father drove up the block, they passed by Pop Star Girl, and her icy disposition didn't seem so cold anymore. She appeared to be more of a loner type without Sneaks and Q-Tech, but she still had that eye-catching junior pop-star glam about her. Mayfair and her father also drove past Jonathan Chang, who was sitting outside, in front of his house, with his little brother Timothy, who swung annoying karate kicks over Jonathan's head while they waited for their grandfather.

"Twenty-eight, twenty-nine, thirty! Ugh!" Timothy said, and fell to the ground. He looked up at the sky, which no longer held the floating wisps of pale pink clouds, and yawned, followed by another loud yawn, and drifted off to sleep.

Maverick Elem was just across the street, and Jonathan watched all the action going on as children were being dropped off and parents were yelling "Good-bye!" and "I love you!" along with the monstrous sounds of two colossal yellow school buses that pulled up in front of the school as children plopped off. Jonathan looked down at Timothy, asleep on the ground, and wished he could've just stepped over him and walked away. It would've only been a forty-five second walk to school if he jaywalked it, since his house sat perpendicular from Maverick Elem, and probably a whole minute if he used both of the crosswalks.

All his grandfather had to do was stick his head out of the front upstairs window or just stand outside by the front gate and watch his grandsons get to school, like everybody else in the Curbside Block-Watch Program, but for protective and strict safety measures, their grandfather was their travel escort, and Jonathan hated it! Timothy didn't mind being overprotected so much, but as he'd get older, especially in his later teen years, his rebellious nature would shift into gear and kind of spiral out of control, like when he'd destroy the second set of brand-new tires on his car after completing a figure-eight donut swerve in one of those midnight sideshow battles, when he'd turn eighteen.

Finally, after what seemed like forever, their eighty-year-old grandfather stepped out and said, in Mandarin, "Come on. Let's go." He probably understood English more than he could speak it, and curiously looked down at Timothy, who was snoring like a puppy. "Is he asleep?" he asked, and pulled out a cell phone from his pocket and snapped a picture. "Come on, Timothy. Wake up. It's time to go to school," Grandfather said, and chuckled.

Jonathan gave Timothy a hard shove, and he groggily sat up and rubbed his eyes. The boys dutifully followed their grandfather to the short end of the block, crossed both crosswalks, and then up the street to the main entrance of the school. Grandfather patted each child on the head, told them he'd be back to pick them up after school, then he shuffled away, back down the block towards home.

# Chapter Three

When Richard kissed Mayfair good-bye, the kitty-cat panic attack came back and tried to sit on top of Mayfair's head, but she swatted it off, and two little pesky butterflies took its place and bumped around inside of her nervous stomach when her father drove away. She wasn't sure which way to go, so she decided to ask the gentle old woman who was giving out great-big hugs to the children that ran up to her, and got swept up in a scoop of children, while Mrs. Hocklock squeezed. She smelled of a tropical-scented perfume mixed with just a hint of spray starch, and she looked at Mayfair with the warmest smile.

"Your freckles are just lovely. They match your exquisite auburn-colored hair. I don't think I've seen you before. Are you new?"

"Yes, I'm new," Mayfair said.

"What is your name, dear?"

As Mayfair introduced herself, she wondered how old Mrs. Hocklock was because the tips of her fingers were arthritic and she wore thick orthopedic stockings. But her fierce blue eyes that sat behind a pair of elegantly framed glasses, still had fire in them.

"It's nice to meet you, Mayfair. I'm Mrs. Hocklock, and I'm your principal," she said as a few children ran up for a hug.

"I'm not sure where I'm supposed to go," Mayfair said, and handed Mrs. Hocklock her classroom assignment.

"Ah, Mr. Marci is your teacher. I think you're going to like him," Mrs. Hocklock said as she waved good-bye to the colossal yellow school-bus drivers. "Just go right inside through the front entrance and ask for Ms. Mothped. She'll show you where to go."

Mayfair thanked her and went up the front steps of the school and disappeared inside.

The lobby of Maverick Elem was quiet except for the loud clicking noises of someone typing on a keyboard. Mayfair followed the sound over to the front office and peered in. The bright glare of sunlight bounced off of the walls in the office, and the different-colored bouquets of Ranunculi that sat in ornate vases on the windowsills seemed to sparkle in the sunlight. There was Ms. Mothped, sitting underneath a large collage of the children's drawings and paintings that were posted on the wall right above her. Mayfair thought she looked like an art teacher instead of a school secretary, in her bright-red framed glasses and the precise, blunt, bobbed hairstyle she rocked.

Ms. Mothped took a sip of her coffee and noticed Mayfair spying on her.

"Oh, hello," she said. "Can you tell me..." Mayfair turned around and was startled to see Rachel Ward quietly standing next to her.

Ms. Mothped smiled at the girls and thought they were just a darling pair, with Mayfair in her denim outfit and her cute pink high tops, and Rachel in her layered black and gray Tatum Nicole ensemble that was a spin on the parochial schoolgirl look.

"Who's your teacher?" Ms. Mothped asked as she took another sip of coffee.

"Mr. Marci," Mayfair said.

"And what about you, dear? Who's your teacher?"

Rachel quietly replied, "I have Mr. Marci, too."

"Well, what do you know? Both of you are in the same class. And what are your names?"

As Mayfair and Rachel introduced themselves, Tayla Reynolds, a fifth grader in Ms. Mack's class, came through the front entrance.

"Hey, Ms. Mothped," Tayla said as she passed by.

"Oh! Tayla! Come here. I want you to take these two young ladies to the Upper Yard. This is Mayfair and Rachel."

Tayla was a pretty girl with light-brown eyes and light-brown hair that was flat-ironed to the bone. She had a down-to-earth personality and instantly took to the girls.

"Okay, Ms. Mothped. Come on, y'all," Tayla said. Mayfair and Rachel followed her up to the second level of the school to the Upper Yard. It was crawling with kids. "I'm going to take you to Mrs. Stone, and you guys sit with her, okay? And when the bell rings, I'll come back and take you to your classroom. Okay?" Tayla brought the girls over to Mrs. Stone, who was sitting on a bench by the kick-ball court.

"Well, good morning!" Mrs. Stone said, beaming.

"Good morning, Mrs. Stone. This is Mayfair and Rachel, in Mr. Marci's class. I'm coming back to get them when the bell rings," Tayla said, and quickly walked away.

"Please, have a seat." Mrs. Stone was always glad to have company. Mayfair and Rachel sat down on either side of her. "Do you know each other?" Mrs. Stone asked.

"No, not really. This is my first time at this school," Mayfair said.

Rachel said the same thing but barely above a whisper. It was becoming clear that Rachel Ward was extremely shy.

"I bet the two of you will be friends for a long time to come," Mrs. Stone said, as a kickball bounced over Mayfair's head and she ducked out of the way. A boy who looked to be about twelve, but was a fifth grader, with dark hair, dark eyes, and was rather handsome, ran up and grabbed the ball that landed near Mrs. Stone's feet.

"Wait a minute, Thad. I'd like to introduce you to Rachel and Mayfair."

Thad flashed a smile that was so spectacular that Mayfair thought, dare she even think it, this Thad was better looking than her TV star-crush, Dennis Dean?

"Hey!" Thad said, and took off with the ball.

Mayfair leaned over and saw Rachel peering back at her, and they gave each other knowing smiles.

"Yes, that's Thad, and the other boys out on the kickball court are his teammates. You'll probably meet them too, I guess. They sure do love their game," Mrs. Stone said.

The boys did love their game and were very particular as to whom they allowed on the kickball court. All of them pretty much ignored the girls in their class, except for Thad, who was practically in love with Pop Star Girl. He had been keeping one eye on the game and the other eye on the doors that led out to the yard, hoping she'd come through at any minute.

The Snootish Girls were looking out for her, too. Known for their stuck-up ways and their clever sense of style, The Snootish Girls descended upon the yard in all of their Maverick Elem school status, and struck exaggerated poses that said *Yeah, we VIP. We light this place up. We lit!*

"Where is she? I don't see her," LaRae Davis said, who sported the latest hairstyle called the Side Shave or the Half Hawk, with one side of her head lined and shaved, while the other side was full of long hair that was pulled in a side ponytail.

"I don't see Kiara anywhere," Shandelina Smith said, who sported a flawless manicure, with each nail painted in a different color.

"She better not be wearing her pink Marie shirt when I told her not to. I'll pop her upside her head if I catch her with it, 'cuz she knew I was gonna wear my blue Marie shirt, and I ain't about to look stupid over it!" Starmesha Collins said, who rocked a pair of Snug as a Bug designer jeans with her blue Marie shirt.

The girl they were looking for, Kiara Campbell, was nowhere to be found, but when Pop Star Girl finally walked by, The Snootish Girls stared so hard at her that it's a wonder they each didn't get a headache.

"Oh my GOD! She's got those new Spitfires with the matching notebook!" Naomi Braithwaite said, who was like the preppy Banana Republic one of the group.

Pop Star Girl wasn't as dressed to impress and "see and be seen" as The Snootish Girls, but it was that seemingly icy undertone about her that kept everyone believing she had something more than what she actually had.

Mayfair spotted Pop Star Girl, too, and watched her sit down on a bench across the yard and open up a book. Thad saw her, left his outfield position on the kickball court, and wandered over.

"C'mon, man! On the first day? Really?" Thad's outfield partner, Phron Thompson, loudly said as he threw his arms up.

"He'll be back. He just gotta go check with his girl first," a boy named Keem, near second base, said.

"Oooh, look at Damarcus," Shandelina Smith said.

Damarcus was at home plate in his signature kickball position, and slammed the ball across the yard, which landed over by the monkey bars, which was where Kiara Campbell was.

"Oh, wait! I see her!" Skyy Jones said, who wore a pair of Sugar Swag sneakers with a Branded Box pursette strapped across her body.

The girls headed over to the monkey bars.

The Upper Yard bubbled over with third, fourth, and fifth graders, with Mr. Marci's second-grade class sprinkled in with them. The children played at the tetherball court, on the monkey bars, at the basketball court, and sat with each other in small groups, on the benches that outlined the perimeter of the yard; or they played their own games, like High Jump and One Fly Up. By now, The glowing-spiritual Father Sun sat comfortably in the morning sky, and the weather heated up to 75 degrees, with the bubbly sounds of happy children that echoed to the outskirts of the Ranunculus District.

And then, right before the first bell rang, a fight broke out.

# Chapter Four

It started over by the monkey bars, and before anyone could see who it was, a crowd quickly formed.

Big Julius, who was squatted behind home plate at the kickball court, spotted it first. "Hey, look! I think it's a fight," he said, and all the boys turned and looked.

"A fight on the first day of school?" Damarcus asked.

The boys took off running.

Mrs. Stone got up and did a walk-trot across the yard. Mayfair and Rachel inched their way over. Neither of them had ever seen a school yard fight before, and it was actually quite thrilling, with everybody trying to see just who it was that had the nerve to get into a fight on the very first day of school!

Mrs. Stone pushed her way through six feet deep of rubbernecking children, all trying to have a look-see, with lots of grabbing, pushing, shoving, and yelling. Mrs. Stone pulled out her bullhorn and turned on the car-alarm siren that made everybody cover their ears and glare at her, while some of the children shouted, "Dang, Mrs. Stone!"

The first bell rang, and as if on cue, everything stopped.

"Will everyone move out of the way?!" Mrs. Stone yelled through the bullhorn.

The children peeled back until they got to the bottom, and finally saw that it was a fifth-grade girl named Nosha, who was balled up with the leader of The Snootish Girls, Kiara Campbell. The children shouted lots of sarcastic "oooohs" and let out loud gasps as Mrs. Stone grabbed the two girls up by their armpits, each refusing to let go of the other.

"I said break it up, NOW!" Mrs. Stone said, but it only made Kiara pull even tighter on Nosha's hair. That's when Nosha burst into tears and broke free of Kiara's grip.

The children had spread a wide semi-circle around the girls and Mrs. Stone. Mayfair and Rachel stood just a few steps outside of it, and Mayfair noticed Pop Star Girl standing on the bench, on the other side of the semi-circle, trying to see.

"You two come with me!" Mrs. Stone said as she led Kiara and Nosha through the crowd. "You two should be ashamed of yourselves, fighting on the first day of school!" Mrs. Stone said, and when she saw Mayfair and Rachel, she held up the bullhorn. "TAYLA!" Tayla came running. "I want all of the students who are in Mr. Marci's class to come over here and line up with Tayla." One by one, the second graders trickled out of the fight circle and lined up behind Mayfair and Rachel. "Is that everyone? Okay, Tayla, take them inside."

Tayla led them away, looking like a mother hen with her baby chicks in tow. OMG, it was sooo cute!

* * *

Across the street and a couple of houses down from Maverick Elem, Nestor, Green Eyed Mike, and Jeorgie casually trekked their way towards the school, hardly concerned that they were running terribly late.

"There's Big Bomb Tom, X-To-Da-Next, Paul Sweet, Kunta Okeke, and I think The Maraud Brothers," Nestor Reyes said, who was already handsome at seven years old, with his jet-black hair, lined and styled against his smooth, earthy, indigenous brown complexion.

"Yeah, but you forgot The Highway Man," Green Eyed Mike Morrison said, who was a cute, caramel-colored child with eyes the color of grass.

"Oh, yeah, I forgot about The Highway Man, but he's kinda old. They should put him with Tox Taylor, though," Nestor said.

"Or, what about everybody in the Duper Super Slam Bam Jam against everybody in the Liquidator Downtown Throw-Down?" Jeorgie Sterling asked. He had a serious yet goofy way about him, and sported a nicely roasted summer tan on his olive-Caucasian skin, with a haircut similar to Nestor's.

The boys had been friends since kindergarten, in Mrs. Owyong's class at Maverick Elem, and were also in Ms. Chatcuff's class for first grade. Now they were together for second grade, in Mr. Marci's class.

Jeorgie's little sister, Little Laura, who was caught up in her own little fairytale land, quietly sang nursery rhymes to herself as she trailed behind the boys. She was so delightfully adorable—like a freshly sprouted Ranunculus with early-morning dew sprinkled on its petals.

"Hey, let's go up to the skate park after school. We probably won't have any homework anyways," Jeorgie said.

"I probably can't go. Unless Davina lets me, but she won't," Green Eyed Mike said.

"Davina's cool! She'll let you go," Jeorgie said.

"No, not gonna happen. She likes some boy who hangs out up there," Green Eyed Mike said.

"So what? She can hang out with him and we can skate," Jeorgie said.

"No, it'll take her two hours to get ready, and everybody will be gone by the time we get up there," Green Eyed Mike said as he picked up a rock and mindlessly threw it at the chain-link fence they walked by.

But that chain-link fence that was seemingly of no importance was, in fact, *the* chain-link fence that restrained the Ranunculus District's most dangerous dog that ever lived near a public school. Nobody knew her name, but they all called her Monster. The very second Green Eyed Mike's rock casually hit the fence, Monster appeared out of nowhere and let loose a round of incessant barking, with vicious growls that were so terrifying that it paralyzed the boys into utter fear.

But what a treat this was for Monster! The only thing she had planned that day was her morning walk, but she never anticipated having a bit of fun, teasing the boys. Quite honestly, it made her look just awful. Monster was a beautiful black sable German Shepard, and she had absolutely no idea how the unpleasant barking and snarling, and the baring of her teeth, made her look, with her nose all twisted up and her ears flattened out, as she peeled back a set of snarling fangs.

How she got the name Monster had to do with the urban legend that connected her to the ugly scar on the mailman's leg. Something about how Monster's owner, Mr. Mean Old-Man Jones, kept getting the neighbor's junk mail, got really sick and tired of telling the mailman about it, and finally got fed up and let Monster loose on the poor guy. Nobody ever really knew how the mailman got that horrid scar on his leg, but however he got it (motorcycle accident), the children steered clear of the dog.

"How are we going to get to school?" Green Eyed Mike asked.

"We could turn back and go past the S&K on the other side and walk up Orchid Ave.," Nestor said.

It never occurred to the boys to just cross the street, but Monster's reign of terror, with gut-wrenching sounds like she was gnawing on a leg, had scrambled their brains, and she started charging at the fence.

"But if we go back the other way, it'll take too long," Jeorgie said in a brave, courageous voice.

The boys sucked up their fear, and on the count of three they took off running. But something crossed Jeorgie's mind, and he suddenly came to a screeching halt.

"Oh my GOD! Jeorgie! What are you doing?! You better run for your life!" Green Eyed Mike yelled.

"I just thought of something. Why should I be afraid of a dog that's behind a fence?" Jeorgie said as he sized Monster up.

"Jeorgie! She could tear it down and get you!" Nestor screamed.

But Jeorgie defied his fear and put his face right up to the fence, with his nose almost touching it. Monster's barking became hoarse, as foam spewed from her mouth, and the neighbors peered out from behind curtains and blinds. The other children, who were also running terribly late to school, watched the whole thing go down, in sheer terror, from across the street.

And just when a Curbside Volunteer was about to say something, Monster's owner, Mr. Mean Old-Man Jones, yelled from the crack of his front door, "You boys get away from my fence and leave my dog alone!"

The boys strained to get a look at Mr. Mean Old-Man Jones because no one had ever seen him.

"The next time you mess with my dog, I'll call your principal and have you suspended!" Mr. Mean Old-Man Jones said, and the boys took off running.

"When has Monster ever been on the loose?" Jeorgie asked as he slowed down and caught his breath. "She's never been on the loose, so it's okay," he said.

"No, that's not true. What about the mailman?" Green Eyed Mike asked.

Just as the boys were about to cross the street, just as Jeorgie was about to take his foot off of the curb, the most horrific, blood-curdling scream that sounded like something out of a slasher-horror film, shattered Jeorgie's moment of victory, and the boys slowly turned around.

Nestor was the first to see her and said, "Jeorgie! You forgot your little sister!"

Jeorgie had indeed forgotten all about Little Laura, and he almost shoved Nestor for reminding him. Little Laura didn't dare take one step past Monster, for if she did, she would've peed all over her brand-new khaki-colored Capri pants. Jeorgie could see the terror in her eyes and became rigid with anger that was fueled with embarrassment, and reluctantly went to fetch her.

Tears streamed down Little Laura's face as she hysterically wondered: how in the world could her brother just run off and forget her like that?

"Jeorgie!" Little Laura yelped, which turned into one of those high-pitched wails, which turned into another blood-curdling scream. It was times like this that Jeorgie wished Little Laura was a Little Luke or a Small Steven, or whatever, because a little brother could roll with stuff like running past a vicious dog.

"Why can't she just grow up?" Jeorgie mumbled to himself as he stomped past Monster, who went full throttle on her ferocious attack.

Jeorgie grabbed Little Laura by the wrist and dragged her right back past the vicious dog as her legs turned to noodles. She was on the verge of a fainting spell, while her vivid imagination took over. The dog suddenly grew fifty feet high as her barking broke the sound barrier, shattering windows of parked cars, all of it followed by a big gush of dog-breath wind. Little Laura hoped that if she didn't die a terrible death when she opened her eyes, she'd be back home, in front of the television, watching her favorite *Trinkles* DVD.

Suddenly, there was a loud, quick whistle, and Monster abruptly stopped her attack, sprinted towards the house, and disappeared inside, followed by a loud door SLAM!

Little Laura looked up into Jeorgie's evil glare and gave him a such pitiful look that his expression softened. How could he stay mad at his little sister, who was like a freshly sprouted Ranunculus with morning dew sprinkled on its petals? He took her by the hand, and they quickly walked the rest of the way to school.

# Chapter Five

Even though Rachel didn't say much, Mayfair was glad to have someone to walk with, and Rachel was comfortable with Mayfair, but their classmates seemed to know each other. Mrs. Stone could still be heard outside, fussing and calling out classes on the bullhorn as Tayla led the children down to the end of the hall and had them line up outside of Mr. Marci's classroom. Soon, Ms. Deckey's third-grade class came lumbering in, and Mayfair was surprised to see Sneaks and Q-Tech.

Ms. Deckey's classroom was right across the hall, and when Q-Tech spotted Mayfair, he started to crack on Sneaks when he said, "Yo, there goes your girl..." But when Q-Tech's eyes landed on Rachel, he was suddenly struck by her shy prettiness, and became just as awkward and confused by his feelings, as they grabbed him up by the collar and dared him not to say another silly word about Sneaks's crush on Mayfair. When the girls looked their way, the boys fumbled and clumsily darted into their classroom.

Pop Star Girl's class was the last one called to go in, and as she walked down to Ms. Plan's classroom, there were a few curious eyes on her, mostly Thad's eyes, who spied on her from Ms. Mack's class across the hall. When she glanced his way, Thad's heart skipped a dozen beats, and he wrote a poem in his mind:

When I look inside your eyes,
and when you look back at me,
It's us and we,
you and me.

Maybe one day he'd write it down.

Maybe one day he'd give it to her.

"I brought your kids in," Tayla said when she entered Mr. Marci's classroom.

"Oh, good morning!" Ms. DeMauvé-Pflume said in an eloquently enunciated tone that flowed like soft classical music with just a hint of hood in it.

"You're not Mr. Marci," Tayla said.

"Oh, no indeed! I am Ms. DeMauvé-Pflume, my dear."

Pronounced de-mahh-veh-floom, Ms. DeMauvé-Pflumé was Mr. Marci's classroom volunteer aide, and everything about her said style and sophistication. She wore a classic St. John pantsuit and smelled of an expensive perfume that should've floated around her like an invisible fog, but the aromatic notes just clogged up the room.

"And what is your name, dear?"

"Tayla."

"Tayla, what?"

"Tayla Reynolds."

"It is a pleasure to meet you, Tayla, but you should always properly introduce yourself, my dear. Two names are always a much better introduction than one," Ms. DeMauvé-Pflume said.

Tayla wasn't sure how to respond, so she kind of curtsied and left the room.

"You all may sit down now. Anywhere is fine," Ms. DeMauvé-Pflume said with a gracious smile.

Mayfair sat down at a desk in the front of the class and looked at Rachel, who wanted to sit with her but was too shy to say so.

"We can sit together," Mayfair said, and Rachel gladly sat down, relieved that Mayfair seemed to understand her even though they just met.

The classroom was nicely set up for lots of learning, especially with the mini computer lab in the back of the class with brand-new computers. The pictorial history of the U.S. presidents that hung above the dry-erase boards was lively to look at, since all of the first ladies' portraits were underneath them.

"Is Mr. Marci coming?" a boy named Kade Bondshea asked.

"Oh, yes. Mr. Marci should be back in just a minute," Ms. DeMauvé-Pflume said.

"Back from where? Where did he go?" Kade asked.

"He went down to the copy room."

"Oh. Who are you?"

"I'm Ms. DeMauvé-Pflume."

"Yeah, but why you here?"

"I'm the classroom volunteer aide. I'm here to assist Mr. Marci and all of you."

"Oh, aiight."

"Ah-what?"

"Aiight."

"Aw-ight? What is an, aw-ight?"

Another boy named Deshawn Sanders raised his hand and said, "He's saying all right."

Ms. DeMauvé-Pflume had such a perplexed look on her face. Trying to make the translation of all right into aiight bothered her deeply. "Young man, if you're going to say all right, then say what you mean instead of using that slang language."

Kade looked at her and said, "Oh, okay...aiight."

When the second bell rang, Mr. Marci suddenly appeared in the doorway, and a hush fell over the children.

"I made it!" Mr. Marci said, and closed the door with a neat stack of copies in his hand. "Good morning! I am Mr. Marci, and welcome to second grade! Welcome to your new classroom for the next nine months."

The children just stared at him. They were expecting a much older man, not some guy in his thirties who looked like a well-seasoned rock star, with long rock-band hair, in a pair of hand-sanded jeans and brand-new biker boots, standing before them. He also had an armload of tattoos that he tried to hide underneath a nice dress shirt, while some of the rather spectacular-looking tats near his neck tried to peep out around the collar.

"I'm sure all of you have met the lovely lady in the back of the classroom, our volunteer classroom assistant, Ms. DeMauvé-Pflume."

Every head turned and looked back at her, and she gave them another generous smile. Mayfair thought she looked like one of the older women in her mother's sorority chapter, who always arrived dressed to impress at the monthly meetings.

"So, let's find out who everyone is and take roll. Just say, 'here,' when I call your name," Mr. Marci said, and pulled out his roll book. "Demetrius Applethorn."

A few of the boys quietly chanted, "D-D-D!" in low tones as Demetrius raised his hand and said, "Here!"

Well, the class just about fell out in spills of laughter, because not only did Demetrius Applethorn look like a little pipsqueak bookworm with a side of dapper, glasses and all, but he sounded like one, too.

"Man, y'all wrong for that," Demetrius said under his breath.

When Kade Bondshea's name was called, he replied by saying, "What up?" Everything about him was cool, popular, mouthy.

When Xembi Bower's name was called, both Rachel and Mayfair tried not to stare at the girl. They had never seen someone so beautiful, with her tortoise-shell-colored eyes against her dark complexion that was like smoothed bark from an ebony tree, and her hair that was braided in tiny cornrows that wrapped around her head and cascaded down her back in a loose, curly ponytail. Mayfair became envious and wanted her own hair braided the same way.

Trendy Brown, who sat next to Xembi, had a bubbly light of friendly sunshine about her. Jonathan Chang shared a desk with Leah Olomua, who was a little tomboyish, and the tallest girl in the class. There was Lydia Jackson, a plump little girl who rocked a pair of slick afro puffs and sat next to Sandra Jang, who wore a pair of bright-pink rimmed glasses that popped against her jet-black hair. Erica Ross and LaDera Levitt sat together, who were junior versions of The Snootish Girls and had been BFFs since Mrs. Owyong's kindergarten class.

When Green Eyed Mike Morrison's name was called, Kade Bondshea liberally pointed out, "Michael? Who calls Green Eyed Mike, Michael?"

Probably the only time Green Eyed Mike was ever called Michael was when he was at home.

Mr. Marci took a closer look at Green Eyed Mike's eyes and was amazed at how grassy-green they really were. "Okay, Green Eyed Mike it is."

Ryan Keefe, who sat next to Green Eyed Mike, sported a mini high-top fade with a signature part that made him look like he played in the NBA.

Nestor sat with Jeorgie, and Jeorgie had to correct Mr. Marci when he called his name. "Uh, I don't really go by James, Mr. Marci. Everybody calls me Jeorgie."

"Yup! That's right! Nobody calls him James. Who calls him that? Sounds weird," Kade Bondshea blurted out.

"Jeorge it is," Mr. Marci said.

"No, not Jeorge, it's Jeorgie."

When Rachel Ward's name was called, she found it hard to respond, so Mayfair did it for her. "She's here. She's sitting next to me," Mayfair said, and wondered why it was so hard for Rachel to speak up.

And James Yoro, who sat next to Kade Bondshea, reminded Mayfair of Sneaks and Q-Tech, but without so much of the Blerdiness.

"Is that everybody? Did I miss anyone?" Mr. Marci asked.

Deshawn Sanders, who sat next to Demetrius Applethorn, raised his hand.

"That's Deshawn!" Kade Bondshea said.

"Oh! Deshawn Sanders. Sorry about that," Mr. Marci said, and checked off Deshawn's name in his roll book.

There were eighteen children in Mr. Marci's class, and he was glad that he didn't have twenty or more students, like some of the other teachers did. "Now that we're all accounted for, let's do a meet and greet."

Most of the children seemed to already know each other, but Mr. Marci had them get up and go around and talk to each other anyway, introducing themselves with a handshake. It was clear that Deshawn Sanders, Kade Bondshea, and Ryan Keefe were friends. They kept bouncing off of each other with silly comments and cracking up, like when they shook hands with Leah Olomua and said things like, "She got a grip like a dude!" and "She bring the pain with her handshakes. Almost broke my hand!"

Erica Ross and LaDera Levitt barely spoke to anyone, and kept to themselves.

Mayfair and Rachel tag-teamed their introductions, with Mayfair doing all of the talking, introducing Rachel to everyone, who never said a word.

Once the children were acquainted with one another, somehow the girls ended up on one side of the room, while the boys bonded on the other side, like a stuffy, formal school dance.

"But what about you, Mr. Marci? We don't know anything about you?" Kade Bondshea said.

"Well, I studied to be a teacher at State University. I ride a motorcycle, and I play bass guitar in my brother's band."

"You got a lot of tattoos. Can we see them?" Kade said.

The children gathered around, and Mr. Marci unbuttoned the wrist of his shirt and slowly rolled up the sleeve to reveal an armload of colorful tats. The coolest one was a very lifelike image of a 1969 black Cadillac Coup DeVille convertible, and it looked like it was driving right underneath his arm!

"Well, what do you think?" Mr. Marci asked.

The girls were impressed, and the boys were in awe of their cool-looking teacher.

"Ooh! I'm gonna get me a Bugatti when I grow up! And I'm gonna put it right on my arm, too!" Kade said. It was becoming clear that Kade Bondshea didn't have any problems speaking up or freely saying what was on his mind.

The bell suddenly rang for the mid-morning recess, and the children filed out and headed for the school yard.

* * *

For the most part, things were pretty much the same at recess as they were before school started: children at play. The girls in third through fifth grade kept an ear out for the gossip about the fight, and an eye out for Kiara Campbell. There was a ton of talk going around about why she got into it with Nosha, and everybody especially wanted to know what The Snootish Girls were thinking, since Kiara was like, the boss of them. Most of the girls on the yard didn't really bother too much with Kiara Campbell and The Snootish Girls because they were so stuck-up, and kinda mean.

Tayla was seething mad when she found out it was her girl Nosha who was tangled up in the fight with Kiara Campbell. Nosha didn't bother anybody, and Tayla knew the real reason why Kiara picked a fight with her. Actually, all of the girls Tayla ran with—Sekoya, Channen, Penelle, Kenda, K'Lixia, Rezen, Nosha, Taronka, Simonay, and Tandra—knew why Kiara picked on Nosha, but none of them would say it out loud. It had to do with a little yellow polka dot heart. Nosha's mother shopped at the thrift store for school clothes, and she always managed to make the used clothing look brand new. Nobody ever concerned themselves about Nosha's recycled style until it was indirectly pointed out that she had on a pair of jeans that clearly used to belong to another girl named Wandasia, who was in Ms. Mack's fifth-grade class last year. The jeans had a distinctive yellow polka dot heart on the back pocket, and everybody knew for a fact that those jeans had belonged to Wandasia. Nobody else on the Upper Yard had a pair, not even in a different-colored polka dot heart. This didn't mean that Nosha got everything from the thrift store, but generally all it took was just one little thing, like a pair of used jeans, and it turned into something scandalous.

So when Kiara saw Nosha over by the monkey bars, she made some indirect, snide remark like, "I bet yo' mama even got yo' nasty underwear from the thrift store too! With your used up, ugly-looking, tryna-be, wannabe, brand-new school clothes!"

Tayla and her girls, Sekoya, Channen, Penelle, Kenda, K'Lixia, Rezen, Nosha, Taronka, Simonay, and Tandra, waited for Kiara by the monkey bars, but she never came out for recess.

Mayfair and Rachel hung out by the kickball court with Mrs. Stone, and got an invitation to play a game of High Jump with Xembi, Lydia Jackson, Trendy Brown, and Sandra Jang. Everybody else in class was scattered about on the yard except for Jeorgie and his two best buds, Green Eyed Mike and Nestor, who were fixated on the One Fly Up game.

"I always heard about this thing, but seeing it in person is amazing!" Jeorgie said as Green Eyed Mike and Nestor readily agreed.

They watched from a corner sideline near Mrs. Stone's bench and were in total awe of the One Fly Up Crew, as TyRhaj, who was in the pitcher's circle, spun a perfectly rounded pitch, and Damarcus flawlessly kicked the ball that floated over the kickball court. Terrell, who was in the outfield, effortlessly caught the ball, and Jeorgie wanted in.

"Okay so, let's go in the outfield and spread out," Jeorgie said, and they took off.

Keem was up at home plate and kicked a stunning flying-saucer ball that zoomed in the direction of Nestor, and when he stretched his arms out to catch it, Chance, The Boy with the Golden Arms, ran past Nestor and snatched it away, inches away from Nestor's fingertips, and tossed it to Phron Thompson, who was the shortstop. When Keem kicked the ball again, it went flying towards Jeorgie, and he thought he almost had it, but Terrell grabbed it out of his reach, then grabbed it again when the ball almost hit Green Eyed Mike in the face.

At first the boys didn't see what was going on until it slowly dawned on them what the One Fly Up Crew was doing. They were being blocked from playing this repetitive yet glamourous game and didn't understand why.

Jeorgie took a time out and debriefed on the situation. "It's a lockout, guys. They're locking us out," Jeorgie said.

"Did we do something wrong?" Nestor asked as the ball came hurling towards them.

When Jeorgie tried to catch the ball, it was like the whole thing happened in slow motion when he jumped up as high as he could to catch the ball, and just as it was about to safely land in his hands, Phron Thompson grabbed it. It was like Jeorgie did a layup, going in for the slam dunk, and Phron Thompson jumped up and slapped the ball away. The boys weren't sure what to make of this "lockout," but Jeorgie was going to get to the bottom of it, and walked right through one of TyRhaj's spectacular pitches.

"Who's in charge around here?" Jeorgie asked.

"Who's in charge?" Mrs. Stone replied.

"Yeah, who's in charge of all of this? Because we want to play, and they won't let us."

Mrs. Stone took Jeorgie's claim very seriously. "Who won't let you play? You tell me who it is, and I'll make sure they won't make that mistake again!"

Jeorgie gave a dramatic wave of his arm and said, "Them. They won't let us play ball with them."

Mrs. Stone got up in a huff. "Why won't you let them play? The kickball court is free to everybody," Mrs. Stone said to Damarcus, who was the closest one to her.

"But we're using it right now, Mrs. Stone," Damarcus said.

"So let them get in on the game."

"But Mrs. Stone, you don't understand. We can't just let anybody play One Fly Up. We have to see what their skills are like."

Mrs. Stone had been the Upper Yard monitor for about a year, and it never occurred to her that the boys who played on the kickball court every day, rarely, if ever, allowed anybody else to play with them. It was always them and nobody else. By now the whole One Fly Up Crew surrounded them.

"No disrespect, Mrs. Stone, but we have, like, a system going, and if your skills aren't good, then it messes everything up," Keem said.

"This isn't a private kickball court. You're not paying to play on it. It belongs to everyone," Mrs. Stone said.

"If he can kick and catch, then we'll let him play," Damarcus said.

The other boys seemed to agree, but Mrs. Stone was a little taken aback by their arrogance. Most of the boys had been playing on the court since third grade, and none of them knew what else to do with their lives except play a game of One Fly Up.

Jeorgie was up for the challenge. "I'll take their test."

The crew already knew he'd fail just by looking at him.

"Can I take the test now?" Jeorgie asked, but the bell rang and mid-morning recess was over.

"Come back at lunchtime. You can take your test then," Mrs. Stone said. "But you don't have to do this. They can give up the court for lunch," she said, and the crew groaned.

"No, it's okay. I'll take the test. Thanks, though," Jeorgie said, and left with his best buds.

Mrs. Stone was somewhat appalled at how the One Fly Up Crew had been hogging the kickball court, but the boys were creatures of habit, and if they were forced go somewhere else on the yard, their well-oiled system would dissolve into a void of nothingness and wreak havoc in every part of their lives. They thought like a collective, traveled like a posse, and rolled deep. A bit dramatic, but basically, it would just mess them up.

"Jeorgie, I don't think you should take the test," Green Eyed Mike said.

"It'll be fine. I can kick pretty good, and I can catch the ball if the sun's not in my eyes, so I'm good," Jeorgie said.

But after everything Green Eyed Mike just saw, he knew the One Fly Up Crew were like professionals, with championship rings and Hall of Fame jerseys, and he didn't understand how Jeorgie wasn't intimidated by them.

"Well, if you make the team, me and Nestor will come to all of your games."

# Chapter Six

Aside from teaching, playing in his brother's weekend rock band, and a cool tattoo collection, Mr. Marci also collected interesting and unique children's picture books. Most of them were favorite books from his childhood, and he'd probably end up adding a few books that his students liked, to the collection. When Mr. Marci would retire after fifteen years of teaching, he'd start a new career in writing his own children's picture books, like *Boys and Their Capes* and *Are Mosquitos Like Vampires?* But the one called *What's Khalil Eating Today?* would be his most popular book.

So when the children got back from recess, Mr. Marci had them talk about their favorite books.

"You can spend a few minutes writing down what you'd like to say."

The girls were thrilled. Some of the boys, not so much. Most of the girls had a favorite book or two, but the boys didn't have anything in mind. It wasn't like they didn't have a favorite book; they did—or rather, they used to. Video games had replaced the books in their lives, which left the books sitting somewhere at home, in their rooms, collecting dust.

"But what if you don't have a favorite book?" Ryan Keefe asked.

"See if there's something in the back that you like," Mr. Marci said, and Ryan Keefe, Deshawn Sanders, Kade Bondshea, and James Yoro all got up and headed to the little library bookshelf in the back of the classroom.

"If he said talk about your favorite video game, shoot, I could write about *Fortnite* all day!" Kade said. He thought he'd be slick and parlay the game into his presentation. "See, I like this book because it's about some dinosaurs at a store, and just like in *Fortnite*, you can buy some dinosaur skins for battle. So that's what makes it a good book."

If Kade had taken the time Mr. Marci gave everyone to read, for those who picked a book from the library bookshelf, instead of flipping through it, he probably would've actually liked the story of *Big Harold and the Boys*, about a group of used toy dinosaurs for sale in a thrift store who throw a going-out-of-business party when the store closes.

Jonathan Chang tried to explain how the main character in his favorite book, *Pud the Spider*, had to find his way out of being trapped inside of a house. "Well, Pud gets stuck in the bathroom when he slips and almost falls to his death through a crack in one of those windows that's on the ceiling."

"Does he ever make it out?" Mr. Marci asked.

"Yeah, but it's on the other side of the house, so it takes him a while to get out."

"Sounds kind of boring to me. Don't think I'll read that book," Kade said under his breath.

Mayfair talked about why she liked *Oh My, Ms. Fly* so much. "Because she's cool and her friends are cool, and they rhyme when they talk. And the four horseflies named Glitch, Ditch, Itch, and Stitch are funny."

Rachel Ward's favorite book was *A Girl and Her Flute*, and she didn't have much to say about it other than, "It was nice to read."

"Still don't know what it was about," Kade said to himself.

Demetrius Applethorn's favorite book was *Can a Bug Get a Shower Around Here?* Erica Ross and LaDera Levitt both wrote about the same book, *Girls Are Like Cats*.

"My favorite book is called *The Lonely Cloud* because I like how the cloud makes friends and isn't lonely anymore," Sandra Jang read to the class.

"My favorite book is called *The Little Yellow School Bus*. I like it because it's a bus for kids in special wheelchairs and it turns into a party bus on the way to school," Trendy Brown said.

"My favorite book is *The Stench That Came from Marvin's Closet*," Nestor read aloud.

"Hey! That's the book I just picked out!" Deshawn Sanders said, as if Nestor had stolen the book from him. Deshawn didn't like it.

"Dang, Nestor, why you gotta take Deshawn's book for?" Kade asked.

"How was I supposed to know? I actually have this book at home, so Deshawn stole the book from me!" Nestor said.

Deshawn went from zero to sixty and darted across the room and got up in Nestor's face. The boys squared off.

Mr. Marci jumped in before they started pounding each other. "One book. Two students. Different reasons why they like the same book. Just like Erica and LaDera. No need to fight over it. Nestor will go first."

"Well, I liked it because Marvin was scared that a real monster was in his closet, because of the stinky smell."

"What was the smell?" Mr. Marci asked.

"Well, I really don't want to say what it was—but trust me, it's awful."

Deshawn glared at Nestor and looked down at what he wrote. It was practically identical to everything Nestor had said, except that he was going to reveal what the awful smell was that was hiding in Marvin's closet. "I was going to say the same thing. He stole what I was going to say!" Deshawn said as he cut his eyes at Nestor.

"There must be something else about the book that Nestor didn't talk about," Mr. Marci said.

"Well, I guess I liked the pictures in it. I liked looking at them when I was reading the story."

It wasn't what he wanted to say, but Deshawn remembered another book he liked, *When Wug Turned into Doug*, and wrote about that while James Yoro talked about the book he found on the library bookshelf, *Bring Your Pet to School Day*.

"Mr. Marci, I have another book I wrote about," Deshawn said as he stood up. "The best thing about *When Wug Turned into Doug* was when Wug turned into a cat!" Deshawn said. He looked at Nestor and said, "You can't steal that book 'cause you probably never heard of it."

Actually, Nestor had in fact heard of it because he had a copy of the book at home, and he wouldn't have given away the mysterious plot like Deshawn did.

\* \* \*

Lunch was pretty much uneventful, except that Kiara Campbell was seen hanging out with her Snootish Girls near the far end of the basketball court, while Tayla and her girls, Sekoya, Channen, Penelle, Kenda, K'Lixia, Rezen, Nosha, Taronka,

Simonay, and Tandra kept their distance. (Yes, it's annoying to see all of Tayla's girls whenever they're mentioned, but you gotta recognize each one of them, cuz that's how they roll, always holding each other down. Like line sisters in a sorority. Eleven Sides of a Situation. Airtight. Ride or fly.) Both cliques kept an eye on each other, just in case anybody got any ideas of going in on another round with Nosha. But the headliner for lunch was the main event on the kickball court between Jeorgie and the One Fly Up Crew.

When Jeorgie stepped onto the yard, he was ready for anything, until he saw the One Fly Up Crew. They were lined up along the fence near Mrs. Stone's bench, in a unity of silence, with their game faces on, looking all athletic and serious, and the pit of Jeorgie's stomach did a backflip down into the depths of his gut, and his confidence floated away. He wasn't expecting the guys to be so serious. It was just a game of kickball, for crying out loud, and for a second, he almost changed his mind about the whole thing.

The One Fly Up Crew got into action, as Big Julius squatted at home plate while TyRhaj patiently waited in the pitcher's circle. The crew's best outfielders, Terrell and Golden Arms Chance, were on opposite sides of the school yard.

"Are you ready?" Mrs. Stone asked.

"I guess so," Jeorgie said as he went over to home plate and got into position.

TyRhaj handed out the first pitch: nice and smooth, easy on the eyes, and went down like the best vanilla milkshake in the city. The pitch was so ridiculously perfect! Jeorgie fumbled a bit but managed to get the ball up in the air and almost forgot about the "test" as he watched Golden Arms Chance seamlessly catch the ball with one arm.

"Well, that could've been cool if he hadn't caught the ball like that," Jeorgie said to himself, then traded places in the outfield with Chance and Terrell.

Damarcus went up to home plate, and TyRhaj didn't waste any time pitching the ball. Jeorgie wasn't ready. He thought he was, but he really wasn't. When Damarcus kicked the ball, it shot out into orbit, over TyRhaj, like a speeding comet, and bounced off the top of Jeorgie's head, almost knocking him out cold. To his relief, none of the boys snickered, smirked, or openly laughed out loud at him. Even when it was the silliest thing to see that ball bounce off the top of Jeorgie's head, with his hands stretched out like he was going to actually catch the darn thing, the One Fly Up Crew kept it one hundred and gave props to Jeorgie for his hustle and nerve. And then, it was over.

The One Fly Up Crew resumed their perpetual game as if they hadn't been interrupted. Jeorgie and his two best buds slowly walked away. Jeorgie hoped that somebody in the crew would see potential in him and give him another shot. He looked back at Terrell and wished he'd hear him yell out, "Hey, kid!" Jeorgie would turn around and say, "Yeah?" and Terrell would say, "Kid, you got a lot of spunk. Come on back and we'll train you." But instead of the happy ending, Jeorgie heard, "Leah's up after Keem."

Jeorgie turned around and saw his classmate, Leah Olomua, go up to home plate and kick a well-rounded hoofer that skidded across the court. "What the?! What is going on?! They let Leah play? Just like that, and not me?!" Jeorgie was in complete shock. "Did they make her take a test?" he asked.

"I dunno. Maybe they did and she passed?" Nestor said.

The boys watched in disbelief until a voice behind them said, "She's legacy."

They turned around and looked up at a kid who was probably the biggest kid at Maverick Elem, bigger than Big Julius, and his name was Derrick Bay.

"What does that mean?" Jeorgie asked.

"It means that she gets to play because of Matu," Derrick Bay said.

"What's a Matu?!" Jeorgie asked as he looked at Derrick Bay like he was insane.

"What's a Matu? A legend."

Jeorgie took a moment to think, and still came up confused. "What in the world is a Matu?"

"Matu Kapu. He used to be the best ball player at Maverick Elem—kickball, basketball, tetherball, two square, four square, you name it. Whenever Hunter Smith would bring his football to school, Matu was good at that, too. Legendary, almost a god," Derrick Bay said as he casually watched the One Fly Up game.

Jeorgie curiously examined Derrick Bay, and thought he looked like a big ol' lovable, huggable, giant teddy bear with lazy eyes. Green Eyed Mike and Nestor stared up at him and seemed to think so, too.

"But why does Leah get to play because of the Matu?" Jeorgie asked, still not understanding that Matu was an actual person.

Derrick Bay took his eyes off the game and looked down upon Jeorgie and his friends like an ancient and wise philosopher. "How long have you been coming to Maverick Elem?" Derrick Bay asked.

"Since I was in kindergarten."

Derrick Bay rubbed his chin while trying to put the pieces together. "Is this your first year on the Upper Yard?"

"Yeah."

"Okay, now I get it," Derrick Bay said as he took a moment to gather his thoughts. "Leah gets to play on the kickball court because Matu Kapu is her cousin."

"So you mean I gotta have a cousin to play with them?" Jeorgie said.

Derrick Bay let out a big sigh. Ever so patient was the elder with the young one with the kooky questions. Derrick Bay nodded towards the kickball court, and Leah practically murdered the ball when she slammed it across the yard near the tetherball court. It was rather impressive, but Leah was done for the day.

"I don't feel like playing anymore," she said, and walked away.

"Not only is she legacy, but she also knows how to kick a ball," Derrick Bay said.

"So where's the Matu now?" Nestor asked.

"He's at Glick Mid," Derrick Bay said.

"How come you don't play with them?" Green Eyed Mike asked when Golden Arms Chance kicked a ball that bounced near them.

Damarcus ran over to get it and made eye contact with Derrick Bay. It lasted about five seconds, but there was definite tension between the two boys.

"I don't play with them because they don't play with honor. They act like ballers instead of ball players," Derrick Bay said as he put his hands in his pants pockets and walked away.

"Who was that guy?" Jeorgie asked.

"I'm Derrick Bay." Apparently, he had supersonic-bionic hearing skills.

* * *

Mr. Marci spent the afternoon on math lessons and spelling words, and after the children's P.E. time, it was three o'clock, when the last bell of the day finally rang. Mayfair's first day as a new student wasn't so bad. She was happy she made friends with the other girls in class, not counting LaDera Levitt and Erica Ross, and she didn't mind that Rachel Ward had quietly attached herself to Mayfair when they exited the school together. But Rachel was grateful for Mayfair. She was so afraid that she'd just blend into the classroom walls because of her debilitating shyness. She never expected to gain a full friendship on the first day, and was relieved when she spotted her father waiting for her down by the main entrance of the school. She quietly told Mayfair goodbye, and Mayfair watched as Rachel and her father chatted for a moment, as he probably asked how her day was. Then he led her away as they held hands and walked home.

Jonathan's grandfather was there, too, and patted him on the head with a smile. Mayfair saw that his grandfather didn't have very many teeth, and the ones that he did have were gold.

Timothy did a stealth karate move on Jonathan, and Jonathan said, "Well, good-bye..." to no one in particular.

Kade Bondshea and Deshawn Sanders got on one of the colossal school buses, while Erica Ross and LaDera Levitt got on the other one. The other children in class, Sandra Jang, Ryan Keefe, Trendy Brown, James Yoro, and Lydia Jackson all left together, but when they crossed the street near Monster's house, all of them suddenly went their separate ways.

When Leah Olomua's brother walked up, Demetrius Applethorn looked up at the man-child and said, "Whoa!" Leah's brother, Loto, was almost five feet, seven inches tall, with pubescent facial hair and built like a fullback. He was only in the seventh grade, but he looked like a Native Sophomore at Local High.

"I wonder if that's the Matu," Jeorgie said when he left with his best buds, with Little Laura in tow as they crossed the street, looking for Monster.

Soon there was a low-sounding, repetitive thud heard several blocks away, as the sound came closer and louder. The thud had a ton of bass in it, and the children could feel its vibration as it fell in step with their heartbeats. Finally, a car rolled up, and the front passenger window eased down, along with the bass. "Yo, D! C'mon, man!" said the voice from inside the old-school Oldsmobile Cutlass Supreme. The car was painted in a matte gray primer, propped up on twenty-two-inch chrome rims.

"See you guys tomorrow," Demetrius Applethorn said, and climbed in the back seat.

Once the door closed, the bass went back up full throttle, and Demetrius and his uncle rolled off. The only ones left waiting for their ride were Mayfair, Xembi, and her little sister, Peppertina.

There was a bit of awkward silence among them as the after-school noises evaporated into soft sounds of chirpy birds and light traffic off in the distance. Mayfair tried not to stare, but she was captivated by the tiny corn rows that swerved around Xembi's head, that were gathered in a ponytail of braided curls. Xembi admired Mayfair's cute pink high tops and wondered if they came in red. Mayfair also noticed how Peppertina and Xembi didn't look anything alike, except for the same style of their braided hair. Peppertina didn't have Xembi's beautiful mass of eyelashes that featured the tortoise-shell color of her eyes against her flawless dark-brown complexion, which was like a rich blend of Dutch chocolate. Peppertina was cute, but Xembi had a regal way about her, as if she were the heir to a royal kingdom, and Mayfair wondered if Xembi knew just how pretty she really was. Xembi thought the same thing of Mayfair, with her earthy, light-sienna complexion against her long auburn-colored hair, with the smattering of freckles around her nose.

When Mayfair's mother arrived, she got a little concerned about Xembi and Peppertina, and asked, "Is someone coming to pick you up?"

"Our mother is picking us up," Xembi quietly said. She was just as shy as Rachel Ward.

"Okay, but I don't want the two of you waiting by yourselves. So we're going to sit here until she shows up," Roxanne said, despite seeing the two Curbside Volunteers, who were right across the street. She gave Xembi a quick once-over and thought she was exquisite. When Xembi's mother finally pulled up, everyone said their goodbyes and drove off.

* * *

The girls didn't say much to each other that day, but they eventually forged an easy friendship through their time together after school while they waited for their mothers to pick them up. And when Mayfair and Xembi got home that evening, they sat around their dinner tables and held their families captive with their fascinating stories and the details of the day. There were reactions of shock and horror about the fight between Kiara Campbell and a girl named Nosha, and the varied descriptions of Mr. Marci were utterly mesmerizing, as their parents tried to erase the picture of a balding, middle-aged white man replaced with a young, thirty-something teacher with rock-band hair and killer tattoos.

Mayfair talked endlessly about Pop Star Girl with those cold, languid eyes and the fact that she walked to school every morning with a kid named Sneaks and his friend Q-Tech. Mrs. Hocklock was the nicest principal ever, and Mayfair put her in a special place in her heart, just like every other child at Maverick Elem who ran up for morning hugs. And then there was Ms. Mothped's abstract sense of style. "I don't know how to describe it, but her clothes were like art," Mayfair tried to explain. Between Xembi and Rachel Ward, Mayfair thought Rachel was the shyest, but her eyes were full of language.

The whole One Fly Up thing was just a glorified game of kickball, and Mayfair didn't see what the big deal was. Mrs.

Stone was like a soft cushion that you could just lean up against and take a nap on. But the best part of Mayfair's day, after seeing Demetrius Applethorn leave in his uncle's loud, booming car with the shiny hubcaps, was finding out that Xembi and Rachel Ward were new students, too, just like her.

And thus began the Maverick Elem school year as it rolled itself out into a daily routine. The glowing-spiritual Father Sun began to lower his temperatures as the earth rotated away, and the spring-like weather became cooler and aligned itself with the fall season. The skies of the hazy-blue summer turned into butter-colored autumn skies, and the children looked forward to the upcoming Harvest Moon Potluck.

"Keep a look-out for the new Harvest Moon, children. I might look like a cookie or a cracker, so please, try not to reach out and grab me for a bite! But for now, sleep tight. Good night," Brother Moon said as he phased himself out.

It seemed like he was gone for so long that the children began to worry. They kept an eye out for him in the moonless night sky, but sure enough, the oven-baked Brother Moon reappeared and slowly emerged as the gigantic Harvest Moon and radiated in a buttery-orange encrusted glow.

"Don't be afraid, children. It's me! I am the new Harvest Moon, no longer wrapped up in my silver-lined cocoon. I will give you extra light during the night, just in case you have to stay up late to read a book, finish your homework, talk on the phone with a classmate, or maybe even roller skate!"

# Chapter Seven

It was a such beautiful evening for the Harvest Moon Potluck, which was Maverick Elem's annual Parent-Teacher/Meet-and-Greet Open House. Everyone was expected to bring an appetizing dish from home, and with growling appetites, the children couldn't wait to eat! Most of the parents of the children in Mr. Marci's class were eager to finally meet him and said things like, "Oh, we've heard so much about you," and "You really do look like you're in a rock band." The children showed off their artwork, where they sat in class, the inside of their desks, and introduced their parents to their friends.

When Mayfair was officially introduced to Rachel's father, Mayfair thought Rachel resembled him a little bit and could see where she got her soft, silky-brown hair from. Normally, he had a top-level executive look about him, but for this event he was relaxed, with his tie loosened around his neck.

When Mayfair asked about Rachel's mother, Rachel quietly said, "Well, my mother passed away..." A bit stunned by this tragic information, never expecting Rachel to reveal something so devastating, Mayfair wasn't sure what to say, so she introduced Rachel to her little sisters. Myla and Makayla gave Rachel squishy love-hugs, and the whole class just about fell in love with them.

The ever-dapper Demetrius Applethorn spied Mayfair's father's sense of style, and took mental notes on Rachel's father's relaxed CEO look. Demetrius was there with his Uncle Ced, who dressed for the occasion and sported a pair of brand-new Timbs, a pair of pressed denim jeans that sat just below his waist but high enough not to show any underwear with his butt sticking out (which Demetrius made sure of), and a black blazer over a plain white T-shirt.

"Hey, little ladies. What's up?" Uncle Ced said to Mayfair and Rachel.

They were so flattered that he acknowledged them.

"Demetrius, how come your parents didn't come?" Mayfair asked.

"I live with my uncle," Demetrius said.

Mayfair and Rachel expectantly waited for a further explanation, but Demetrius didn't want them to know *all* of his business. They didn't need to know that his mother was really young when he was born and gave him up as baby, and that his father, who was Uncle Ced's younger brother, was currently incarcerated and wouldn't be out of prison for quite some time.

Green Eyed Mike's parents were there, and it was clear where he got his celebrity-colored eyes from. His mother, who looked like she could've been a Miss Black America pageant queen, had a pair of stunning grey eyes, while his father, who was shaped like a pro-football player, had a pair of solid blue eyes that were striking against his sandy-brown complexion.

Nestor was there with his mother, his father, his older brother, Raymundo, who was a Native Junior at Local High, and his two older sisters, Michella and Ingrid, who were in their early twenties.

Demetrius spied Raymundo's cholo-esque attire and admired his baggy, khaki pants and the solid white sneakers he wore with them. "Yeah, that's tight. That's tight," Demetrius said to himself.

Nestor's older sisters came dressed like they were gonna hit up the club after the potluck. Erica Ross and LaDera Levitt took mental notes on Michella's hip-hugger designer jeans and Ingrid's red-bottomed high heels.

"Mija! Mira que lindo son! They're so adorable!" Michella said. She thought Nestor's classmates were just the cutest little things.

When Ingrid took one look at Mayfair's little sisters, it was pre-K cuteness overload. "They're coming home with us! Uno para mí y uno para usted!" Ingrid said.

Jeorgie brought his mother, his grandfather, Little Laura, and his older brother, Arnie, who was also a Native Junior at Local High.

"Hey, where's your grandfather? I thought he was going to be here, like he always is," Jeorgie said to Jonathan Chang.

"He's at home watching a movie, I think," Jonathan said.

The children were so used to seeing Jonathan's grandfather that it was like Jonathan was missing a body part when he wasn't with him. Jonathan's mother came to class while his father was downstairs in Ms. Baylee's class with Timothy. Jeorgie was disappointed that Jonathan's grandfather wasn't there because he had big plans for their grandfathers. He wanted to introduce them to each other so that they could become best friends and hang out, talk on the phone, and do stuff.

"S'up?" Nestor's older brother, Raymundo, said to Jeorgie's older brother, Arnie.

"Hey," Arnie said in a dull tone.

The two of them had known each other for so long that it was like they were distant relatives.

"Man, look at the teacher," Raymundo said.

Arnie, who had been totally zoned out, bored out of his mind, didn't know where to look.

"No, over there." Raymundo pointed across the classroom at Mr. Marci, and Arnie was shocked! It was as if Raymundo had attached a pair of jumper cables under Arnie's armpits that quietly gave him a spark that took him out of his inner-gloomy teenage zone.

"That's the teacher?"

"Yup. Don't look like any teacher I ever had."

"Yeah, I know. I was there. In class. With you. Kindergarten to now," Arnie said in a sarcastic, robotic tone.

Most of the teachers at Maverick Elem were women, except for Mr. Douglass, who taught one of the first-grade classes, and Mr. Washington, who taught one of the kindergarten classes. Arnie had never seen anything like Mr. Marci, and now he was the one taking mental notes.

LaDera Levitt and Erica Ross's mothers were so nice and friendly. It was confusing. How could mean girls like Erica and LaDera have really nice parents and not know that their girls were terrible to be around?

Xembi finally arrived after her parents met Peppertina's teacher, who also had Ms. Baylee for first grade. Mayfair finally got a better look at Xembi's mother, since she was always in the car after school, and saw how much Xembi resembled her mother, with the same flawless, dark-brown complexion and the beautiful tortoise-shell eyes. Peppertina, on the other hand, not so much. She had the same Afro-centric touches that her mother exuded, but Peppertina didn't have any of her mother's likeness, and barely favored her father, who had more of a golf-weekend-getaway look about him. Mayfair wondered if Peppertina was adopted and wanted to ask questions, but she knew it would make Xembi uncomfortable.

Everyone was there except for Kade Bondshea, and Deshawn Sanders knew Kade hated that he couldn't be there. "He said he was coming, but I dunno what happened," Deshawn said.

"Wonder why he didn't come," James Yoro said.

"I dunno, but he's gonna hate that he missed it. And he hates missing stuff," Deshawn said.

He was right, because Kade didn't go to school the next day. He couldn't bear being left out of any of the inside jokes among the boys, about anything interesting that happened the night before, so he pretended he didn't feel well and stayed home.

After the parent-teacher/meet-and-greets were done, everyone was herded down to the cafeteria for the epic potluck buffet.

* * *

There were tuna and chicken casseroles, pans of lasagnas, big wooden bowls of salads, and fried chicken galore. Someone brought a massive pan of Thai pad noodles and an even bigger pan of meatballs with spaghetti drenched in marinara sauce. There were several pans of egg rolls and lumpia, enough to feed an army, along with enchilada pies, pho burritos, and the racks of Hawaiian and Korean barbequed ribs and chicken were endless. The first dish that was gobbled up was the crab mac and cheese. God, it was so good! The children seemed to stay away from the mashed potatoes and brown gravy that had a beautiful veneer, served with a side of a delicious turkey meatloaf that all of the parents ate up. And there wasn't a drop left of the humongous pot of fresh chicken gumbo, but there was enough for seconds of the red beans and rice with corn bread, and that didn't last very long, either. The potluck dinner was an all-out stately feast!

"Welcome to the 30th Annual Harvest Moon Potluck at Maverick Elementary. I am Mrs. Hocklock, the school principal here at Maverick Elementary—or as the children say, Maverick Elem—and we are so happy to see all of the familiar little faces out here on this celebrated evening."

Mrs. Hocklock stood at the podium that was on a platform, in front of the stage. The cafeteria fluttered in the children's artwork of the Harvest Moon, as orange and yellow moons hung from the ceiling.

When Ms. Mothped appeared, Mayfair's mother was surprised at how abstract she really was, "Oh, wow! She does look like a piece of artwork," Roxanne said.

Mr. Dalewood, Maverick Elem's janitorial custodian, got a big surprise when Mrs. Hocklock and Ms. Mothped gave him an honorary award for his thirty-five years of service as the resident janitor.

"Wasn't expecting this...I truly love my job here, with all the kids..." Mr. Dalewood said as he got all choked up with tears.

Mrs. Stone and the Lower Yard monitors were appreciated for their time and service, and some of the One Fly Up Crew ran up and hugged a few tears out of Mrs. Stone.

There was a bit of entertainment when the curtains were drawn open on the stage, as Mr. Dalewood rolled out the piano and set the mic up. The first act was the fifth-grade teacher, Ms. Mack, and the fourth-grade teacher, Ms. McQueen, who sang a jazz duet accompanied by the third-grade teacher, Ms. Deckey, on the piano. Then Mrs. Hocklock read some of her favorite poems, and the first-grade teacher, Ms. Baylee, conducted a sing-along with everyone, which was a lot of fun. When Mr. Marci got up on stage with his amplifier and a set of speakers, it was his guitar-solo interpretation of famous nursery rhymes that rocked the house that night, and the children went absolutely nuts over it! That was also the moment Jeorgie's older brother Arnie, who had been spying on Mr. Marci ever since Raymundo had pointed him out, made a life-altering decision to become a teacher.

It was Mr. Marci's wicked rendition of "The Wheels on the Bus" that opened the gateway to the unlocked potential Arnie never knew he had. Arnie was bored with his life, was an average student, lacked motivation, and was probably depressed. Mr. Marci was the coolest thing Arnie had seen in a long time, and in that electrifying moment, he was suddenly inspired and couldn't wait to get started on his life. When he found out that Mr. Marci rode a motorcycle and played lead bass guitar in a band, Arnie started growing his hair long and decided he would no longer waste his life on video games (even though he was really good at it and probably could've made a living as an eSports athlete). He got a job after school and on weekends, at the drugstore, and started saving for a motorcycle of his own. He'd eventually learn how to play the guitar and read music, and still thought about becoming a teacher. After he'd transfer from City Community College and go to State University, Arnie would make the biggest decision of his life and study music recording and studio engineering, instead of becoming a teacher, and eventually have his own recording studio. Thank goodness his mother pulled him away from his video game and threatened to donate his Xbox if he didn't go with everyone to his little brother's Harvest Moon Potluck that night, or else he would've missed the biggest life-altering event of his life. And who knows how long it would've taken him to figure it all out. So, thank goodness for fussy mothers.

As the children were all stuffed and satisfied, Maverick Elem's 30th Annual Harvest Moon Potluck ended at seven o'clock on the dot. By the time the children got home, the Harvest Moon's buttery-orange encrusted beams of moonlight began to taper off and eventually disappear, never to be seen again, until the arrival of the next autumn equinox season of fall.

# Chapter Eight

Mr. Marci was turning out to be a rather grassroots, earthy kind of teacher. He gained the children's trust and respect by listening to their ideas, questions, frustrations, and disagreements. Mr. Marci was also learning a lot from Ms. DeMauvé-Pflume. Always in an elegant pantsuit with stunning jewelry (all of it real), impeccable in style, and her saturated signature body spritzes that kept the back of classroom smelling like a downtown department-store perfume counter.

As nice and helpful as Ms. DeMauvé-Pflume was, the children found out rather quickly that she did. not. play. Oh, sure, she gave off an effervescence of a dignified disposition, with strict punctuations and classical bourgeois affectations, with all of her *agains* pronounced *ah-gain*. She had high expectations of the children and kept them on their toes; however…if you tried to *play* Ms. DeMauvé-Pflume, trust and believe, she'd *cross* you! And Kade Bondshea was the main culprit in class that could bring out that hint of hood in her.

"Let's get one thing straight, Mr. Kade Bondshea! Today *is not* the day to act a fool up in this here class-ah-rooom!" Ms.

DeMauvé-Pflume would say with her manicured, glossy-red index finger positioned, with a no-nonsense traditional neck roll. Sometimes Kade would cut up just to hear her say *class-ah-rooom*, and he'd gag for air trying not to laugh. Then she'd say, "What's so funny?! I know you not trying to be a joker up in this here *class-ah-rooom!*" Sometimes just the words *up in this here* would start a round of bottled-up giggles and snorts from the boys.

Kade Bondshea was popular, always up for fun, and always looking to get into sumptin.' Even when he wasn't trying to cut up, he'd cut up. Like the time he and Deshawn Sanders ran down to the S&K after they got off of the school bus, before school, and bought one of those horrid pickle loafs and ate it on the way back to school. Everything was fine until the inside of their stomachs started talking to each other, with loud, volcanic bubbling and gurgling sounds, as Kade tried to ease his farts out in stinky squeaks and hisses that were sticky and foul, while Deshawn let it rip like a round of rapid machine gunfire and stunk up the classroom. The can of aerosol that Ms. DeMauvé-Pflume used to cover it up only made it worse.

Ms. DeMauvé-Pflume refused to put up with Kade's mess, but Mr. Marci allowed it. His approach was that if he tried to stifle Kade's seemingly disruptive behavior, it would've made things worse, and he had to find a way that worked for Kade instead of punishing him. Kade was allowed to crack a joke, do some spontaneous pop-locking when he got a correct answer, give deadpan side commentary on anything, like when Leah Olomua got up to sharpen her pencil one time, and Kade quietly observed, "Man, she done squeezed the life outta that pencil sharpener. Put that grip on it." After that, he was a well-behaved child.

Since the kickball court was off limits, Kade and his buddies hung out on the basketball court during recess and lunchtime with the other boys in class, and with some of the older boys like

Sneaks, Q-Tech, and Derrick Bay. Sometimes they'd hang out and talk shop, or they'd play a game of hoops, but for the most part the basketball court was used to play football. Derrick Bay was totally in awe of Deshawn Sanders's athletic abilities, and he'd always say, "His mama named him right! He got the name of champions! Can't lose with a superstar name like Deshawn Sanders!"

This encouraged Deshawn all through elementary and middle school, and by the time he got to Local High, he decided to play football and ended up going pro in the second-round draft pick from State University. He always gave his props to Derrick Bay, even when they were old men with a lifelong friendship.

But the boys on the basketball court weren't quite the well-oiled system, and the tight-knit tribe like the One Fly Up Crew, yet they created their own little village that allowed other children on the yard to hang with them or come and go as they pleased. The One Fly Up Crew *lived* on the kickball court, and never, ever got tired of their unending game. Jeorgie always kept an eye on them, always with a plot in mind on how to play with them. He even wrote a short essay on it for a homework assignment, in hopes that it would bring him closer to his goals:

### Kickball Is My Dream

One day the guys on the kickball court will see me at Deepoe Park (he meant Depot) playing kickball with my friends. It will be the best ball kicked they have ever seen. And then they will ask me to play with them at school.

### The End

Demetrius Applethorn was the most particular child in class, who had a dapper dress code and kept his swag rotation with a fresh haircut, nails trimmed, shirts always tucked in, and his shoes clean. Even had a different colored handkerchief to clean his glasses with each week. His Uncle Ced always picked him up on time after school, in that low-bass booming car of his that sat up on those chromed-out twenty-two-inch rims. It's a wonder Demetrius wasn't hard of hearing with all of that sub-woofing going on. God, it was so loud!

Leah Olomua hung out mostly at the basketball court because she really liked sports. Trying to hang with the girls in class and play their game of High Jump wasn't much fun. She hated being called a tomboy and could deal with it from the boys, but when it came from the girls, mostly from Erica Ross and LaDera Levitt, it always hurt her feelings, which was never easy to deal with. Jeorgie would occasionally bug Leah about her connections to the One Fly Up Crew, always asking if he could go with her to the kickball court whenever she went over to play.

"Jeorgie, give it up. You don't have the skills," Leah would say, before she'd go and her kick her one ball for the day.

Jeorgie would just shake his head and mumble under his breath, "What a waste." He'd say it every time Leah would do that, and one day, Derrick Bay overheard him.

"Waste of what?" Derrick Bay asked.

Jeorgie had gotten used to Derrick Bay's stealth, ninja-style ways and had stopped flinching whenever Derrick Bay would quietly slide up beside him. "She can kick, but it makes me so mad that she just wastes it! Man, if that were me, I'd be on the court before school and I'd try to get the guys to play after school. It's like she's wasting *their* time. I know I wouldn't."

Derrick Bay took in Jeorgie's frustration and gave a wise smile. "Now you're getting it. It's not about the players. It's not about the crew. It's about the game."

Erica Ross and LaDera Levitt were like two little stuck-up peas in a rotten pod, with a pair matching attitudes that were on the verge of being cruel. Erica and LaDera hung together so tight that they were like conjoined twins connected at the hip, in their own little rude and obnoxious world, and they treated the other girls in class like they were totally beneath them. Just because Xembi rocked a *My Name Is Cool* lunch bag, just because Mayfair still watched the *Trinkles* with her little sisters, and just because Trendy Brown giggled a lot, did not mean they had to be so ridiculously stuck-up to them. They were especially cruel to Leah Olomua, never to her face but always loud enough to hear behind her back. Erica and LaDera were just two little girls who thought they were grown, trying to be all up in grown folks' business, which was the business of Kiara Campbell and her Snootish Girls. Desperate for their attention, always twenty steps behind them, Erica and LaDera constantly searched for that camouflaged magic portal that would allow them to slip inside the world of Kiara Campbell and stay a while.

After the fight with Nosha, Kiara Campbell and The Snootish Girls kept their distance from Tayla and her girls, Sekoya, Channen, Penelle, Kenda, K'Lixia, Rezen, Nosha, Taronka, Simonay, and Tandra, but always with an eye on each other. Kiara and her girls never missed a beat in their Monday through Friday ready-to-wear-to-school looks. Their style demanded attention, and sometimes on the rarest of occasions it even got Pop Star Girl's attention, who always had her head down, inside of a book. She was a Savanah-Hannah-Ashley girl with just a hint of a hip-hop diva in her look, clueless to the fact that she was considered a style icon at Maverick Elem, and probably didn't care, but her unconcerned sense of fashion set the tone. Thad still had his crush on her, was probably in love with her. Every day he'd spend as much time with her as she allowed him to, which was usually a few minutes, and every day he was that much closer to a friendship with her.

But yeah, there weren't any more fights between Kiara and Nosha.

Still didn't like each other though.

Jonathan Chang couldn't seem to find his place among the boys. Not that he wasn't allowed to hang with them but he just felt so self-conscious around the guys because of his hovering grandfather. It really bothered him, especially when he'd see Jeorgie, Nestor, and Green Eyed Mike without any parental supervision after school. Some days he'd sit with Mayfair and her friends for lunch; other days he'd try to hang with the guys at the basketball court; and sometimes he'd sit near Mrs. Stone and watch the One Fly Up Crew. Jonathan was so hard on himself, yet he was a really cool kid and easy to be around. But unlike Leah Olomua, who was labeled a tomboy, nobody ever called Jonathan a girl just because he hung out with the girls sometimes. The fact was, nobody even noticed.

As for his grandfather, he wasn't all dull and boring and embarrassing, as Jonathan believed him to be. After he'd walk his grandsons to school, Grandfather would shuffle down to the bus stop and catch the number seven that would take him downtown. He'd get off near the Kaleidoscope Building, walk two blocks down to the assisted-living facility, and stop by the coffee shop next door for a cup of chai-matcha green tea first. He'd sign in at the front desk at the assisted-living facility, wave hello to everyone who seemed to know him, take the elevator up to the third floor, walk down to room 310, and there he'd find his wife, Jonathan's eighty-year-old grandmother, resting in her hospital bed.

Grandfather would pull up a chair and press the remote control attached to the bed, which would raise her up just enough to spoon-feed her the chai-matcha green tea. Jonathan's grandmother was such a sweet woman, and when she spoke, her voice was so soft and delicate. It was light as a feather and matched the white wisps of thinning hair around her face. Grandfather would read the community newspaper to her that was written in Mandarin, show her pictures of the grandchildren on his cell phone, chit-chat, and watch TV for a while. Then he'd gently kiss her on the forehead and head out. He'd walk several blocks into Chinatown and stop by the dim sum shop for lunch, or he'd go to the park and meet up with a few friends on their bench. Sometimes Grandfather would go get a haircut or his nails trimmed, depending upon whether it was needed. Sometimes he'd stop by the library in Chinatown and check out a Hollywood blockbuster movie that was either subtitled or voiced-over in Mandarin, or he'd stop by the grocery store for a few things that were imported from China, like his favorite beer or a bag of his favorite shrimp chips. Then he'd make his way back down to the Kaleidoscope Building and catch the bus back to the Ranunculus District, just in time to pick up Jonathan and Timothy.

Timothy, Little Laura, and Peppertina were all in Ms. Baylee's first-grade class, and on more than one occasion, Peppertina had to set Timothy straight when he tried to cut up in class by doing karate moves when he was supposed to sit still in his reading group on the carpet.

"Timothy, if you don't sit down and hush-up, I'm gonna karate chop your head off!" Peppertina would say, in a tone that was way beyond her six years on Earth, sounding like a grown woman who didn't put up with foolishness. Most times Timothy would do as she said, and didn't have the kinds of hang-ups that Jonathan had about their grandfather.

Sneaks and Q-Tech kept their long-distance crushes on Mayfair and Rachel, and Sneaks was glad that Mayfair carpooled to school every day. It meant that he'd still see her every morning from a quick, moving distance, but whenever he'd see Mayfair on the school yard, he'd try to block her out. He couldn't be thinking about girls when he was with his friends, especially that one over there with the long pretty hair and freckles, and the cool shoes. Whenever he'd find himself near her, Sneaks would totally ignore Mayfair, even if she was looking at him dead in his face. When she wasn't looking, Sneaks would watch her with the most pitiful, lovelorn googlie eyes, the same ones Thad had for Pop Star Girl, except Thad's were more mature.

Mayfair really wanted to let Mr. Fariq know what she thought about that pack of NowLaters he gave her, but she never made another trip back to the S&K, since her father drove her to school every morning. She relied on her friends, like Trendy Brown and Sandra Jang, who walked to school, to hook her up with a stash of candy when she could give them a couple of dollars to buy stuff for her. The girls had created their own little school yard clique of sorts, by bonding over lunchtime cafeteria talk, helping each other in class, or when they'd babysit Little Laura, if she was waiting for Jeorgie after school.

Just like the One Fly Up Crew's game of perpetual kickball, High Jump was their game. Mayfair wasn't so good at it, since she was new to it, but the other girls were veterans at it. The game required a six-foot rope of connected rubber bands that involved different levels of jumping over it, kind of like a pole vault without the pole. The hardest level of High Jump was the skyscraper jump, where the rubber band rope was held high above the head, arms straight up in the air. The only person on the yard who could do it was one of Tayla's girls, Sekoya.

She always obliged whenever she was called on to make the spectacular jump, and would always say, "Don't worry. I'ma get it!" before she'd back up about ten to fifteen feet, to get a running start. When she'd make the jump, it was Olympic gold. When

Sekoya got to Local High, she could've trained to participate in the decathlon, but she preferred to be on the girls' track team. She even had a scholarship to run track at State University, but in the middle of her junior year at State University, Sekoya had a baby, broke off her engagement with her boyfriend, and enlisted in the military.

Although Mayfair and Rachel Ward were really good friends, Xembi was the one that became Mayfair's best friend, as their friendship developed during their time after school. Xembi was shy, but once she got to know a person, she was super cool to be around and could talk about all kinds of stuff. When Rachel became comfortable with all of her new friends, she still didn't say very much.

# Chapter Nine

Soon, Halloween arrived with the parades and costume contests, and the S&K threw a Halloween Block Party with a DJ and everything! Mr. Akrahm and Mr. Fariq would say it was one of the best Halloween parties they ever had, but they said that every year.

"We're also building up our brand and our community outreach," Mr. Fariq would tell the parents, who were out trick-or-treating with their children. Their Instagram page was on fire, and the YouTube channel their niece and nephew operated had thousands of likes. It was just video tutorials of Mulesha, who was known for her pretty face underneath bright-colored hijabs, and her glossy manicures; and Yohannis, who was just as handsome, making the S&K's signature club sandwiches with their special saucy condiment they referred to as "secret ganache from the old country."

Picture Day at Maverick Elem was an unofficial yet mandated requirement that each child come dressed to the nines for their school portraits. On that particular day, it rained, so the children were kept inside, but it didn't stop them from doing a spontaneous flash-mob fashion show during lunch, as the girls strutted and slayed their stuff while the boys bragged and dragged their swag down the catwalk that was stretched down the second-floor hall. Kade Bondshea and his boys took a turn, and so did Erica Ross and LaDera Levitt, hoping they'd get noticed by Kiara Campbell and her Snootish Girls. But Demetrius Applethorn stole the show. He killed it in his jeans and sports jacket, with a pimp-walk strut and a side-long, gangsta-lean pose. He sure was sharp that day! Couldn't tell him nuthin'.

After the Thanksgiving holiday, the children couldn't wait for the Christmas break. Mr. Marci's class had their first field trip to the Symphony Orchestra Hall for the annual Christmas-holiday show, and Ms. DeMauvé-Pflume planned the whole thing. The children had to really dress up for the event, and the boys weren't too excited about it, since it was a classical-music concert.

"It ain't my thing, but my mama said I had to go," James Yoro said to the guys as they watched Kade Bondshea do a layup down the basketball court in his brand-new suit, and ended up getting scuff marks on his shoes and tearing his slacks at the knee. Ms. DeMauvé-Pflume fussed at him so bad that for once in his life, Kade didn't find anything funny about it.

"Sorry, Ms. DeMauvé-Pflume," Kade said with pitiful eyes.

"I don't want your sorry excuses, Mr. Kade! You knew better than to rip a hole in your dress pants! I don't even have time to fix it! Now go get your sorry behind on that bus!"

But instead of one of the colossal yellow school buses, Ms. DeMauvé-Pflume arranged for a motor coach, and riding across town in such luxury was so exciting!

When they arrived at the Symphony Orchestra Hall, Ms. DeMauvé-Pflume pulled all of the boys aside before they got off the bus. "Let's get one thing straight. If *any of you* try to act a fool up in this here symphony, if y'all start that rough-housing business, with all that loud talk, and are disrespectful to either me *or* Mr.

Marci...I will shut it down! I will shut it down in the middle of the show! Just try me and see what happens. Cuz I will act a fool up in this here symphony! If one of you cuts up, *all* of you will be in double trouble!" It was hard not to laugh when she said "double trouble." "Be on your best behavior!" Ms. DeMauvé-Pflume gave the boys such a cold-blooded look that it made them feel guilty for just standing there.

"I'ma fall asleep, up in, this-a-here, orchestra place. That's what I'm gonna do," Kade said under his breath, but loud enough for the other boys to hear, which made them snicker.

Once inside the orchestra hall, Ms. DeMauvé-Pflume didn't have to worry about anything because the boys were well-behaved, surprised that they knew most of the holiday songs, and had to admit that they were glad they were forced to attend the concert. As tempting as it was to crack jokes at the other funny-looking children who were there with their schools, Kade kept it all business, and Ms. DeMauvé-Pflume was proud to say that not one boy in Mr. Marci's class acted a fool, up in that there, symphony orchestra hall that night.

* * *

The remaining school days that led up to the last day of school before the holiday break were restless. In the mornings, Mr. Marci would give his lessons, and after lunch he'd set the mood by plugging up his aromatherapy vapor mist that filled up the classroom with the aromatic odor of pine trees, pumpkins, and peppermint. The children did so much holiday arts and crafts that the classroom was like an explosion of Christmas decorations, as things were posted all over the walls and hung from the ceiling, with little paper and clay doodads of Santa Claus, reindeers, elves, and Christmas trees. The classroom door became the Hall of Fame of Christmas Wreaths.

The children also prepared and rehearsed for Maverick Elem's annual holiday program, and on the last day of school, before the break, Mr. Marci's class performed the song "Christmas Time Is Here," with Mr. Marci on guitar. It was just lovely. Ms. McQueen's fourth-grade class sang "Jingle Bell Rock," and both of the fifth-grade classes, Ms. Mack's and Ms. Plan's classes, combined their performance and brought the house down with "All I Want for Christmas Is You," with everybody in an ugly Christmas sweater. They thought they had the best performance until Ms. Deckey's third-grade class performed a moving rendition of "The Little Drummer Boy," and the children sang it like a tabernacle choir on Christmas morning.

After the Christmas program, the rest of the afternoon was all abuzz in Christmas parties. Mr. Marci had the children sipping on cups of chocolate milk and sparkling cider, and they sang Christmas sing-along songs on the CD player. Ms. DeMauvé-Pflume served soft peppermints dipped in chocolate, handed out samples of her favorite perfume to the girls, and gave the boys samples of an expensive men's cologne. "Just dab a little here and dab a little bit there." Ms. DeMauvé-Pflume instructed to the girls as they dabbed the scent behind their ears and on their wrists.

"Oh, great, now we all smell like her," Sandra Jang said in a dour tone.

"This don't smell like Polo. I know cuz my dad wears Polo. She got us smelling like an old man in an old suit," Kade Bondshea said under his breath as the boys slapped the decrepit-smelling cologne on their necks and faces.

Mr. Marci had the children do Secret Santa, and pretty much everyone gave each other the three-dollar gift card from the S&K that had completely sold out. Other gifts were exchanged, such as when Thad gave Pop Star Girl the new book that his older sister recommended, *The Pretty Daydream on Stardust Drive*. He gave it to her teacher, Ms. Plan, before school started that day, and asked Ms. Plan to give it to her during their party. Thad would never know how much she appreciated his gift until many years later, but for the moment, all he could do was hope that she liked it.

When the final bell rang for the day, the children were off to two weeks of complete and utter holiday joy. They gorged themselves on sleeping in and staying up late, playing outside, playing video games until odd hours late in the night, and just being bored in anticipation of Christmas Day.

*** * ***

Mayfair and her friends sent each other Christmas cards, and she got her first one from Trendy Brown that had a picture of a cute little Santa Claus sitting on top of a house that had collapsed underneath him. When Mayfair exchanged addresses with Rachel Ward, she never really looked at it until she got a card from her and noticed on the return address that Rachel only lived a few blocks away, so Mayfair surprised her. She showed up at her house one day and gave her a copy of her personal favorite book, *Oh My, Ms. Fly*, and another picture book she thought Rachel would like, called *The Story of Becco, A Most Interesting Life of a Doll*.

Even at home Rachel was shy. Mayfair thought she'd be more outgoing in her own house, but she was just lonely for her mother and missed her so much. A play date was set, and Mayfair's mother took them to the mall with Myla and Makayla. They ate tangy fish and chips with lemon claws, while a pair of icy-cold aquamarine eyes across the food court seemed to be spying on them. As much as Mayfair wanted to turn around and look at the other set of icy-cold aquamarine eyes, which belonged to Pop Star Girl's mother, she decided not to. Mayfair hoped that by the time they got up to leave, she'd be able to get a good look, but Pop Star Girl and her mother were gone. It was one of those times where Mayfair wished that Xembi was there, too, so they could thoroughly talk about the Pop-Star-Girl sighting, since Rachel wasn't a chatter box, and figure out why she was at the mall. Actually, she was there trying to find a gift for Thad, but he would've been happy if she had written the word *hello* on a Sticky Note.

The weather stayed frosty and clear during the break, and on Christmas Day, the early-morning sky was filled with lines that looked like geometric linear equations, left behind from the drifting contrails of the airplanes. Mayfair and her friends each got an authentic Pursette from the Tatum Nicole Collection, and made plans to carry their Pursettes to school on the first day back. The one gift she was hoping for but didn't get was a brand-new cell phone. When she tried to ask her mother about it, Roxanne said, "Who are you going to call? Your friends? You see them every day at school." The fully loaded tablet made up for it. Mayfair also got a nail-art kit, a realistic doctor set with a stethoscope and a blood pressure strap, from her Auntie Raquel, and a computer-coding tech-lab kit from her other auntie named Raquel (yes, she had two aunties named Raquel—her mother's sister and her father's sister). Mayfair wasn't really into video games, but somehow she managed to get one of those game consoles that all the boys in class had, along with that popular video game called *Flutter Glow,* and that other one called *Sugar Socks,* which was kind of cool, once she figured out how to play them. She got some new clothes, all from the Tatum Nicole School Collection, a couple of new dolls, a pair of roller skates, a *My Name Is Cool* trivia board game, and she was surprised to get a copy of that spectacular illustrated edition of *The Boy King, Mother Queen,* which was the same book that Pop Star Girl was reading, after she had finished all the books in *The Princess Snow*

*Frog* series, except her copy of *The Boy King, Mother Queen* was just a regular paperback book.

After the gifts were opened, the twins played with their new toys, while Mayfair's mother started to prepare dinner and her father headed out to the airport to pick up relatives who flew in for Christmas. Mayfair settled down on the sofa and was curious to read the first chapter of *The Boy King, Mother Queen*. She wanted to know what Pop Star Girl found so interesting in the books she always had her head in.

# The Boy King, Mother Queen
## Chapter One

**M**s. Helene had been hiding behind the stacks of papers on her messy desk all morning. She just couldn't be bothered with her boss, Mr. Blithers, who had been trying to secure a story with Roland Ryder, the handsome young man who had just been drafted to the Calico Blades. Roland Ryder had received the largest contract ever given to a Ulama player, $60 million dollars, to be exact, with a $25million dollar endorsement from his one and only sponsor, a manufacturing company that produced headbands. And for anyone unfamiliar with the extreme Ulama sport, it's the game of the ancient Mayan kings and Aztec warriors, which was recently re-introduced to the $21^{st}$ century, with a major fan base in South America.

    Ms. Helene had no way of knowing whether or not the handsome young man, Roland Ryder, was obnoxious or polite, but she definitely knew that she didn't want to produce an interview with him. She was burned out and so tired of producing empty interviews over the years, even though the television show she worked for specialized in newsworthy stories. Ms. Helene wanted something she could connect with, and have it connect with the millions of viewers who watched the show each week. She was no longer interested in winning awards; she just wanted to feel something, something to rejuvenate her spirit.

There was a knock at her office door as Ms. Helene sunk behind her desk, trying to hide. "Ms. Helene? Helloooo? Ms. Helene, are you in here?" It was Marge, Ms. Helene's co-worker, who also produced shows.

"Marge, is that you?" Ms. Helene asked as she slowly peered over the tall stacks of papers on her desk. "Oh, it is you. Close the door."

Marge moved a stack of binders off a chair and sat down. "Hiding from Mr. Blithers?" Marge asked.

"He wants me to do an interview with that good-looking kid, Roland Ryder, and I don't want to do it," Ms. Helene said in a tired voice.

"I'll do it," Marge said.

Shocked by this, Ms. Helene perked up a bit. "You will? Why?"

"Because I came in here to ask if you wanted to switch segments. I'll do the Roland Ryder interview," Marge said as she started looking through a stack of magazines on Ms. Helene's desk.

"So, what will I get?" Ms. Helene asked.

"A trip to Rukique," Marge nonchalantly said.

"Where?"

"Rukique." Marge said it like she had said Rhode Island.

"Where in the world is that?" Ms. Helene asked, totally confused.

"It's a little island in the Pacific Ocean. It sits right on the equator," Marge said.

"And you don't want to go, because. . .?" Ms. Helene asked as her eyes narrowed on Marge, over the papers on her desk.

"I dunno. I just wanted to meet Roland Ryder."

Ms. Helene went silent.

She and Marge had done this sort of thing before, swapping interviews to produce. Ms. Helene thought about it while Marge picked up an old copy of Tout Magazine and flipped through it like she was at the laundromat with a load of clothes in the dryer.

"What's the story?" Ms. Helene asked.

"Something about an eleven-year-old boy-king who lives on the tiny island-nation of Rukique. Something about how he succeeded his parents, the king and queen, who both died in a plane crash," Marge said.

"He's an eleven-year-old king? And the whole nation is on an island?" Ms. Helene asked.

"With a population of close to a thousand servants to rule over," Marge said as she ogled over a hunky T-shirt model and tore the page right out of the magazine. "I think I'll make him my screen saver."

Ms. Helene thought some more about the story and decided she didn't want to do a story about an eleven-year-old boy-king. It meant she'd have to make an international trip to the equator, get her passport, take a long plane ride, and hire an interpreter. "Do they speak English in Rukique?"

"They sure do," Marge said, buried in the magazine.

Well, at least she wouldn't have to hire an interpreter. But then there was the international time difference. Ms. Helene lived in New York City, and there was no telling what the time was in Rukique. Whatever it was, it could only mean that her sleep would get all out of whack. And what about money? What was the exchange rate for whatever the currency was over there? This was starting to seem like way too much work, this story about a boy-king. Roland Ryder probably wouldn't be such an agonizing interview after all.

"You can stop over in Hawaii for a couple of days on the way back. It's not that far," Marge said in a casual way, which was the hook that changed Ms. Helene's mind.

"Well, Hawaii would be nice for a couple of days, I guess. Okay, I'll swap with you."

And so it was to be, that the boy-king of the tiny island-nation of Rukique would forever change the course of Ms. Helene's life.

※ ※ ※

Everybody else in the Ranunculus District spent the day playing their new video games, such as *Light Bulb Socket* and *Detention After School*, watching new DVDs, playing games on new tablets, riding around on new bikes, and wearing new shoes (Sneaks got five new pairs of sneakers for Christmas!). But the most coveted gift was the classic Green Machine. It performed like a pint-sized Ferrari, sat low to the ground like a pimped-out '67 Ford Impala, did spin-outs like a race car on a speedway track, and Ryan Keefe was in complete shock when he saw the Green Machine with a big red bow tied around it, parked in his garage. He was the envy of his neighborhood when the children lined up for a spin. But things went completely left when Sheena Watson, who was in Ms. McQueen's fourth-grade class, took too long on her turn, and Jason Tides, who was in Ms. Mack's fifth-grade class, got mad about it and tried to push Sheena off while she was still riding it. That's when Sheena's older sister, Sharice, who was a seventh grader at Glick Mid, came outside and tried to handle Jason when Sheena went home and told her sister what Jason did. But Ryan's father broke it up before things got completely out of control. After that, Ryan's father took him to the vacant parking lot over at the old Dime and Five Storehouse, so that Ryan could ride in peace.

As Christmas Day settled down into a warm hearth of being with family, a quiet somber fell over the Maverick Elem student body on December 26. Each Maverick Elem household received a letter in the mail addressed to: **The Parent(s) of:**

Dear Maverick Elementary Parent,

It is with the deepest regret and profound sadness that we must inform you of the passing of Maverick Elementary's principal, Mrs. Hocklock. She quietly passed away on December 21$^{st}$, at her home.

Dr. Geoffrey Nickeldime will be the interim principal at this time, until the end of the school year. There will be a memorial in Mrs. Hocklock's honor on January 4$^{th}$, at 10 a.m. Parents and other Maverick Elementary alumni are welcome to attend. If there are any questions, comments, or concerns, please feel free to contact my office with Ms. Felicia Foster: f.foster@cw-usd.com.

Sincerely,

*Ethan Glassman*

Ethan Glassman, M. Ed
Superintendent
Citywide Unified School District


Mayfair remembered when she met Mrs. Hocklock on the first day of school.

"How do you feel about all of this?" her mother asked.

"I don't know. She was really nice, and she smelled like an ironing board and fruit."

# Chapter Ten

Mrs. Hocklock had just finished packing her little suitcase and set it by the front door as she waited for her sister, Betty Sue, to pick her up. Mrs. Hocklock had become accustomed to spending the holidays without her husband, Harold, since his passing a few years ago, but she always had the good fortune of spending it with her sister, Betty Sue, and their cousin, Sara. Every year they'd rotate Christmas dinner at each other's home, and this year it was going to be at Cousin Sara's house, who lived just outside of the city. Christmas dinner at Cousin Sara's house was always fun because she had so many people over; it was like an old-fashioned family dinner. So while Mrs. Hocklock waited for Betty Sue to pick her up, she sat in her easy chair, listened to Christmas music on the stereo, and flipped through one of her *House and Home* magazines. When she suddenly put her hand to her chest, the magazine slipped from her hands, and she quietly passed away.

The news of Mrs. Hocklock's passing spread from Maverick Elem over to the student body at Glick Mid, to Local High, and the students, staff, instructors, and professors at State University. It even made it on the local news, with a story about how Mrs. Hocklock had become an extraordinary figure that was synonymous with the Ranunculus District.

The first day back at school after the holidays was a cold, dreary, rainy day, and aside from the shock of Mrs. Hocklock's passing, the children were very interested in finding out who this Dr. Geoffrey Nickeldime was, and managed to contain their excitement so they wouldn't disrespect the day of not having Mrs. Hocklock anymore. The kindergarten and first-grade classes seemed to be the only ones who were completely distraught by her death. To them, she was like their special grandma who gave out warm hugs that were like fresh batches of baked cookies right out of the oven.

* * *

The Snootish Girls were all decked out in their new clothes they got for Christmas. They met up near Ms. Plan's class so they could check out what Pop Star Girl had on, who was in the classroom reading a book.

"She think she cute, but she ain't all that!" Starmesha Collins said as she sucked her teeth and twisted up the side of her mouth.

Actually, it was the cross-strap Branded Box mini satchel that gave them the stank attitudes. It was a real, live Branded Box purse, and not one of those lousy, fake, cheap ones.

"She always be readin' a book. Look like the same book she been reading," Shandelina Smith said, like there was something wrong with that.

When Pop Star Girl looked up and put her cool, steel gaze on the girls, they quickly moved on, and another pair of eyes peered in. It was Mayfair, trying to discreetly get a look-see. But wait a minute. What was this? Did those cold aquamarine eyes slightly brighten up when they saw her? Like, were they actually happy to see her? It was weird seeing those ice-cold eyes turn sunny.

Mayfair forgot all about the mall sighting, but apparently Pop Star Girl got a kick out of seeing Rachel Ward, Mayfair, her little sisters, and her glamourous mother. Then the girl did something Mayfair didn't see coming: she waved hello. Mayfair waved back, then practically ran down the hall to class, wondering why the girl waved at her. She wanted to find Xembi so they could examine the whole thing, inside and out, but the One Fly Up Crew was in the middle of a dance battle, battling it out to Fred Choi's tribal remix of "Category."

Some of the boys had grown a little taller over the break, all spiffed up in their new school gear, with fresh haircuts and new kicks.

Terrell was in the center of the cypher circle, pop-locking until he pointed to Keem and called him out.

"All right, then..." Keem said as he stepped into the circle with an Apache Top Rock move.

"Keem locked you out, T!" Big Julius said as Fred Choi's tribal remix of "Category" changed into Dirty Cash's clean version of "Stank on da Bank" that pumped from somewhere out of Q-Tech's solar backpack. The song was so hype that Big Julius couldn't stand it anymore and jumped in the circle with his rough, busted-up moves.

"Ooh, girl, look! She got a Tatum Nicole Pursette!" Skyy Jones said as the other girls looked at Mayfair.

"Is it a real one?" Starmesha Collins asked.

"I think so. What do you mean is it real?" Mayfair asked.

"Don't worry about it. You got a real one. Look at the strap." Skyy said, and quickly lost interest and turned back to the dance battle.

Mayfair didn't know of such things yet, whether or not her purse was real, but when she'd get home she'd ask her mother about it, for sure. She spied Skyy's black rain boots that had such a sheen to them that they looked like black sparkled patent leather, and Mayfair wondered if they were real, whatever that meant.

Keem finished his set with an Air Flare that pushed Big Julius out of the circle.

"You got smoked, son!" Damarcus said to Big Julius, who waved him off.

"Who's next?" Terrell yelled to an empty circle.

The children looked around at each other, and then out of nowhere, the fourth-grade teacher, Ms. McQueen, jumped in the circle and started doing old-school moves that were so unusual that everyone was looking around at each other like, "Um, okaaaaay, Ms. McQueen."

"I put that shabba-DAB-ba on ya!" Ms. McQueen said, out of breath.

Big Julius moved back in the circle and started dancing like her. "I got your shabba-dabba, Ms. McQueen. Watch this!" He took her shabba-dabba and turned it into a South-Side Bounce, and the children went wild over it!

"Oh, okay! It's like that?" Ms. McQueen said.

"Been like that," Big Julius said.

"Boy, don't get me started!"

"Don't start nuthin', won't be nuthin'!"

Ms. McQueen leaned back with raised eyebrows like *I know he's not talking to me like that!* "Oh it's on, now! Move out the way!" Ms. McQueen said, and started dancing like she was on Soul Train from like forty-five years ago, doing the Funky Chicken, The Robot, and The Bump.

But when the song switched to "Auto Tomic," the children went completely NUTS and simultaneously did the Harlem Shake, flash-mob style. It was such a sudden rush of spontaneous dance adrenaline that even Rachel Ward, of all people, was dancing! Can you believe it? RACHEL WARD! Wow!

In that moment, everyone forgot that it was the first day back at school, to an unknown future, with a new principal, and the devastating loss of a loved one, until the sound of the first bell jarred everyone's somber memory. Q-Tech turned off the music and shuffled in with everyone to class.

* * *

After spending two solid weeks away from the classroom, the children had forgotten about Ms. DeMauvé-Pflume's personal, aromatic smell that hovered in the classroom like an invisible thick fog that hit them across the face like a backhanded slap.

They were also completely caught off guard by Mr. Marci's new look.

"Yeah, I needed a change," Mr. Marci said as the children stared at him, mouths open. Gone was the rock-band hair. He had it all chopped off and sported a laid-back, bushy pompadour with a side part. He also grew a beard over the break that was manscaped and trimmed very nicely. His jeans and biker boots were replaced with slacks and casual dress shoes, with a vest over his dress shirt. He had gone from a metal-rock god to a slick city hipster.

"I hope everyone had a good holiday break. What did you get for Christmas? Anything good?" Mr. Marci said, and Demetrius Applethorn's hand shot right up. He was so excited about the new designer socks he got for Christmas!

"My grandmother got me a new bike, and my uncle got me some new socks from Urban Status!" He got up, positioned his foot on his desk, and showed off a brand-new pair of kicks, by the way, so that everyone could see his bright-orange socks.

"Man, those socks are on fleek! Now I want a pair of orange socks!" Kade Bondshea said.

Who knew that a pair of bright-orange designer socks would have such an impact on Demetrius? He became so infatuated with them that he'd hand wash the socks after he'd finish his homework and create a particular look around them so he could wear them every day. He started saving his allowance and bought two more pairs of orange socks when he wore out the first pair. When he got to middle school, Demetrius started sketching out his own clothing designs, and that's when his grandmother would buy a sewing machine. Once he taught himself how to sew, Demetrius started making clothes for his grandmother. When it got out that he wanted to be a fashion designer, Demetrius was bullied about it, and Kade Bondshea, Ryan Keefe, Deshawn Sanders, and James Yoro would take up for him whenever they could. When he graduated from Local High, Demetrius was selling his signature polo shirts with his logo of an orange sock trimmed in gold on the back of the shirt, just below the seam of the collar, out of the trunk of his car. After fashion-design school, he'd go to State University and graduate with a degree in business that would help him start up his own clothing line with his own shop called The Orange Sock.

The other boys in class talked about new bikes and video games, but they all wanted to hear about Ryan Keefe's Green Machine. "A fight almost broke out over it," Ryan said as the boys listened with excitement in their eyes.

"Oh yeah, I heard about that. I heard Sheena Watson's sister almost kicked Jason Tides's butt," Trendy Brown blurted out, and blushed with embarrassment when everybody looked at her.

"But what does the green thing do?" Erica Ross asked, not understanding what a magnificent piece of engineered machinery the Green Machine was.

That's when Jeorgie let out a loud, dramatic gasp. "Oh my God! The spin-outs are insane, and the drifts are sick! It's a Green Machine, for crying out loud, so it makes total sense why a fight broke out over it! SHEESH!" Jeorgie said, as if he were a salesman down at the Green Machine dealership.

The children weren't all that interested in Mr. Marci's dull holiday vacation that he spent at home. They were even less interested in Ms. DeMauvé-Pflume's story of her world-famous eight-layer Christmas cake she made for her sister's Christmas dinner.

The children were given construction paper to make condolence cards to give to Mrs. Hocklock's family.

"What does condolence mean?" Nestor asked.

"It's when you understand what a person is going through when they are sad about the death of someone they loved," Mr. Marci said. "So take this time to write something meaningful, and don't forget to sign your name." Mr. Marci turned on the CD player, and jazz music filled the room while the children worked on their cards before they headed down to the cafeteria.

"But why we gotta take our coats for?" Kade asked.

"Because part of the service will be held outside," Mr. Marci said as he grabbed his jacket and wool hat.

When they lined up outside of the classroom, Ms. Deckey was herding her third graders down the hall, and the other classes were already leaving. It was crowded on the first floor, near the entrance of the cafeteria, and once inside, it was like entering the threshold of a bereavement wonderland. The hard, metal folding chairs were replaced with soft, padded ones, and huge off-white Ranunculus flower arrangements and sprays hovered near the stage. The lights were dimmed, the programs were trimmed in gold, and the ambient music that floated around seemed to be in an off-white tone. Ms. Mothped and her blunt, symmetrical haircut were spotted up front; Mrs. Stone was way in the back; Mr. Dalewood stood near the kitchen, with the cafeteria ladies; Jonathan Chang's grandfather was there, near the front; a large group from Local High was there; an even larger group from Glick Mid was there; and a bunch of older Maverick Elem alumni were all there to pay their respects.

A large framed picture of a younger Mrs. Hocklock was projected onto the pull-down screen above the stage, and the children were surprised to see that she had dark hair as a young woman. When the programs were handed out, the children were even more surprised to read that Mrs. Hocklock's first name was Mary Kay. It was so weird because, to them, school principals didn't have first names. Crazy. The podium was dazzled in white Ranunculi, and when the ambient music faded, there was lots of silly shushing from the children, as Mrs. Hocklock's sister, Betty Sue Jingold, stepped up to the podium. Everyone strained to look at her, and Mr. Dalewood gave a complimentary, low-toned catcall whistle and quietly said under his breath, "Would you look at those gams?"

Now, if Mrs. Hocklock was showing signs of being elderly at sixty-four, then her sister, Betty Sue Jingold, was the exact opposite at fifty-nine. Betty Sue was a stunning, statuesque woman, with an old-school Coke-bottle figure, and she glowed in a tropical San Tropez tan, as if she had just flown in from the French Riviera. No wonder Mr. Dalewood was near the front of the cafeteria. He couldn't keep his eyes off of her.

"Good morning. I'm Betty Sue Jingold, and I'm Mary Kay's youngest sister. She was my big sister and I loved her dearly. Actually, I had two big sisters. Patti Jane, who was in the middle, passed away a few years ago, and now I'm the only one left."

Quiet gasps and surprised looks flew around the cafeteria, with murmurs of "That's Mrs. Hocklock's sister?"

"Or should I refer to her as Mrs. Hocklock? It's nice to see so many of you, who have come to honor her today," Betty Sue said, while she took a moment to gather her thoughts.

Mayfair tried to see if Betty Sue resembled Mrs. Hocklock, and she came to the conclusion that, unfortunately, Mrs. Hocklock looked more like Betty Sue's mother than her sister.

"Did you know that my sister was on the rowing team in college?" Betty Sue asked. She knew the children would get a kick out of trying to imagine their beloved principal rowing a boat, and she got the surprised reaction she was looking for. "I bet you also didn't know that she had a chicken named after her." A sea of heads all shook no. "Would you like to hear about it?" Betty Sue asked, and the children gave lots of nodding and bobbing of heads. "Well, it was during one of the Thanksgivings we spent with our grandparents. I must've been around six years old, and Mary Kay would've been eleven. Kind of hard to imagine her at eleven years old, I bet. My grandparents lived on a huge patch of land that had a fishing pond that was filled with big ol' catfish. Sometimes we'd see turtles going for a swim in the pond, and sometimes we'd see a pair of geese in the water, before they'd fly away. My grandma had a couple of chickens and a rooster, and on that particular Thanksgiving, she asked Mary Kay to go down to the chicken coop, pick a chicken, and handle it for plucking." Betty Sue paused for effect and thought the children were captivated with the story, but they were more enthralled with her glamour.

"Grandma always prepared a fresh chicken with one of her roasted turkey dinners, which I hadn't realized until that particular Thanksgiving. Grandma felt that Mary Kay was old enough and up to the task to slaughter a chicken. Usually it was Grandpa-pa who did the slaughtering, but when Grandma said to 'handle it,' we both knew Mary Kay couldn't bring back a clucking chicken. But Grandma didn't know that I had watched over those chickens like they were my babies, and I didn't want any of them to end up on the dinner table, so I followed Mary Kay down to the chicken coop, and she didn't waste any time. She grabbed up the one I named Mona, and boy, did I ever start crying. I said, 'But that's MY BABY!' So she let go of Mona and asked, 'What about that one?' and I said, 'Noooo! All of them are MY BABIES.' Mary Kay said, 'Betty Sue, Grandma said I gotta handle one of these chickens.' And I cried, 'BUT THEY'RE MY BABIEEEEEES!'"

An uproar of silly laughter filled the cafeteria.

"Mary Kay knew what she had to do, and she grabbed up another chicken by the neck, the one I named Fifi, took one look at her, and burst into tears. She just didn't have the heart to do it. We sat out there at the chicken coop for so long that Grandma came looking for us, wanting to know where her chicken was. When Mary Kay told her that we couldn't have chicken for dinner because all of them were my babies, Grandma looked at me like I was crazy, and then she started to laugh. When she found out that I had given each chicken a name, Grandma laughed so hard that she turned red and wiped her eyes. Let's see, there was Dottie, Fifi, Tulip, Carol, and Mona, but I changed Mona's name to Mona Mary Kay, since Mary Kay didn't have the heart to handle her. So, that Thanksgiving we had fish with our turkey dinner. Sounds strange, I know. And you know what? Grandma never laid a finger on those chickens. She kept them for their eggs, and just about all of them outlived ol' Jessup, Grandpa-pa's dog, who lived to be about thirteen. And that was how my sister, Mary Kay Hocklock, had a chicken named after her. God bless her soul. Love you, Mary Kay."

The cafeteria erupted in a rousing applause, as three elderly women, each dressed in a vintage, sequined sweater, got up and carefully made their way to the podium, with Mr. Dalewood's help. Mayfair instantly recognized them as the Ladies of Yesterday

Way, who lived in the house with the long driveway. The three of them held each other up, in their sequined outfits, while the aroma of their ancient Far East perfume gently drifted through the cafeteria. It smelled like a time-forgotten era of elegant ladies in hats and gloves. Mayfair was beside herself and tried to see if Pop Star Girl was just as excited as she was to see the Ladies of Yesterday Way, but she couldn't find her.

"Hello. We're the Birch sisters. I'm Lucinda Birch. This is my sister Fidelia and my other sister Parentha." The Birch sisters each wore a different-colored sequined tam and smiled through their glammed-out sparkle.

"Mary Kay was such a dear friend of ours, going back at least, what...fifty, sixty years of friendship?" Parentha asked.

"No, I think we've only known her for forty years," Lucinda said.

The children could barely comprehend how long a forty-year friendship was but figured it must've been close to a hundred years, in their little minds.

"Oh, yes. That's when we had our little jazz club called The Rose Petal, and by the time we met Mary Kay, we had already been in business for twenty years or so," Parentha said.

"Mary Kay used to work at The Rose Petal while she was in college and helped us around the club," Fidelia chimed in.

"She loved to hear us perform 'Why Don't You Sing for Me?'" Lucinda said.

"Oh, yes! That was her favorite! And we're going to sing it here, today, just for all of you," Fidelia said.

"But it's too bad we don't have our band anymore," Parentha said.

"We're too old to have a band!" Lucinda said.

The children laughed at this and collectively thought the Birch sisters were a riot.

"This is for you, Mary Kay. Somehow, we always figured one of us would go on to that restful journey before you. But then, what do we know about such things?" Lucinda said.

"Absolutely nothing!" Parentha said, which got another good laugh.

"Love you, Mary Kay..." Fidelia quietly said.

The sisters took a moment to harmonize, and the cafeteria fell silent.

*"I was somewhere, where I can't remember, but I think you were there...*

*Laughter, smiles, dancing, were you there?*

*Maybe you could hum a little tune?*

*Yes, that's it.*

*Why don't you sing for me?*

*The memories are nice.*

*So long ago.*

*So far away.*

*Why don't you sing for me?"*

The Birch sisters still had a catchy vocal range at their elderly age, and the children gave the sisters a roaring applause as Mr. Dalewood helped them back to their seats.

Then it was Ms. Mothped's turn. She took a deep breath as she stepped up to the podium. "I've been at Maverick Elem for a little over ten years now, and I considered Mrs. Hocklock a dear friend."

Ms. Mothped was such a loyal secretary that when she had the opportunity of a new career with a better salary, Ms. Mothped decided to stay because she knew that she'd never have a place like Maverick Elem. Working there allowed her to do her art. It allowed her to travel and do the things she loved.

Ms. Mothped wanted to say all of this, but all she could do was wipe at her tears and finally say, "I will certainly miss my friend. Always know how much she cared for each and every one of you. She truly loved her students...."

It was so quiet that you could hear a pin drop. Ms. Mothped took a moment to compose herself. The children weren't used to seeing the adults at their school get so emotional.

"And now, I'd like to introduce you to Maverick Elementary's—or Maverick Elem, as the children call it—new interim principal, Dr. Geoffrey Nickeldime."

There was applause, but you could feel the silence in it, as excitement ran through the children like lightning when they all laid eyes on their new principal. When Dr. Nickeldime stepped up to the podium, his presentation did not disappoint. He was dressed in a classic, dapper suit that was so sharp that Xembi thought of her Uncle Bender, who would always say, "Clean as a clock that goes tickety-tock-tock!"

The very second Demetrius Applethorn laid eyes on Dr. Nickeldime's smart sense of style, he completely geeked out over it and kept saying under his breath, "Man, that's tight! I like that, fo' sho'!"

Dr. Nickeldime wasn't a tall man, but his energy gave off a height at a strapping six foot, five inches tall, that demanded your attention, and the children couldn't take their eyes off of him. He was refined, well-dressed, and the designer eyeglasses he wore said he was all business. In spite of his stern and serious appearance, there was a heart of gold underneath all of that no-nonsense.

"Good morning," Dr. Nickeldime said in an authoritative voice. "Thank you, Ms. Mothped, for your introduction. I'd like to give my deepest condolences and sympathies to the family of Mrs. Hocklock, and to the faculty and staff of Maverick Elementary. Most importantly, I am truly sorry that the students had to return to school from a holiday vacation with such sad news, faced with uncertainties. I'd like to do a question-and-answer session with the students, so if anyone has a question they'd like to ask of me, please step over to the microphone that has been set up over there." He pointed to a standing mic near the front of the cafeteria, and Demetrius was already making his way towards it.

A murmur erupted as Demetrius stepped up to the mic.

"Could you please tell me your name?" Dr. Nickeldime said.

"It's Demetrius Applethorn."

Someone yelled, "Big D!" which was probably Kade Bondshea, and the children erupted in explosive laughter.

"Okay, let Mr. Applethorn ask his question."

"Um, why are you called Dr. Nickeldime? Are you a doctor like at the hospital kind of doctor?"

"That is an excellent question, Mr. Applethorn. Am I the kind of doctor that you see at the hospital? No. My title is Dr. Nickeldime because I am someone who has spent a large amount of quality time doing research in the field of education administration, as well as teaching, which has given me an advanced, comprehensive understanding of the public-school system. I received my doctorate degree in college, which is vastly different from going to medical school to become a medical doctor." He paused for a moment, to see if Demetrius was listening, and he was. "A medical doctor does his or her studies and research in a hospital, but I did my research through thorough study, high volumes of intense reading and application, and I wrote a lengthy and detailed book report of sorts. Does that answer your question, Mr. Applethorn?"

"Yes, thank you," Demetrius said, and returned to his seat.

"Is there anyone else who'd like to ask a question?"

Tayla Reynolds stood up and made her way to the mic. "Hi, Dr. Nickeldime. My name is Tayla Reynolds, and—" A loud shriek followed by an insane applause from most of the Upper Yard girls, ran through the audience.

"Yes, Miss Reynolds, what is your question?"

"Well, I just want to know about your family."

"Good question, Miss Reynolds. I grew up in a family of boys. My mother had five of us and kept us all in line. I don't think any of you are old enough to remember when Mrs. Nadine Nickeldime, my mother, taught English at Local High..."

Some of the adults in the cafeteria gave a light applause, who actually did have her as their teacher.

"...And my father, Mr. Clark Nickeldime, worked the evening shift at the Foster-Pruitt Power Plant, working with heating and cooling systems. My two older brothers are both professors at State University. My brother Nathan, the oldest, is a tenured professor of African-American literature in the School of Ethnic Studies, while my brother Clarence teaches chemistry in the Edward J. Stranton School of Science..."

There was another round of applause from those who had taken classes with both of them.

"My brother Howard, who is a few years younger than I, recently graduated with a law degree, also from State University, and is currently studying for the bar exam. My youngest brother, the baby of the family, Tyrone, is also at State University, studying to be a—actually, I don't know what he's doing. He hasn't figured it out yet."

Everyone was just mesmerized by Dr. Nickeldime's eloquent way of speaking, and he wasn't as stuffy as he appeared to be. The children were impressed with their new interim principal and wanted to hear more of whatever he had to say.

"I'm a middle child, and as you can see, I come from a family of academics, the arts, and higher education." Dr. Nickeldime waited to see if anyone else had a question, and Derrick Bay got up and headed towards the mic.

"Hello, good morning, Dr. Nickeldime. My name is Derrick Bay, and I wanted to know about your last name. It's uh, kind of different."

"Yes, it is, Mr. Bay," Dr. Nickeldime said as he took a moment to gather his thoughts. "The surname Nickeldime is a very old name on my father's side, originating from an ancient great-great-great grandfather, undoubtedly an origin of some variation of a pre-Civil-War enslaved name, carried down through the ages and generations of the young men in my family." Dr. Nickeldime took another moment to gather his thoughts. "Mr. Bay, your question has given me an idea that I'd like to propose for Black History Month, but I'll elaborate more on it as we get closer to February."

"Oh, okay. Thank you, Dr. Nickeldime," Derrick Bay said, and went back to his seat.

"Is there anyone else with a question they'd like to ask of me?" Dr. Nickeldime scanned the cafeteria, and Big Julius raised his hand and hurried over to the mic, and the cafeteria erupted in silly laughter.

"Hey, Dr. Nickeldime, my name is Julius Anderson, and my question is, why do you call everybody by their last names, like we grown?"

"Good question. Well, I like to formally address my students because I have found that it gives a sense of maturity and responsibility. All of you will soon develop into young men and women, and I believe it to be vital to not only treat your teachers with respect but also treat each other with respect, even when there are disagreements. You should always handle yourself with a sense of responsibility rather than wild abandonment." Dr. Nickeldime took the time to elevate the children to his level and not talk down to them. Big Julius appeared to look as if he understood, but he really didn't.

Soon, Ms. Mothped signaled that it was time to wrap things up and head out for the last part of the ceremony. That was Mr. Dalewood's cue to bring out the butterflies that were held in little boxes with air holes, as the lunch ladies handed them out to the children.

* * *

The Lower Yard looked so different from the Upper Yard, and Mayfair felt like she was at a totally different school. The morning was still gray, cold, and wet from the rain, with everyone huddled together, bundled up. The Birch Sisters were looking fierce as all get-out, in their well-kept vintage faux fur coats, while Mrs. Hocklock's sister, Betty Sue Jingold, sported a full-length parka.

Dr. Nickeldime stepped up to the platform that sat in the middle of the school yard in a very classy double-breasted pea coat. "Can everyone hear me?" Dr. Nickeldime bellowed.

On the count of three, just as the children opened the little boxes to release the butterflies, the dark, gray clouds suddenly opened up a pocket of sunshine right above them, and a brilliant patch of blue sky sat smack-dab in the middle of those somber gray clouds. When the butterflies were released, half of a rainbow appeared that looked like part of a watermelon rind, and the only thing missing was just a spectacular unicorn with dazzling, gigantic wings, to guide the little butterflies that flapped and fluttered away.

"Well, would you look at that?" Fidelia Birch said in astonishment.

The children and everyone else were amazed at this sudden outpouring of sunshine. Betty Sue Jingold and Ms. Mothped hugged each other and dabbed away happy-sad tears.

Dr. Nickeldime was just in awe of it all, and quietly said to himself, "Glory be..." Then the blue patch of sunshine in the sky closed up, and the gray clouds drifted together for a light rain. Everyone ran back inside, and the service was over.

It was the end of an era at Maverick Elem. Life would go on, and Mrs. Hocklock would be memorialized with an oil-painting portrait that would hang in the lobby of the school, where she'd still be able to keep a loving eye on the children.

# Chapter Eleven

Dr. Nickeldime seemed to be a perfect fit at Maverick Elem. The children respected him, and the teachers and staff liked his leadership. Soon it was February, and Dr. Nickeldime used the idea sparked from Derrick Bay's question about his last name, and Tayla Reynolds's question about his family, and Maverick Elem celebrated Black History Month by having the children write a short blurb about their families, and had their stories and family photos posted on the walls of the school.

Mayfair wrote about how she inherited her auburn hue from her great-grandmother on her mother's side, and had a side-by-side picture of her great-grandmother when she was a little girl and Mayfair's school photo, and the resemblance between the two of them was just mind-blowing. Mayfair looked just like her, freckles and all.

Rachel Ward wrote about her mother and all the things they did together, like helping her mother make a cake or brush her mother's hair sometimes, never mentioning that she had passed away.

Jonathan Chang wrote about his grandfather. He really didn't want to write about his parents because they drove him nuts. He didn't want to talk about his older sister Tina because she was so annoying, and he definitely didn't want to write about Timothy, so he shared how his grandparents were actually his great-grandparents who immigrated from Beijing, China, before Tina was born.

The children also had the option to write about a historical person instead of their family for Black History Month. Pop Star Girl wrote about one of her favorite authors, Memory Fellowes, who wrote the classic middle-grade book *Cream Cone Ice*. The One Fly Up Crew all wrote about their favorite Saturday-morning sportscaster, Dego Parker, who was an iconic figure in the local news scene. Weird, though, because it seemed like they would've chosen some major sports star instead of a local sportscaster.

Valentine's Day was typical, with the parties and the greeting cards. Thad gave Pop Star Girl a small box of chocolates, by way of Ms. Plan again. Sneaks happened to see it when Thad gave it to her the day before Valentine's Day, so he thought he'd do the same thing for Mayfair. He found a special Valentine's Day card just for her, and snuck down to Mr. Marci's class before school started and slid it under the door. Later in the day, Sneaks couldn't understand why Mayfair pretty much ignored him, didn't even give a knowing glance his way about the card. It wasn't until he went to bed that night and went over it in his mind that he suddenly remembered he forgot to sign the darn thing. Mayfair never knew who gave her the card. Even with the pair of sparkly high tops on the front of it, she never guessed it was Sneaks.

* * *

After the Easter holiday and Spring Break, things were status quo at Maverick Elem. Around this time, Mr. Marci was preparing his students for their week with a substitute teacher. He was going on a week-long retreat that involved his accreditation towards getting his Master's degree in education (he had just enrolled in a program that would start during the summer), and the children couldn't wait to let loose and cut up, despite promising to be on their best behavior.

So, first thing on Monday morning, as the children headed to class, everybody was in high spirits, with lots of loud talking and laughing. Kade Bondshea led the way and said, "Up in this here! Miz De Mauvé-FLOOOOM!" when he entered the classroom, but he was thrown off by the look on her face that said, "Boy, you better hush it up!" through clenched teeth. Kade just stood there for a moment, as the party behind him came to a screeching halt and the children bumped into each other as the laughter and smiles quickly faded. There was a very interesting man, whose complexion was almost of an African, sub-Saharan Congolese, sporting short dreads, standing next to Dr. Nickeldime.

"Good morning!" Dr. Nickeldime said, invigorated like he was ready for a 5K marathon. The children took their seats and stared up at their new, temporary teacher. "Is everyone settled in? Good. I'd like to introduce you to your substitute teacher for the week, Mr. Freelander," Dr. Nickeldime said, and Mr. Freelander gave the class an incredibly awesome smile. "He comes highly recommended by Mr. Marci, and I expect all of you to be on your very best behavior while Mr. Freelander is your teacher for the week. Do not disrespect him, Mr. Marci, Ms. DeMauvé-Pflume, and most importantly, do not disrespect yourself."

Kade Bondshea raised his hand.

"Yes?"

"What do you mean, 'do not disrespect yourself?'"

"When I say do not disrespect yourself, it means, first and foremost, that you must respect Mr. Freelander. If you do not, then you are not only putting embarrassment and humiliation on Mr. Marci and Ms. DeMauvé-Pflume, but you will also be an embarrassment to your classmates and, more importantly, to the whole student body, faculty, and administration of Maverick Elementary. So, therefore, out of the disappointment to your peers and such, as a result of your illicit behavior towards Mr. Freelander, you are actually disrespecting yourself while everyone else is on their best behavior. Do you understand?"

Kade nodded his head in all seriousness, pretending to understand, hoping Dr. Nickeldime would leave before he gave another long-winded explanation of something else.

"Very well. Good luck to you, Mr. Freelander. I know your students—yes, all of you are Mr. Freelander's students now—will rise to the occasion and be on their best behavior," Dr. Nickeldime said. Then he left.

Mr. Freelander surveyed the children while they stared back at him, waiting for him to say something. If Mr. Marci's new look was a well-coiffed and bearded upscale hipster, then Mr. Freelander had an eclectic earthiness about him that was neo-soul bohemian and tribal. The children couldn't stop staring at him. Finally, Mr. Freelander said, "Well, shall we get started?" and from that moment on, the children were just as polite and accommodating, did their assignments from Mr. Marci's lesson plan for the day, dutifully worked on their projects, did their Language Arts work, and lined up single-file when the bell rang for recess—and did it again for lunch. Mr. Freelander was impressed with the children, and Ms. DeMauvé-Pflume was thoroughly pleased, until....

It was during the math lesson. Mr. Freelander was going over the answers, and Kade Bondshea dropped a bomb, and it wasn't another one of those gassy pickle-loaf fart bombs. He was excited about getting the answers right to the math problems and got all caught up in his celebration, when he blurted out a spontaneous curse word. It was so bad that Deshawn Sanders, who was usually down for anything that Kade was up to, looked at his friend from across the classroom with his mouth opened in shock. In fact, the whole class heard it, mouths all open and eyes wide as saucers. But what made it even more shocking was that Kade didn't just drop the infamous F-bomb like it accidentally fell out. Instead, the word causally rolled itself out like a finely crafted, whistled tune, and before Mr. Freelander could say or do anything, Ms. DeMauvé-Pflume was already on it, and jumped on Kade like she had a switch in her hand, ready for an old-school butt whuppin'.

"Get up! I'm taking you to the principal's office NOW!" Ms. DeMauvé-Pflume said. It was the first time she didn't fuss at Kade, so it probably meant she was really upset. Kade noticed it, too, and got up and left with her.

"Ooh, Ms. DeMauvé-Pflume took him down to the principal's office. Dang! If it was Mrs. Hocklock, she'd probably sit with him in detention, but Dr. Nickeldime? Shoot, he might make him stay after school for a whole week!" Deshawn said.

Turned out that it was worse than getting detention for a whole week. Kade's parents had to have a parent-teacher-principal meeting about the F-bomb incident, and the last thing on Earth Kade wanted was his mother to take off from work, come to school, and talk about what he said in class. It would get ugly for everyone involved. The meeting was scheduled for Thursday. After that happened, Ms. DeMauvé-Pflume stayed on the children and watched them like a hawk.

But there was something brewing on the school yard.

❋ ❋ ❋

It was just like any other normal day during lunchtime at Maverick Elem, on the Upper Yard: the never-ending game of One Fly Up on the kickball court, Jeorgie and his two best buds trying to figure out a way to get in on the game, Pop Star Girl on a bench with her head buried in the book Thad gave her for Christmas, while Thad was in the outfield with one eye on the game and the other one on her. Derrick Bay was throwing around the football on the basketball court with Deshawn Sanders, James Yoro, Ryan Keefe, Demetrius Applethorn, and Jonathan Chang, minus Kade Bondshea, who had detention during lunch. Sneaks and Q-Tech played their own made-up, tech-infused games with a few other boys in their class at the basketball court, both of whom had one eye on Mayfair and Rachel Ward, who were across the yard caught up in a game of High Jump with Xembi, Trendy Brown, Lydia Jackson, and Sandra Jang.

It was Tayla Reynolds and her girls, Sekoya, Channen, Penelle, Kenda, K'Lixia, Rezen, Nosha, Taronka, Simonay, and Tandra, who first broke the news like it was urgent BREAKING NEWS about what had just gone down with Kiara Campbell and The Snootish Girls.

Well, for reasons unknown, except for the people involved, Kiara Campbell was suddenly relieved of her duties as leader of The Snootish Girls, and was kicked out of her own clique. When word hit the yard that Kiara was out, the rumors began to swirl like crazy, everyone trying to figure out what had happened, none of it making sense. It was just that Skyy Jones, Starmesha Collins, Naomi Braithwaite, Shandelina Smith, and LaRae Davis no longer wanted her around. They had nothing else to say to her. They no longer needed Kiara's status symbol, and no longer needed her friendship. The real deal was Kiara's nasty attitude: the girls were sick of it! Now that Kiara no longer had a crew to run with, she stood there in front of the water fountains and watched as The Snootish Girls were just smiling and laughing over by the basketball court, having a good time without her. Come to think of it, that was probably the first time in a long time The Snootish Girls had smiles and laughter.

When Kiara was "runnin' thangs," it was all business and no fun. But Kiara wasn't mad. Well, she was mad, but she needed another group to boss around, a new entourage, a new fan base, as she scanned the yard and landed on Mayfair and her friends in the middle of their High Jump game. Lydia Jackson was about to do a hip-level jump when Kiara appeared and plopped down on the bench. Confused by her presence, the girls cut their eyes at each other and tried to act normal. The news of Kiara getting kicked to the curb hadn't reached them yet, and the mood quickly turned cautious. Sandra Jang nervously scanned the yard and saw The Snootish Girls over by the basketball court and wondered why in the world Kiara wasn't over there with them. Things got even more strange when Mayfair finally said, "Hey, Kiara." But Kiara was so focused on glaring at The Snootish Girls that she didn't even hear Mayfair. And the more she glared at them, the angrier she became at seeing her old clique having a good time without her.

By now, the news had gone almost full circle; even the One Fly Up Crew had heard about it. This was Erica Ross and LaDera Levitt's opportunity to get in with Kiara, and they plopped down on the bench next to her. Mayfair and her friends were even more confused, because Erica and LaDera never paid any attention to them. They thought the other girls were a bunch of babies who still wore pre-K-looking clothes, drenched in embarrassing motherly love.

Mayfair didn't mind Kiara, so much, only because she really didn't know her, but the way Erica and LaDera swooped in like a pair of greedy seagulls was just downright scandalous, with their gloating smirks and knowing eyes, as if to say, "Yeah, WE runnin' thangs now!"

When lunch was over, Mayfair and her friends overheard the news about how The Snootish Girls had kicked Kiara to the curb, and Trendy Brown said, "Wonder why they stopped being her friend?"

"Who knows?" Mayfair said.

"So are Erica and LaDera her friends now?" Trendy asked.

"Oh, God, I hope not! They're the worst people ever!" Sandra Jang said.

The girls were about to find out what Kiara had in mind.

* * *

When the children got back from lunch, they were surprised to see a set of conga drums at the front of the class, with a weird-looking man they had never seen before, and a guitar strapped across Mr. Freelander's body. Lots of "Is that your guitar, Mr. Freelander?" and "Who's that?" and "Are we going to do music now?" and "Can I play the drums?" questions were asked, and the children got excited.

"I want to share with you one of my favorite books, which is called *The Sunset Is My Friend*," Mr. Freelander said as Ms. DeMauvé-Pflume handed out copies of the book to the children. "There's a song in the story that I'd like all of you to learn, and I'm going to sing it, with the help of my friend Bodhi, who will play the conga drums."

The children stared at Bodhi and his hippie appearance. Most of them had never seen a white man with dreadlocks, and Kade Bondshea blurted out, "What up, Bodhi?" and Ms. DeMauvé-Pflume shushed Kade with one of her mama-across-the-room glares. Bodhi gave the class a handsome smile.

"Would you like to know why *The Sunset Is My Friend* is one of my favorite books?" Mr. Freelander asked. "Because I wrote it."

The second he said that, everyone picked up their copy and saw, right there on the front cover, Mr. Freelander's name. Then came the questions: "Your first name is Trevor, Mr. Freelander?" and "Can we call you Trevor now?" and "How did you write this book?" and "How long did it take you to write it?" The book was lush with illustration. More questions and comments came: "Did you do the drawings, too?" and "I want to write a book, Mr. Freelander."

"Okay, settle down, everyone. Open your books and follow along with me," Mr. Freelander said as he slid his guitar around and began to strum it, while Bodhi quietly started a soft, mellow tune on the congas.

> Gather around, everyone. Gather around the campfire.
> Is everyone comfortable?
> Good.
> Do you see what I see?
> Look at the sky.
> Do you see the sun setting?
> Isn't it a beautiful sky?
> Have you ever wondered why the sun sets each night?
> I know why.
> Let me tell you the story.

The sound of twenty pages turning, was loud and silly.

It's the story of how the moon and the sun tried to be as one. A very old story that has been passed down through the ancestors, who bore witness of it.

It started when the moon would rise with the sun each morning, while the sun glowed with the moon each night. They did this sort of thing for eons, as the earth formed and the rains came that created the oceans.

And as the earth began to populate itself, a traveling comet passed by, with its extraordinary burst of light and energy that propelled it through space and time.

And it caught the sun's attention.

The sun got curious and followed the comet and stayed away so long that the moon worried if the sun would ever come back, lonely for its friend.

The moon waited for what seemed like an eternity for the sun, and drifted away into its own space and time, and decided it would only shine at night, hoping the sun would see the light of the moon.

When the sun grew tired of the comet, and returned, the moon was nowhere to be found. The sun looked everywhere, but the moon was gone, and now the sun was lonely.

It should've told the moon it was coming back instead of just taking off when it saw the comet.

The sun was heartbroken yet determined to find the moon, no matter how long it took.

And that was the creation of the sunset.

Each evening, the sun would show its appreciation of the moon in the form of a beautiful sunset, hoping the moon would see it around the world and know how much the sun honored their friendship, hoping to be bonded again, as one.

Everyone closed their books, and Mr. Freelander began to strum his guitar.

*"The sun and the moon were one.*

*Now they are far from each other, one in search of the other.*

*When the sun goes down in the evening, it leaves a blueprint in the sky.*

*The moon sees it and wonders,*

*'Does anyone else appreciate the gift of the sun as much as I do each night?'"*

The children gave Mr. Freelander and his friend Bodhi a rousing round of applause, and even asked Mr. Freelander to sign their books. Bodhi let the children play on the congas, while others tried to strum on Mr. Freelander's guitar. It was a nice way to end the afternoon before school let out.

# Chapter Twelve

So just what was the deal with Kiara Campbell? Always with a resting snooty-face, why did she always have such a snarky little attitude? She was a pretty little thing, fashionably on point, with a head full of beautiful kinky-curly-textured hair, the color of bronze, that her mother always kept nicely styled. She had eyes the color of golden tree bark, and a light-brown complexion that was brown-sugary smooth.

Once the rumors settled down about Kiara getting kicked to the curb out of her own clique, the one truth that kept coming up had to do with Blake Daniels. She beat him up in second grade. Blake Daniels liked Kiara a lot, even gave her a note in class and told her that he liked her a lot, but when she caught him two-timing her at lunchtime with Stephanie Reed, Kiara beat him up. After that, Stephanie steered clear of Kiara, and Blake moved away after third grade. Everyone wondered if that had something to do with Kiara and The Snootish Girls, but it was just the usual conversation that always came up when anything strange happened with her.

The thing was, Kiara was heartbroken. It had nothing to do with a boy, and everything to do with her father. She was the clichéd apple of his eye, a total daddy's girl, spoiled rotten to the core with his love, time, and attention. They were kindred spirits, just like two little peas in an adorable little pod, and Kiara loved her father so very much. Her life at home was somewhat similar to Mayfair's, except that Kiara was an only child. Her parents doted on her and made sure their daughter was exposed to the endless possibilities that life had to offer, which allowed Kiara to dream and believe in herself, with all the love that a close-knit family could have.

It was when Kiara was in the second grade that her parents' marriage started to quietly unravel. She knew nothing of her parents' daily squabbles, heated arguments, and heavy silent treatments. They did a good job at shielding her from their problems, but the day finally came when they sat Kiara down and told her, "Daddy is going to move out of the house." Kiara couldn't believe it. She heard the words, but the shock of it scrambled her understanding. She thought everything was fine. She never saw them argue. Never saw her parents be mean to each other. Nothing. She looked to her mother, who had the fine grace of a beautiful prima ballerina, as she dabbed at the tears in Kiara's eyes. She looked to her father, who was a strapping man with strong black-action-movie-hero movie-star looks, and kind eyes that matched his heart as he reached for Kiara's hand.

"But, why?" Kiara said as tears streamed down her cheeks.

"Well, Mommy and Daddy don't get along like we used to, and it's hard for us to live in the same house now," her mother said.

Kiara was devastated. She buried her face in the nook of her father's arm and just cried and cried.

The very next day at school was when she beat up Blake Daniels. Just an easy excuse to vent her anger over what was happening at home. When her father moved out, he did everything he could to maintain the relationship he had with his daughter, and it was hard for Kiara not being able to see him every day. They settled into a routine that seemed to work, until her father met Shavonne, and Kiara went from being a sad but perky little girl into an angry, prickly child.

* * *

On the first day of school, Kiara expected her father to pick her up for their new tradition he had started with her back in third grade, which was breakfast together with a goodie bag of cool school supplies and a new designer book bag. When she called to find out why he was running late, he should've just told her that he had a morning meeting at work, but he was en route to Ebonetha's school, since it was close to where he lived, and couldn't make it back in time to see Kiara off to school. Who was Ebonetha? She was Shavonne's ten-year-old daughter. Shavonne's relationship with Kiara's father had gotten serious when they decided to move in together and found a nice little place way on the other side of the city. This meant that Kiara didn't get to see her father as much as she did when he lived just ten minutes away. It also meant that Ebonetha was now getting all of Kiara's father's time and attention.

Kiara hung out with Ebonetha a few times when her father and Shavonne took them out to dinner or to the movies. Ebonetha was *aiight*, and Shavonne seemed to be nice enough, but Kiara didn't like that she had to share her father, especially with another little girl who wasn't technically his. When Kiara realized that it was Ebonetha who was probably getting breakfast with a goodie bag of new school supplies and a new designer book bag on the first day of school, when it should've been her, in her mind she knew she had been replaced, and that's when Kiara snapped and found herself taking all of it out on a girl named Nosha.

So when she started to notice how much Xembi looked like Ebonetha—Xembi was prettier than Ebonetha, but they both had the same dark complexion—before she could stop herself, Kiara was all up in Xembi's face during lunchtime, and suddenly shoved her to the ground. She hated Xembi simply because she looked so much like the girl she really hated.

Mayfair and the other girls were in shock. Too stunned to move. Erica Ross and LaDera Levitt were just as surprised, as Xembi looked up at Kiara with a mix of confusion and total terror. Kiara got into position to pounce, but then the bell rang, which kind of broke her out of her sudden rage, and she calmly walked away. Mayfair helped Xembi up, and Erica and LaDera went running after Kiara.

"What happened? Why did she push you like that for?" Trendy Brown asked.

"I don't know. I didn't do anything. I was just standing there," Xembi said.

"I wish we could get rid of her, like her old friends did," Lydia Jackson said.

That was Tuesday.

✻ ✻ ✻

When the girls got back to class, they noticed how Erica and LaDera's attitudes had shifted a bit. Normally, they were in their own little BFF world, but now they spied on the girls, and kept a special eye on Xembi.

"Why are they looking at us like that?" Sandra Jang whispered to Lydia Jackson.

Lydia tried to turn around and look at them, but Sandra said, "Don't look at them! They'll know that we know that they're looking at us all creepy."

Xembi couldn't stop thinking about how Kiara Campbell shoved her to ground for no apparent reason, and it started to really bother her. Even if Xembi had an answer, it wouldn't have made any sense, and unfortunately, she'd never know what the deal was with Kiara. She hoped that was the end of it, but she knew better.

Bodhi was back again, with three other young men.

"Mr. Freelander! Who are these guys?" Kade Bondshea asked.

"These are my friends," Mr. Freelander said. "All of you remember Bodhi, who was here yesterday, and this is Kaiholo, Malik, and Will. They teach dance classes at the Goah Arts Center, and today they're going to do a live performance."

The children were riddled with excitement.

"Man, his dreads are tight," Demetrius Applethorn quietly said to himself as he looked at Will, who sported a head full of dreadlocks that he had tied up in a ponytail.

Ms. DeMauvé-Pflume always had an eye for good-looking men and couldn't keep her eyes off of the one named Kaiholo. He was tall, good-looking, and clean-cut, with a smooth, dark, cherry-wood complexion. Malik wasn't bad-looking, either, with his mess of dark, curly hair against his smooth, indigenous, reddish-brown skin.

"We're going to need more space than this, so can we move the desks?" Kaiholo said, and the children went into action and moved the desks around and created a dance floor in the middle of the room. "Has anyone ever heard of a dance called Capoeira?" Kaiholo asked.

Lots of blank stares, followed with "Noooooooo."

"Well, Capoeira is a form of dance combined with the martial arts," Kaiholo said.

"Everyone knows what karate is, right? Well, think of Capoeira as doing skilled karate moves with dancing," Malik said as he got into position and nodded to Bodhi, who started a rhythmic tempo on the congas.

Kaiholo and Malik circled each other like sumo wrestlers, until Kaiholo did an overhead kick just above Malik's head as he spun around and did a power move against Malik's blocking move. They squared off until Malik finally took Kaiholo out, who was flat on his back. The children cheered and wanted to see more.

"Who wants to learn a few moves?" Will asked, and everybody raised their hands.

NowLater bets were secretly made among the boys when Jeorgie and Kade Bondshea sparred with each other, and the NowLater pot got bigger when Leah Olomua squared off with Lydia Jackson. It was close, but Leah took her down when Lydia did a random twirl that got her a little dizzy when she spun around and kinda fell down on her own.

The rest of the afternoon was spent with Brazilian folk songs, dancing, laughing, and fun. Mr. Freelander was turning out to be the ultimate substitute teacher, and the children loved it!

By the end of school that day, Erica and LaDera were still giving Xembi the business when they gave her ugly glares before they got on the school bus. It bothered her so much that Xembi shut down when Mayfair tried to talk to her about it.

Since Mr. Freelander didn't have a car, he walked to the city bus stop and trailed behind Jeorgie and his two best buds, down Timber Avenue, past Mr. Mean Old-Man Jones's house, to get to there. He didn't notice it the day before, but this time Mr. Freelander saw the boys taunting Monster.

"Come on, guys, think you could leave the dog alone?" Mr. Freelander said.

"But she's always barking at us like it's our fault. We didn't do anything except walk by, trying to get home," Jeorgie said.

"Well, you could always cross the street, you know," Mr. Freelander said as little light bulbs clicked on over the boys' heads, realizing that they could've walked on the other side of the street the whole time. Then something caught Mr. Freelander's eye, and he was absolutely floored!

"How many times do I have to tell you boys to leave my dog alone?!" It was Mr. Mean Old-Man Jones, who had snuck up on them. The boys took off running, and Mr. Freelander stared at Mr. Mean Old-Man Jones like he was his long-lost father.

"Hello, there!" Mr. Freelander said.

Mr. Mean Old-Man Jones was so accustomed to fussing at the children that he almost fussed at Mr. Freelander too, but caught himself. "You better—oh, uh—hello..." he said.

"Aren't you John Arrow Ever?"

* * *

Wednesday morning, Xembi and her little sister Peppertina were in line at the S&K. Xembi had promised to buy Peppertina a pack of Jubber Jabs when the new shipment came in.

"If they run out of it, is there anything else you want?" Xembi asked while Peppertina took a moment to think about it. Xembi didn't see Kiara Campbell walk in the store and spy on them. The S&K was crowded, as usual, with Mr. Akrahm and Mr. Fariq manning the counter.

Terrell and Golden Arms Chance, from the One Fly Up Crew, were in line behind Xembi, and Terrell kept looking at Chance and said, through clenched teeth, "Go 'head, man! Whatchu waiting for? Talk to her!"

Chance took a now-or-never deep breath and tapped Xembi on the shoulder. "Hey, what's up?" Chance said, and Xembi turned around.

She looked at Terrell but noticed that Chance had a kind of glint in his eye.

"I was just saying what's up. We see you sitting with Mrs. Stone sometimes," Chance said.

"Yeah, sometimes," Xembi said.

"So you're in Mr. Marci's class?" Chance asked.

"Yes."

"He seems like he's pretty cool."

The closest Chance had ever been to Xembi was usually several feet away, but now that he was standing face to face with her, the glint in his eyes slowly turned into lovesick googlie ones, and he couldn't stop staring at her.

Terrell could see that the conversation was going nowhere, so he stepped in to help. "Do you know each other?" Terrell asked.

"No," Xembi said.

"Well, this is Chance," Terrell said, and Chance held out his hand.

"And you are?" Terrell asked.

"My name is Xembi." She gently shook Chance's hand, and Terrell gave an impatient sigh of relief.

"There. Now you know each other." Terrell's job was done.

Wow! Who would've thunk it, that the boy with the golden arms, who went by Golden Arms Chance, had a crush on Xembi?

When his mother took him to see the city's Major League Soccer Team for a special meet-and-greet event downtown, the first star sighting Chance had was when he spotted the paper boy (yes, *that* paper boy) casually chatting it up with none other than Algernon Blystone, who was the midfielder on the team.

"Mom, look! It's the paper boy! Oh my God!"

Chance was probably more excited to see the paper boy than Algernon Blystone, but when he recognized Xembi with her family, and Brenton Bruger (pronounced *bru-shair*), who was the wingback on the team, Chance became intrigued and wondered who Brenton Bruger was in relation to Xembi. After that, the more he spied on her, the more he started to feel some kind of way about her. He noticed that she was shy; he liked how her hair was braided; and now that he was standing face to face with her, those big tortoise shell eyes of hers that were layered in a pretty mass of eyelashes, had Chance's affections all aflutter. The only person he could tell this to was Terrell, because Terrell could keep a secret and took things like a mad school yard crush very serious.

Chance was just about to ask Xembi about Brenton Bruger, when Kiara Campbell suddenly cut the line in front of her. "And you better not say nothing!" Kiara said, and turned to Mr. Akrahm and asked for a pack of Shellbombs.

"I saw what you did. That's not very nice. Either you get to the back of the line or you leave the store," Mr. Akrahm said.

Kiara stood her ground with a *I wish you would try to make me get out of line* look on her face. This defiant stance infuriated Mr. Akrahm.

He came from behind the counter, and everyone in line immediately went silent, with lots of loud shushing, because Mr. Akrahm never, ever came from behind the counter. "Young lady, we don't allow this kind of rude behavior in our store. You cut the line. Either you go to the end of it or you leave my store, NOW!"

When he emphasized the word *now*, the children jumped. Mr. Akrahm and Mr. Fariq were the most upbeat people the children knew. They were always happy to see a child come in their store, whether it was to purchase something, to chit chat, or to just say hello. No one had ever seen either of them upset, so when Mr. Akrahm came from behind the counter, with a tone of anger, it kind of frightened the children. Nothing worse than seeing a perpetual upbeat adult turn angry.

Kiara was so wrapped up in her own self-centered state of lashing out that she didn't bat an eye. She held her own and calmly walked out of the store. In her later years, that same defiant stance would help Kiara on her path to becoming a prosecuting attorney, but in this moment, it made her look like a mean-girl bully.

Exasperated, Mr. Akrahm turned to his brother and spoke to him in Farsi. "I can't believe this child made me so angry! She just walked right up and cut the line. Nobody cuts the line!"

"Let's have a freebie. It'll make you feel better," Mr. Fariq replied.

The children watched as the brothers communicated in their native language, totally mesmerized by the private exchange. Mr. Akrahm took a deep, dramatic breath, mumbled a prayer in Farsi as he closed his eyes for a moment, and when he opened them, he was the Mr. Akrahm the children all knew and loved.

"Okay, everyone. Listen up! Free bars of Flatbacks for everyone!"

The children cheered.

"And for you, young lady, anything you want, including the Jubber Jabs, on the house," Mr. Akrahm said as Xembi looked up at him, grateful for how he handled the situation instead of turning a blind eye to it.

"Thank you," Xembi quietly said.

"You are most welcome, my dear. I'm glad I was here to help you. But what are you going to do if she gets nasty with you at school? You must stand up for yourself. Never let anybody treat you like that," Mr. Akrahm said, and really took notice of Xembi's prettiness. "She was just jealous of you, anyway. You are much prettier than her. Especially on the inside," Mr. Akrahm said.

Chance beamed with pride, and made a vow to himself that he would do his best to look out for Xembi whenever he could. "So you want to walk to school together?" Chance asked.

Xembi was so embarrassed by what had just happened that she wanted to run out of the store and hide away, but she agreed to Chance's request, and he was on top of the world!

And then everything came to a screeching halt.

Big Julius, Keem, and Damarcus were standing right outside of the store. "Whut's up? Whut-whut!" Big Julius said, all loud and boisterous.

Terrell went over and slapped him five with a bro-hug. Chance's heart dropped to the ground with a resounding PLOP! He didn't want the guys to know about his googlie-eyed crush on Xembi, but he didn't want to snub her either. He was willing to take a razzing from the guys if it meant he could spend a little time with her.

Xembi, on the other hand, felt even more uncomfortable seeing parts of the One Fly Up Crew, and just wanted to get away, so she continued on up the street without Chance. When she glanced back at him, she hinted at a smile, and that was when Chance knew she probably liked him, too.

\* \* \*

Was Kiara Campbell on the warpath? Yes. Was she embarrassed by what had happened at the S&K? Hard to tell. When she walked out of the store, or was thrown out, as she saw it (the second time in three days she was kicked to the curb, by the way), and got to school, she headed straight for the girls' restroom on the first floor. She locked herself up in one of the stalls and had a good, old-fashioned cry. She knew Xembi wasn't the problem, but she reminded Kiara so much of Ebonetha that she couldn't help but want to fight the girl and push her around, the way she wished she could've done to Ebonetha. She had to be honest with herself. She hated that she didn't have her friends anymore, and the person she was really mad at was with her father, but the thought of it made her uncomfortable because she loved him so much. If her anger hadn't blurred her thinking, actually, all she had to do was just open her eyes and start an entirely new school yard clique with Erica Ross and LaDera Levitt, but that never really occurred to her.

When Xembi finally got to school, she went straight to class and was glad to see Ms. DeMauvé-Pflume already there, with the aroma of her perfume filling up the room like smoke from a small kitchen fire.

Kade Bondshea would later say, "Did she have to use the whole bottle today? Oh my God!"

"Good morning, Xembi," Ms. DeMauvé-Pflume said, sounding extra proper as ever.

"Good morning," Xembi said as she looked around the room for Mr. Freelander. "Is Mr. Freelander coming today?" she asked.

"I think so. He should be here in a minute. Don't you just love him? I think he's a wonderful teacher." Ms. DeMauvé-Pflume was thoroughly impressed with Mr. Freelander and his creative teaching style. "We need more teachers like him at this school," Ms. DeMauvé-Pflume said, as a text alert chimed in on her cell phone. "Oh, it's my sister," she said, and went to the back of the class to text back.

Xembi sat at her desk and put her head down. She was so embarrassed by what had happened at the S&K but was glad that Mr. Akrahm didn't let Kiara get away with cutting the line in front of her. And what really surprised her was Chance, the boy with the golden arms. He let it be known that he liked her and wanted to walk to school with her. She hoped to see him at recess.

Once Chance got to school, he went directly over to Mrs. Stone, expecting to see Xembi, and was confused that she wasn't there. When he scanned the yard, he saw the girls she hung out with. But where was Xembi? The One Fly Up Crew got into their positions on the kickball court while Chance stood somewhere between third base and the pitcher's mound in the middle of the court as he scanned the yard.

"Hey, Golden Arms, you trying to play shortstop now?" Phron Thompson yelled.

Chance realized where he was. "Oh. My bad," Chance said, and left for his position in the outfield.

Mayfair was looking for Xembi, too, when she found out what had happened down at the S&K. The girls were huddled around Rachel Ward, of all people, who recounted the story she overheard a couple of third-grade girls telling while she was in the girls' restroom on the second floor. "Then they said that Mr. Akrahm yelled at Kiara and kicked her out of the store," Rachel said.

Sandra Jang and Trendy Brown both gasped, totally stunned by this bit of information. "Mr. Akrahm yelled? Whoa!" Sandra said.

"Then they said that Mr. Akrahm and Mr. Fariq started talking to each other in their own language and gave away free bars of Flatbacks," Rachel quietly said.

"Wow! This is crazy! Why is Kiara picking on Xembi? Xembi never did anything to her!" Mayfair said.

When the girls got to class, they were relieved to see Xembi at her desk and huddled around her.

"Are you ok?" Mayfair asked.

When Xembi raised her head and looked up at her friends, she no longer had the strength to hold it together, and started to cry.

Erica Ross and LaDera Levitt had also heard about what went down at the S&K, all of it Xembi's fault, of course. In their immature, twisted way of thinking, and due to their undying loyalty to Kiara, this was a huge opportunity, and they pounced on it.

"We heard what happened, and you can't talk to her anymore," Erica said.

"Why?" Mayfair asked.

"Because you're part of Kiara's crew now, and Xembi got her in trouble at the S&K, so she can't hang with us," Erica said.

"And y'all can't talk to her, either," LaDera chimed in.

Lydia Jackson, Trendy Brown, and Sandra Jang were tempted to protest but were too afraid, even though they had the upper hand. Strength in numbers.

Nestor noticed Xembi with her head down when he came in. "Hey, what's wrong? Why is she crying? What happened?" Nestor asked.

"She got Kiara Campbell kicked out of the S&K," LaDera said.

"The S&K? Who's Kiara?" Nestor said.

"You know, that girl with the snooty face," Kade Bondshea said.

"Who is that?" Nestor asked.

"The girl who got in a fight on the first day of school," Deshawn Sanders said.

"Oh..." Nestor said, still not sure who Kiara was, because he had missed that epic fight on the first day of school.

"Wait, hold up. She got Kiara kicked out of the S&K?" Kade said.

"Yep. Kiara was in line and Xembi got her put out of the store," Erica said.

"But why did she get Kiara kicked out of the store?" Nestor asked.

Erica and LaDera weren't exactly sure. "I dunno, but she could've said something, and she didn't. She just let Kiara get in trouble," LaDera said.

"Oooh. She shouldn'ta done that," Kade said.

"Well, she did and that's why *nobody* in our class is allowed to talk to her anymore," Erica said.

Xembi could hear everything that was being said about her, and she wanted to run away forever.

"So we can't talk to her because of Kiara Campbell?" Ryan Keefe said.

"Yup, and if she catches you talking to Xembi, you in trouble too," Erica said.

Mayfair got so mad at Erica and LaDera that she wanted to scream at them and say, "You guys weren't even there! So shut-up! And leave Xembi alone!" But she was also afraid of Kiara's wrath, and she knew Erica and LaDera would run back and tattle on her.

"Good morning, everyone!" Mr. Freelander said as he rushed into the classroom just before the bell rang. "Sorry I'm late," he said, and immediately noticed Xembi. "Is she okay?"

The whole class went suspiciously quiet, and Ms. DeMauvé-Pflume rushed over to her, as her trail of her perfume had all the boys pretending to choke and gasp for air. "Xembi, are you feeling okay?" Ms. DeMauvé-Pflume asked.

With her head still down, Xembi shook her head no.

"Would you like to go to the nurse's office?"

All eyes were on Xembi when she finally raised her head and the tears flooded down her face. She couldn't stop crying.

Mr. Freelander got so concerned that he kneeled in front of her and handed her a tissue. "What's going on? Why are you crying?"

The gentle concern in his voice made Xembi cry even harder, because it seemed like he was the only one at Maverick Elem who cared.

"Ms. DeMauvé-Pflume, will you take her down to the nurse's office?" Mr. Freelander asked, and handed Xembi another tissue. "I hope you feel better, Xembi. Whatever is going on, it'll be all right," he said as she got up and left with Ms. DeMauvé-Pflume. "Does anyone know what happened?"

Had Mr. Freelander arrived early to class, and had Ms. DeMauvé-Pflume not been texting with her sister, either one of them could've stopped Erica and LaDera's strong-arm tactics against Xembi. But the damage was done.

Down in the nurse's office, Xembi said she had a headache and was given a cold compress and a cot to lie on. She tried to figure out how all of the trouble started with Kiara Campbell, and came up with nothing. She was too traumatized to go back to class, so she asked the nurse if she could go home.

When Xembi's father arrived, Ms. DeMauvé-Pflume started acting like she was on a dating show, with the batting of her eyes, exaggerated laughter, and a bit of romantic giddiness. Happened every time a good-looking man was in her presence, and Mr. Bower, Ted Bower, was a solid, strapping, athletic man with rugged features, who was so handsome that it almost knocked the wind right out of Ms. DeMauvé-Pflume, and she tried not to swoon.

Xembi's father was at the Harvest Moon Potluck, but Ms. DeMauvé-Pflume couldn't recall meeting him. "So nice to meet you." She shook Ted's hand, and he suddenly sneezed when he got a whiff of her perfume. "Xembi, I hope you feel better. We'll see you tomorrow," Ms. DeMauvé-Pflume said.

Dr. Nickeldime came out of his office and noticed everyone when he passed by. "Oh no, what do we have here?" Dr. Nickeldime said and looked at Xembi. "Not feeling well?" He introduced himself to her father.

"Yeah, she has a headache, so I'm taking her home," Ted said.

Dr. Nickeldime quickly studied Xembi. He looked into those big, beautiful tortoise-shell-colored eyes of hers and could see she wasn't bothered by a headache at all, but something more emotional. He had seen many sick children, as well as a child on the verge of tears over some trivial or petty thing that made it seem like the whole world was going to cave in on them. He also noticed Ms. DeMauvé-Pflume's overpowering perfume and wiped his nose. "You're one of Mr. Freelander's students. I heard he's going to have some really interesting guests today after lunch. I might even stop by and see what it's all about. Are you sure you want to miss that?" Dr. Nickeldime asked. But Xembi just wanted to go home.

Once she got in the car, Xembi debated whether she should've told her father what was really going on. So far, he had been a really good dad and had made things comfortable for Xembi when he dated her mother. When Xembi was three years old, her biological father suddenly passed away from a heart condition. When Ted Bower met Xembi's mother, Binda, on a blind date set up by a mutual friend, the second Ted laid eyes on the beautiful, striking Binda, he knew he wanted to be with her and share his life with hers. Ted's first wife, Peppertina's mother, had also passed away, but we must respect Peppertina's wishes in not discussing the details of her mother's death. May she rest in peace, and God rest her soul.

Xembi's family was ecstatic that her mother had found love again, and most of the women who married in Xembi's family somehow managed to marry men who either had a first or last name with the letter B. So when Binda's family found out that Ted's last name was Bower, they were thrilled. Even Peppertina was given the name Bandi, but she preferred her own name, to honor her mother, which was fine. For a while, Xembi went by her father's last name of Bascōme but decided to add Bower since her new father was such a good guy. So when she decided to tell her father what was really going on, he didn't get mad about it like she thought he would.

"Do you want me to talk to your teacher?" Ted asked.

"I dunno."

"Maybe I can talk to your principal."

"But that might make everything even worse."

Now that he knew that Xembi didn't have a headache, instead of going home, Ted went back to work and brought Xembi with him. He worked at State University in the athletics department, in the sports-nutrition office, primarily as the football team's dietary manager, and they spent the day with the Lacrosse team.

When they got home later that evening, Xembi's mother was very concerned about what was going on at school. "That's it! I'm calling the principal tomorrow!" Binda said.

"But it might make everything worse," Xembi said. She could only imagine what would happen if everyone found out that she told her parents, and that her parents had talked to Dr. Nickeldime about it.

"Yeah, things will get worse if you don't speak up. If you don't want us to intervene, then you've got to stand up for yourself. I don't want you to get into a fight, but if somebody just shoves you to the ground, then you better make sure they don't shove you again! You have a brain connected to your mouth. Use it!" Binda said as she tried to remain calm.

Xembi didn't know how to do a verbal assault. She always wished she could be just like her Uncle Bender, in that way. He always had a way of saying things that could either make you feel good or hurt your feelings. Xembi didn't have the ability to talk smack, but she did have the weapon of a powerful silent treatment. Her silence could be lethal. It felt like she had cut you out of her life, out of your own life, and then you'd start to think that you couldn't care less about Xembi ignoring you, but she was a really cool friend to hang out with, so then you'd be dying to just get back in good with her because Xembi was actually *that* awesome!

"*Please* don't call the principal, Mama. . ."

"Fine! I won't call. But! If things get crazy, I will be down at that school so fast...." Binda said. Binda would've also gone up to the classroom and told the whole class off, including Mr. Freelander *and* Ms. DeMauvé-Pflume. It really was too bad that Xembi didn't have her mother's fire, because she could've handled Kiara Campbell the very second she shoved her to the ground.

So that night, Xembi mentally prepared herself for whatever came her way the next day at school. And if things got really bad, then she'd just ask her parents if she could do home school. Sounded like a good plan when she bounced it off of Peppertina before they drifted off to sleep.

# Chapter Thirteen

Well, as far as Mayfair was concerned about Xembi, she was upset that she had gone home early that day. She wished she could've been there at the S&K when Kiara Campbell cut the line in front of Xembi, but what could she have done? Sad to say, she knew she wouldn't have done anything. She would've been too scared and way too embarrassed, but at least she would've been there with Xembi. And thank God for Mr. Akrahm! Maybe he really did like the children who came to his store. Maybe it wasn't only about selling candy. Maybe he actually cared about his customers. Mayfair cared a lot about Xembi, probably cared more than the other girls. And why was Kiara Campbell hanging out with second graders? Hadn't she been going to Maverick Elem since kindergarten? Hadn't she known most of the other girls on the yard besides The Snootish Girls? It was really too bad that Kiara couldn't hang with Tayla Reynolds and her girls, Sekoya, Channen, Penelle, Kenda, K'Lixia, Rezen, Nosha, Taronka, Simonay, and Tandra, but the thing was, Tayla couldn't stand Kiara, and it was becoming clear that all of the other girls in third, fourth, and fifth grade didn't like Kiara either. And then there was Erica Ross and LaDera Levitt, and Mayfair knew the only reason they were being bossy bullies was because they needed the attention from Kiara. But why?

Right before she drifted off to sleep, Mayfair made up her mind that whatever happened the next day, she was going to do something about it.

No matter what.

* * *

Thursday

The next morning, Mayfair woke up with a mission and a purpose. She got up on time, without having her parents to nag her out of bed. She efficiently brushed her teeth and washed her face, and decided to wear a pair of jeans with a basic T-shirt, her white hoodie that had a gold heart on the front of it, and her worn Nikes to round out the look. Whatever was about to go down, she didn't want to do it in a Tatum Nicole ensemble. Her parents took notice of what she was wearing but said nothing. The twins picked up on Mayfair's warrior-girl vibe that said, "Leave me alone! I got a ton of stuff to do today!" Once Mayfair's mother finished with her hair, and breakfast was over, Mayfair asked her father if they could leave a little earlier than usual.

"Okay, just let me finish up with—"

"No, Daddy, I have to leave now!"

"Well okay then, let's get going," Richard said as he gathered up his things, tucked them in his satchel, and headed out.

Once Mayfair got to school, she went looking for Xembi, and decided to wait for her near the front entrance of the school. The first person she saw from class was Leah Olomua.

"I can't stop thinking about what happened to Xembi yesterday. Man, that was messed up. I'ma still talk to her, though, cuz she cool. I don't like Erica and LaDera, anyway," Leah said, and gave Mayfair a hearty fist bump and headed upstairs to the yard.

Rachel came through, but Mayfair had to send her away. "I have to talk to Xembi, and I need to talk to her by myself. But when we're done, we'll come find you. Okay?"

Rachel understood and headed upstairs and sat with Mrs. Stone.

When Pop Star Girl came through with Q-Tech and Sneaks, she gave Mayfair a fast head-to-toe once-over and seemed vaguely impressed with Mayfair's new look.

Q-Tech practically shoved Sneaks right into Mayfair and sternly, but quietly, said, "Just talk to her! Sheesh!" and ran off.

"Are you okay?" Mayfair said as Sneaks tried not to look too embarrassed.

"Yeah, I'm okay," Sneaks said, and looked at Mayfair as if he were trying to figure out where he had seen her before, trying to lay some game on her. "You're that girl who uh, that girl who, um..." Now his game was just turning lame.

"Everybody calls you Sneaks, but what's your real name?" Mayfair asked.

"Jared. What's yours?"

"Mayfair. Is Q-Tech your brother?"

"No, he's my cousin."

"What's his real name?"

"It's Julian, but he hates it."

In that moment, Sneaks wondered why he waited so long to talk to Mayfair. "I like your hoodie. It's cute," Sneaks said, and he realized he just used the word *cute*. So embarrassing!

Mayfair wanted to ask him all about Pop Star Girl, but Xembi and Peppertina came through. "Hey, Xembi!" Mayfair said, but

Xembi completely ignored her. "I have to go talk to her," Mayfair said.

"Okay, then. I'll see you later," Sneaks said, all giddy, and ran upstairs to the Upper Yard. He was so happy with the exchange he just had with Mayfair that he could've jumped up in the air and clicked his heels three times.

"Hey! Xembi! I need to talk to you!" Mayfair said, but Xembi kept walking and disappeared inside the cafeteria. Was she mad at Mayfair, too, for not saying anything yesterday when Erica and LaDera banned the whole class from talking to her? Mayfair peeped inside the cafeteria and saw Xembi on the other side, way in the back, in the corner, sitting by herself, facing the wall. She looked like a crumpled-up cupcake wrapper, and Mayfair decided to leave her alone. Maybe she could relay a message to her through Peppertina when she saw her coming out of the girls' restroom. Mayfair went after her, but Peppertina was quick, as she ran off and disappeared into the sea of children on the Lower Yard.

The Lower Yard wasn't quite as cool as the Upper Yard; it was more of a kiddie playground. The children looked like goofy animal crackers, still with their daycare and pre-k cuteness, moved around like puppies, and made sounds like they were playing in mud and puddles. Mayfair spotted Peppertina over by the swings.

"Hey, Peppertina, is Xembi all right?" Mayfair asked.

Peppertina started across the yard with the other kids when the first bell rang. "No, not really," Peppertina said off-handedly. "Those girls were mean to her, so she's probably going to go to home school," Peppertina said, remembering the conversation she had with Xembi the night before.

"Wait, what? She's going to home school because of what happened?" Mayfair said. She couldn't believe it. Xembi, her best friend at Maverick Elem, and probably in the whole world, was leaving for home school. It was really too bad Peppertina wasn't able to explain that home school was a last resort if the mean-girl situation wasn't resolved. She left Mayfair standing there in shock.

When Mayfair got to class, she noticed right away that Xembi had a wall up around her that was not only fireproof but it was also fortified with a layer of bulletproof protection that quietly said, "LEAVE ME ALONE!" Everyone felt it, including Erica Ross and LaDera Levitt, who smartly decided not to pick with her. Mayfair wrote Xembi a note that said:

### I hope you are all right. – Mayfair

When Jonathan Chang passed it to her, Xembi read it, then she balled it up and put it inside her desk. Mayfair was crushed.

She almost started to cry because she thought that Xembi thought that Mayfair was just another mean girl, too, and Mayfair was afraid she had lost her best friend forever. She couldn't even concentrate on Mr. Freelander's Language Arts lesson, and was hardly excited for the guests he had lined up after lunch.

During recess, Xembi stayed in class, and Mr. Freelander tried to find out what was going on but hit right up against her wall. "Is everything okay? How do you feel today? Don't you want to go out for recess?" Mr. Freelander tried every which way possible to get Xembi to open up, but nothing seemed to work. "Well, you can stay in here for now, but at lunchtime you will have to find someplace else to go. I have to check on the special guest we're having tomorrow, so..."

The noise in the cafeteria was annoying, so Xembi went to the Upper Yard and sat with Mrs. Stone for lunch. Golden Arms Chance immediately spotted her from his position near the monkey bars, and boy, was he ever happy to see her. Mayfair caught sight of Xembi, too, and didn't want to play High Jump anymore. Playing with Kiara Campbell and under the mean, watchful eyes of Erica and LaDera had turned the game into a lifeless chore. Mayfair's patience was just about used up. She was on edge and could blow at any second. No wonder The Snootish Girls kicked Kiara out. Nothing but a lot of no fun.

Sandra Jang was on a roll, and she surprisingly made the incredibly hard armpit jump, something she hadn't been able to do and was rather proud of herself until she noticed Kiara giving her an ugly side-eye. "Whatever," Sandra mumbled, and restrained herself from rolling her eyes.

Trendy Brown rolled her own eyes for her and mumbled back, "Kiara's just jealous because she can't even do the hip jump."

Truth was, only a few girls on the Upper Yard could get past the armpit jump, and the only one who could do the Skyscraper was, of course, Tayla's girl Sekoya. Rachel Ward was up next and tried to do the armpit jump, but her foot got tangled up in the rubber band rope and she tripped.

It was the chic Tatum Nicole skirt and matching top she wore that made Kiara say, "You have to start over again." Rachel looked really nice in her outfit, and Kiara felt that only *she* could be the best dressed in the group, probably another reason why The Snootish Girls put her out. But that ghetto-fab track suit Kiara wore was fierce!

Rachel started to do the armpit jump again, when Erica grabbed the rope and said, "No! You gotta start *over*-over again!" Erica yelled.

Even LaDera knew that Rachel was allowed another turn, and she'd have to stay at the armpit level until she made it. Those were the rules, but none of it mattered because Kiara made up new rules on the spot, and whatever Kiara wanted, Erica and LaDera made sure she got it. Rachel's feelings were hurt, but she was also mad at Kiara's cheating ways, forcing her and the other girls to play with her every day. She was fed up with Erica and LaDera, and apparently, when Rachel was mad, she came out of her shell.

"But that's not fair," Rachel quietly said, but loud enough for everyone to hear.

The other girls looked at each other like, *Whaaaat? Did she really just do that? No way!* Rachel Ward, the girl who practically never said much of anything, actually said something, in defiance, and wasn't shy about it.

"Girl, bye! Go sit down somewhere!" Kiara said.

Rachel just kind of stood there for a moment and tried to keep the tears in her eyes from spilling out. She started to walk away, and Kiara looked at her like, *I know she's not walking away from me!* and grabbed Rachel by the arm and said, "I didn't say you could leave!"

Rachel wasn't fragile but she was definitely delicate, and when Kiara pushed her down on the bench and said, "Sit yo' butt down! You out the game now!" Rachel couldn't keep the tears from falling down her face, making her look like a sad little lonely doll that was kept in its original box for safe keeping.

The patience that was used up inside of Mayfair had squeezed out its last drop, as her anger bubbled its way to the top and boiled over, and she finally exploded. She was surprised at how level-headed she was when she got up in Kiara's face.

Kiara reared back and said, "What you gon' do, Miss Goodie-Two Shoes?" and laughed in Mayfair's face. She thought it was just the funniest thing to see Mayfair mad, like she wanted to fight.

Mayfair didn't know if she was upset for being laughed at or if her feelings were hurt because she wasn't being taken seriously.

"You can stand there all day, for all I care. You still ain't gonna do nuthin," Kiara said, and took notice of Mayfair's outfit. "Why you come to school wearin' some raggedy-lookin' clothes for and some busted-up shoes? Your mama let you leave the house looking like that? Shoot, I know my mama wouldn't," Kiara said in a lethal tone that knocked all of Mayfair's warrior-girl confidence right out of her. "You gonna stand there all day, May-May?" Kiara had suddenly started calling her May-May, which Mayfair hated, of course. "Go sit down next to your little friend over there. At least she's dressed better than you, May-May."

Mayfair didn't know what to do, so she just stood there, which enraged Kiara, and then she got all up in Mayfair's face.

"I told you to go sit your butt down!" Kiara shouted.

Mayfair snapped back in a nasty tone, "You can't tell me what to do!"

Then Kiara screamed, "GO SIT DOWN!" Then she suddenly grabbed Mayfair by the arm and tried to shove her over to the bench next to Rachel.

Mayfair snatched away from her and screamed, "LET GO OF MEEEE!!!!!!" and shoved Kiara to the ground before she ran off.

"What the...?" Demetrius Applethorn said, in total disbelief. He had just come on the yard and snuck a stick of chewing gum in his mouth, and mindlessly dropped the wrapper when he saw Mayfair shove Kiara Campbell and run away.

Mayfair was so humiliated that she blocked out. It was like the entire school yard that had been buzzing with children, had suddenly stopped, as if everything had come to a screeching halt, as if everyone were frozen in time, and Mayfair was the only one with a heartbeat. She walked across the yard, around the immobile children, and went to the kickball court where Terrell was, in mid-kick, as the ball hung in the air, while the boys all looked up at it. Mayfair looked at the empty spot where Xembi should've been with Mrs. Stone, and scanned the yard and found her sitting on the bench, way down in No Man's Land, near the chain-link gates of the yard. No one ever really played down there, even though there was a four-square box and hopscotch labyrinth. Xembi's crumpled-up cupcake-wrapper appearance was full of sadness, humiliation, and embarrassment, all rolled up into one lonely little girl, looking just as pitiful as ever. When Mayfair approached her and sat down next to her, it was as if she didn't even recognize her friend.

All eyes were on them, everybody from Kiara to Tayla and her girls, Sekoya, Channen, Penelle, Kenda, K'Lixia, Rezen, Nosha, Taronka, Simonay, and Tandra, who were all in position, ready to pounce if things got ugly. Lydia Jackson and Trendy Brown just stood there with their mouths wide open, while Rachel Ward and Sandra Jang kind of held on to each other. Jonathan Chang had his eyes on them while he hid in the tetherball line. Kade Bondshea gripped the football, with Deshawn Sanders, James Yoro, and Ryan Keefe behind him, all squinting to see. Jeorgie, Green Eyed Mike, and Nestor stopped talking kickball shop with Derrick Bay, for a look-see. Golden Arms Chance climbed on the monkey bars to get a better view. Demetrius Applethorn was still at the spot where he dropped the gum wrapper, chewing his gum in suspense. Even Pop Star Girl was looking up from her book.

While the girls sat there, Mayfair took notice of how nice the day was. It was as if it suddenly came to life with sounds of chirpy birds, happy sunshine, and miles of blue sky with clouds in it that floated by like balloons, as it wrapped its arm around Xembi and Mayfair and said, "There, there, little ones. Everything will be all right." There was always comfort in nice weather that was reminiscent of those days long gone by, that only Mayfair's and Xembi's parents could appreciate, where you could walk down to the corner store with your neighborhood friends for missile pops, or for a group bike ride, a day trip to the beach with your family, or just to hang out with your school friends on a Thursday afternoon during lunch time.

Finally, Mayfair said, "So is it true that you're going away to home school now?"

"I dunno. I thought about it. Did Peppertina tell you?" Xembi said.

"Yes, but are you?"

"Maybe next year. I dunno."

"Oh...the way she said it, I thought she meant you were going on Monday, like tomorrow's your last day here."

"Oh..."

"But if it was true, I was going to tell you that I didn't want you to leave because you're my best friend."

Hearing this swelled and mended Xembi's fragile heart, as she wiped away a few tears through a faint smile.

The girls seemed to be insulated from the rest of the school yard, down in No Man's Land, so they were startled when the entire class gathered around them in a collective apology. Everyone felt bad for some reason or another, but mostly for kicking Xembi to the curb when Erica and LaDera told everyone not to talk to her anymore. The boys were sincerely humbled and said sorry, then headed back to the basketball court. Seeing the whole class apologize, Erica and LaDera watched from across the yard and started to feel some kind of way about how horrible they had been to Xembi. They inched their way over and kept their eyes to the ground as they tried to apologize, and then quickly ran off to the girls' restroom. Sandra Jang, Trendy Brown, Rachel Ward, and Lydia Jackson stayed with Mayfair and Xembi, and Leah Olomua looked like she wanted to stay, too. Mayfair grabbed her by the arm and pulled her down next to her so she wouldn't have to decide on her own.

Terrell called out to Golden Arms Chance, "You getting back in the game?"

"Maybe later," Chance said, and wandered down No Man's Land to see Xembi.

When Sneaks and Q-Tech tried to discreetly inch their way over, Mayfair waved at them to join the group, and they gave hearty fist bumps to Chance.

The girls were sick of High Jump, so they sang songs like "Tumble Weed on the Roll," "Sissy Miss Prissy," and the old-school version of that Robin song that started off with, "*We're gonna ring-ring-ring to the rhythm-a-tic.*" Trendy Brown taught them that one.

* * *

Kiara, like everyone else, had been watching Mayfair and Xembi, and she just knew that Erica and LaDera were going to bring Mayfair back when they wandered down to No Man's Land. But when they ran past her and off to the restroom, she was left sitting there, still on the ground, totally confused, especially when Erica and LaDera never came back. It only took a total span of ten minutes for Erica and LaDera to break ties with Kiara, all of it having to do with the little chat they had with The Snootish Girls in the restroom, who, by the way, had missed everything that had just happened, that turned Erica and LaDera against Kiara.

The girls were pretending to take glam selfies in front of the mirror when Erica and LaDera came in.

"So let me ask you a question," Starmesha Collins said in her usual confrontational way. "Why y'all wanna hang out with Kiara for? All she gonna do is run game on you. Y'all don't need her. Shoot! I'm glad we got rid of her," Starmesha said as she inspected LaDera's look.

"Normally, I don't tell anybody who they can be friends with, but Kiara is not your friend. Okay?" Naomi Braithwaite said.

"She cute, but she ain't *that* cute," Shandelina Smith said.

Erica and LaDera were just in awe that The Snootish Girls were even talking to them. They were rather impressed and took heed to what they were telling them. The Snootish Girls were snooty and stuck up, but Kiara was just downright mean. It was right then and there that Erica and LaDera quickly realized they really didn't need Kiara to be popular. They could build their own brand of popularity. And that's exactly what they did, as they developed it at Maverick Elem and Glick Mid, cultivated it at Local High, and utilized it at State University, when they both majored in business and marketing, and became the city's trendiest marking duo, The Ross-Levitt Company, with a very chic clientele.

So it was definitely in their best interest to leave Kiara alone. When Kiara thought she was still the boss of Erica and LaDera, with all of her mystical powers, she was kicked to the curb, *again*! Third time that week.

\* \* \*

Well, after all the high drama during lunch, when the children went back to class, there was a group of Japanese men and a large taiko drum in the middle of the room, along with the aroma of spring rolls. When they saw Mr. Freelander and Ms. DeMauvé-Pflume each wearing a Kamikaze scarf wrapped around their heads, just like the ones the Japanese men were wearing, the children wanted one, too, and saw that they each had one on their desks.

"Everyone, I introduce to you, *Shiro-Chiyoko*," Mr. Freelander said.

One of the young men took a step forward and said, "Good afternoon. We are *Shiro-Chiyoko*. *Shiro-Chiyoko* means third son, child of a thousand generations. This is the taiko drum. We use it to bond with our given birth names and honor our ancestors. YASUO!"

The children jumped when he yelled his name but gave Yasuo an apprehensive applause.

"Wow! That scared me!" Demetrius Applethorn said as he grabbed his chest.

"I am TAMA!" Tama gave a thunderous beat on the drum that made the children jump again.

"I am JIRO!" Jiro took the bachi sticks from Tama and pounded the drum.

"And I am, Naoko." Jiro handed Naoko the bachi sticks, and he softly tapped the drum, at first, and then the drumming became harder, louder, and fast.

Suddenly, everything came to a stop. There was a knock at the door. It was Ms. Deckey. "What in the world is going on in here?" she asked. "We thought it was an explosion or something."

Mr. Freelander promised to keep noise level down to a minimum, and the rest of the afternoon was spent on the ancient tradition of the taiko drum. The spring rolls were so delicately delicious, and the children tried not to get the dipping sauce on their fingers before they were allowed to test the drum.

As three o'clock approached, Mr. Freelander almost forgot that he had to meet with Kade Bondshea's parents, so he and Ms. DeMauvé-Pflume got the children packed up, herded them downstairs eight minutes before the final bell rang, and had them lined up in the lobby by the front office. Kade cracked jokes with the guys to calm his nerves, but when both of his parents walked through the front entrance, the children went silent and stared up at them.

Vonda and Jahiem Bondshea looked like one of those couples on one of those hip-hop shows where there was a lot of arguing, lots of ghetto fabulousness, and blinged-out swag that swirled around in a gluttony of luxury and platinum-gold dreams. Kade resembled his father so much that they looked like twins. Jahiem Bondshea was a young and handsome, lightly caramel-colored man with a soft, deep voice and a gentle swag. He worked long shifts at the airport and rarely saw his son because of it. As soon as he walked in, he gave Kade a fist-bump followed by a quick hug, really wanting to pick him up for a bear hug but he didn't want to embarrass Kade in front of his friends. Vonda, on the other hand, oh boy...she was nuthin' nice!

Ms. DeMauvé-Pflume greeted Kade's parents, and Ms. Mothped arrived and opened the door to the conference room.

Kade's mother responded with curt hellos, like she was irritated, and glared at Kade. "Boy, get your butt in there and sit down! Always gotta cut up! I ought to whup your butt right now, making me come up to the school like this!" Vonda snapped, and Kade bowed his head and slunk inside the conference room.

The children weren't used to seeing Kade so crushed. Normally, he'd have something mouthy to say back, and Vonda made them uncomfortable, so when the final bell rang, the children couldn't get out of the school fast enough.

Everyone sat down at the conference table while Ms. Mothped set up the Skype session with Mr. Marci. Mr. Freelander and Ms. DeMauvé-Pflume could feel the tension between Kade's parents, and whatever was going on with them, Kade was glad they were both there. Well, glad that his father was there.

"Hi, Mr. Marci," Ms. Mothped said as Mr. Marci's face appeared on the large flat-screen TV that hung on the wall at the head of the conference table.

"Hello, Ms. Mothped. I think I see Ms. DeMauvé-Pflume," Mr. Marci said, looking as upbeat as ever.

"Hey there, Greg," Mr. Freelander said.

Kade raised his head, totally surprised that Mr. Marci's first name was Greg, but quickly lowered his head when he saw his mother glaring at him.

"Hey, Trevor. Hey there, Kade," Mr. Marci said.

Kade raised his head and gave a weak, "Hey..."

"Sit up! I said SIT UP!" Vonda viciously said.

"Can you not scream at him? You don't always have to talk to him like that," Jahiem said as he tried to remain calm.

"Well, how else am I supposed to talk to him? He doesn't listen!" Vonda shot back.

Ms. DeMauvé-Pflume and Ms. Mothped exchanged uncomfortable glances. Mr. Freelander wanted to say something to break the tension but decided not to. Everyone sat in the thick moment of silence until Dr. Nickeldime finally arrived.

"So sorry I'm late! Had to take a phone call," Dr. Nickeldime said as he rushed in.

"I'm Kade's father, Jahiem Bondshea."

Dr. Nickeldime shook his hand. "And you must be Mrs. Bondshea," Dr. Nickeldime said.

Vonda gave a lifeless handshake.

"Ah, Mr. Marci! Glad you could meet with us," Dr. Nickeldime said, and looked through his detention notes on Kade.

"Does anyone want some bottled water?" Ms. Mothped asked.

Kade looked up and started to say, "I do!" but Vonda's nasty glare stopped him.

"Okay, so, we are here today because Mr. Bondshea spoke a notorious curse word aloud in class," Dr. Nickeldime said.

Vonda critically sized him up and thought he was a bit uppity, or bougie (boo-jee), as the young people say, while Jahiem had the utmost respect for him.

"I'd like to say something on Kade's behalf," Mr. Marci said, as Kade tried to look at him out the corner of his eye, with his head still bowed. "Well, yes, Kade had an outburst of profanity, but he's more than that incident. He's actually a good student. He's hardly had any absences, and he's an active participant in class, never afraid that he might have the wrong answer. Kade is very social, and he's well-liked by his peers."

Jahiem seemed relieved of Mr. Marci's evaluation of his son. Vonda, on the other hand, was hardly impressed, with a look on her face that said *Are we done yet?*

"Yes, I agree. Since I've been substituting for Mr. Marci this week, I've observed that Kade has a strong curiosity for learning. He didn't use the offensive word towards anyone. He was just excited about what we were doing. But nonetheless, I had to report it because of the explicit language that was used," Mr. Freelander said.

"Notwithstanding the excellent behavioral reports from Mr. Marci and Mr. Freelander, a curse word or words used on school premises warrants a suspension and a week's worth of detention," Dr. Nickeldime said. He paused for a moment to see if Vonda had anything to say, which she didn't, and he was unaffected by her nasty attitude. So he turned his attention to Kade. "What do you have to say for yourself, Mr. Bondshea?"

All of Kade's usual bold swag and confidence was gone and replaced with a cautious little boy.

"Say you're sorry!" Vonda said.

"Sorry..." Kade said, trying not to cry.

"Kade, I'm disappointed in you. You're too young to be using that kind of language," Jahiem said in a calm yet firm tone.

"But Todd and Brian say stuff and Keisha don't be saying anything. And she be cursing at them all the time," Kade said.

Jahiem suddenly began to calmly seethe as he looked across at Vonda. Vonda acted like she didn't notice and was done with the meeting, ready to leave. Kade's parents had been separated for about a year, and Jahiem knew his son was spending a lot of time at his cousins' house but never liked it because he also knew that Todd and Brian weren't always a good influence on Kade.

"Is there anything else you'd like to say, Mr. Bondshea?" Dr. Nickeldime asked.

Kade kept his eyes on the table. When he looked at his mother, she gave him such a nasty glare, something Kade was used to. When he looked at his father, he saw how disappointed he was in him, and it hit Kade in his little underdeveloped core, as tears started to trickle down his face. He didn't want to disappoint his father, but there was also a build-up in Kade that was trying to get out.

He didn't have the words to describe how he wished his father didn't work so much. And Vonda did hair at the very posh Hair Pascal, which kept her busy and with little time for her son. He liked hanging out with his cousins, Todd and Brian, and his Auntie Keisha was all right, but he wanted more time with his parents and wished his mother was cool to be around instead of always mad at him. As curvy and pretty as Vonda was, she was downright mean! She had no joy, no happiness, no fun in her life, no nothing. Everything on the outside about her was perfect, like the expensive hip-hugging jeans she wore, the glossy manicure, her expensive hair weave, the high-end couture handbag, even the car she pulled up in; it was on point! But Vonda's words and nasty looks could cut a person with the precision of a laser beam, and sometimes Kade wondered if his mother even loved him.

"Why are you crying? You got a lot of nerve, sitting up here with tears streaming down your face!" Vonda said. Her words stabbed Kade like a dull butter knife.

Jahiem ignored Vonda's nastiness and put his arm around

Kade. "Son, why are you crying?" Jahiem's concern made Kade cry even harder, and he pulled Kade out of his chair and held him in his lap.

"I'm sorry for cursing in class," Kade said between heaving sobs.

"You're not sorry! You just saying that because you're crying!" Vonda snapped.

That's when Jahiem snapped. "Can't you see that our son is upset? He cursed in class but there's something else going on, and as of today, right now, I'm taking him over to my dad's house. He ain't going to Keisha's house no more!" Jahiem said.

"Well, maybe if you were home, he wouldn't have to go to Keisha's all the time!" Vonda snapped back.

"You know I have to work! And if I didn't, you'd be complaining about that! I am sick of your attitude and how you treat our son! Kade is a good kid, and you act like you can't stand to be his mother!"

The silence that Vonda gave in her response was loud and clear. It was true—she didn't like being a mother. She didn't like that it took up most of her free time, which was why she sent Kade over to her sister Keisha's house, even when Vonda didn't have to work. She loved her son, but she didn't like taking care of him. She just didn't have that nurturing element that most mothers had, and maybe if she stopped pretending that she did, life would've been better for everyone.

Jahiem, on the other hand, loved being a dad and wished he had more time to spend with his son. He didn't mind working those long hours at the airport, but he didn't know how it was affecting Kade.

"Fine, take him to your dad's house. I gotta go anyway," Vonda said as she grabbed her purse, got up, and walked out like she had to catch a hot flight to Vegas. It didn't look like it, but that was probably the best thing she could've done for her son.

Later that evening, Jahiem picked up most of Kade's belongings at Vonda's place and took them over to his father's house. Kade felt a little guilty that he wasn't with his mother anymore but had no problems calling his grandfather Papa and his grandmother Mama. It was the beginning of home-cooked meals every night instead of processed food for dinner, and watching shows like *The Jeffersons* and *Everybody Loves Raymond*, with his grandmother, and Kade discovered that those shows weren't as boring as he thought they were.

Kade absorbed everything at his grandparents' house: the way they cleaned up the dishes after dinner, made him say his prayers before bedtime and say grace before dinner, and learned how to play spades by watching his Papa and his buddies play. He was put on punishment for a week, without his PlayStation, because of the F-bomb he dropped in class. He had to watch the six o'clock news with Papa every night and get his homework done before dinner, and Kade rather enjoyed the new structure and discipline in his life. It was the care and healthy attention he needed from Vonda but never got. Since his grandparents lived near James Yoro and Ryan Keefe, he no longer took the school bus with Deshawn Sanders, and started walking home with James and Ryan. Not long after Kade moved in with his grandparents, his father went to court and got full custody of his son. After that, Kade rarely saw much of his mother, which was fine with him.

Friday

The next morning, Dr. Nickeldime called Kade to his office.

"Have a seat, Mr. Bondshea."

Kade had never been in the principal's office, not even when Mrs. Hocklock was there. He had heard how sunshiny her office was, but Dr. Nickeldime's décor was more masculine, with bold wood grain and blocks of sturdy colors in brown and mahogany.

"How are you this morning?" Dr. Nickeldime asked.

"I'm good," Kade said.

"Well, very good that you're good, Mr. Bondshea. The reason I asked you to my office was to finish up with our conference. I've decided that you will not be suspended, because I believe you blurted out the infamous word in exuberance rather than with malicious intent. So basically, you're off the hook. However, if you blurt out another expletive, in any form or fashion, you will be suspended under the city's school-district guidelines. Is there anything you want to say?"

Kade thought for a moment and finally said, "Thank you, Dr. Nickeldime."

"You're most welcome. One more thing. How are things at home?"

This question caught Kade off guard, as he stared at Dr. Nickeldime. No one had ever asked him about how he was doing or feeling, and nobody ever asked how things were with him at home. After meeting Kade's parents and witnessing how he was in the middle of their ruptured relationship, Dr. Nickeldime decided he'd check in with Kade every now and then. So when Kade stared at Dr. Nickeldime, he could see that he was someone who was genuinely concerned about his well-being, and it deeply touched him, as tears started to well up in his eyes. He thought of his mother, and suddenly missed her. He knew she loved him, in her difficult way, but it still hurt that he wouldn't be with her anymore. "It's all good. I'm staying with my grandparents now…"

"Glad to hear that. And what a commendable father you

have. You should be proud to have a father who is concerned with his son's education, whether it be academic or universal," Dr. Nickeldime said, and handed Kade a tissue as he stood up and shook his hand. "Have a good day today, and no bad words."

Kade had a good rest of the school year.

When Kade went up to the school yard and found his buddies, everything was status quo, except that Kiara Campbell was nowhere to be seen or found. Eventually, it got around that she was absent from school. Even a tough-as-nails child like her could only take so much of getting kicked to the curb, so she faked a nauseating stomachache that allowed her to stay home that day.

Xembi seemed to be all right, still a little weary of Erica and LaDera, but was glad she wasn't being singled out and picked on anymore. During lunch, Chance, Sneaks, and Q-Tech ate with each of their little lovelorn crushes down in the cafeteria, and it just so happened that Jonathan Chang had somehow become a little smitten with Lydia Jackson. He thought her penmanship was pretty, he liked how she neatly kept the inside of her desk, and when he got a glimpse of how neat her Language-Arts homework was written out, he knew he liked Lydia as more than just a friend. All he could do was sit next to her during lunch and hope that maybe she'd get the hint. So that only left Sandra Jang and Trendy Brown without lunch dates, but they were fine with it. Other than that, nothing really interesting happened on the yard that day.

But knowing there was a cultural experience after lunch, the children were excited to see what Mr. Freelander had in store for them. When they tried to ask him about it, Mr. Freelander seemed vague.

"Well, I thought about asking the Tapping Cats to visit us today," Mr. Freelander said.

"Who are they?" Green Eyed Mike asked.

"They're an elderly group who does some dynamic tap dancing," Mr. Freelander said.

"We would've liked that, Mr. Freelander!" Nestor said.

"But then I thought about inviting Ms. Grace Parker, the opera singer, but I figured you guys wouldn't be interested in that."

"Yes we would!" Kade Bondshea said.

"I guess I'm just a little sad because today is my last day, and I wanted to spend it with all of you, so we're just going to have our party and create memories," Mr. Freelander said, disappointing the children.

The whole week was a total blast, and they were looking forward to an exciting end to their week, but little did they know that Mr. Freelander did have something planned, something they would've never expected in a million years.

# Chapter Fourteen

So when the children made their way back to class after lunch, they were really disappointed to see that the classroom hadn't been rearranged and that there wasn't anybody else in there with instruments and weird-looking clothes.

"I was thinking that we could have some free time this afternoon. You can read, draw, or talk quietly amongst yourselves," Mr. Freelander said, as a low murmur of disappointment filled the room.

Xembi and the other girls hovered around Mayfair and Rachel's desks; Jeorgie and his two best buds talked kickball shop with the other boys; and nobody seemed to notice when Mr. Freelander put a chair in the front of the class.

There was knock at the door.

"Oh my God! Who is it?" Jeorgie said as he jumped up from his seat.

"Did you trick us, Mr. Freelander?" Kade asked.

The children watched in anticipation as Mr. Freelander got up to answer the door. When he opened it, there was an old man standing there, holding a guitar case, and when he stepped inside the classroom, lo and behold, it was none other than Mr. Mean Old-Man Jones! The look on Jeorgie's face was priceless.

"What is he doing here?" Jeorgie asked, and gasped like he needed a drink of water.

Mr. Mean Old-Man Jones sat down in the chair in the front of the classroom, and the children were so quiet that you could almost hear a mouse tiptoeing on cotton. Just as Mr. Freelander was about to introduce him, Mr. Mean Old-Man Jones held his hand up. "I got this," he said, and opened his guitar case and strapped a vintage acoustic guitar across his chest. He carefully checked it to make sure it was still in tune and then quietly strummed out a little song.

"Hey, pretty baby...
My, oh, my...
Hey, little lady, you sure do got my eye.
Next time, when you walk by...
Please, don't be shy"

"I call that 'Hey, Pretty Baby,'" Mr. Mean Old-Man Jones said.

He had such a commanding presence that it held the children captive. They were too scared to clap, too afraid to move. Jeorgie couldn't believe it. He couldn't believe that Mr. Mean Old-Man Jones was in his class, at that very moment, playing the guitar!

"My name is John Arrow Ever, but word on the street says my name is Mr. Mean Old-Man Jones. I've lived in this area, in my house, for the last forty-five years, and I've seen all the kids come and go, but it wasn't until I got my dog—by the way, I've heard on the streets that she's called Monster—that I started having a little trouble with some of the kids who come and go, and I see three of them in this classroom."

Jeorgie, Green Eyed Mike, and Nestor all froze. Jeorgie held his breath; Green Eyed Mike just wanted to go hide in Ms. DeMauvé-Pflume's coat that she had hanging up in the back of the class; and Nestor tried to give a brave face but collapsed under the pressure and put his head down on the desk with a *thunk*!

"Come here, young man," Mr. Mean Old-Man Jones said.

Jeorgie looked around the room and pointed at himself.

"Yes, I'm talking to you, son. Could you come up here, please?"

Jeorgie's heart pounded, and if he could've run away, he would've headed straight for the girls' restroom and crawled inside one of the stalls and hid there forever. Jeorgie got up and reluctantly went to the front of the class. He just stood there, looking pitiful as ever, as Mr. Mean Old-Man Jones examined him.

"What is your name?"

"Jeorgie."

"Jeorgie, what?"

"Jeorgie Sterling."

"Do you know who I am?"

Jeorgie pretended like he had no clue who Mr. Mean Old-Man Jones was. "Um, I'm not sure," Jeorgie said.

"Uh-huh. Well, let's just see about that," Mr. Mean Old-Man Jones said, and strummed his guitar.

"This young fella here, don't know who I am.
I said, this young fella here, don't have a clue...
Who I am.
But I see him every morning, almost like he's part of my fam.
He sees my dog and just don't give a da—"

The children gasped in terror but were excited.

**"I said, he sees my dog and never has any ham.**
 **Before I can get to my front door,**
 **When I hear all that flimflam,**
 **This young fella and his friends...**
 **All scram"**

The children wildly applauded, and Mr. Mean Old-Man Jones shook Jeorgie's hand. It was the song that finally broke the ice, and the children wanted to see what else Mr. Mean Old-Man Jones would sing about.

"I invited Mr. Ever as our last guest for the week because I thought some of you would like to meet him. Would someone like to ask Mr. Ever a question?" Mr. Freelander said.

Demetrius Applethorn's arm shot up. "How long have you been singing and playing the guitar?"

"Oh, let's see. I've been playing and singing for a long time. I learned how to play the guitar when I was about ten years old. Been playing ever since."

Leah Olomua raised her hand. "Are you famous? Like, do you play in a band?"

"Actually, Mr. Ever is one of the most renowned blues guitarists in the world," Mr. Freelander said.

"Not as renowned as I used to be, and I don't play in a band anymore or travel like I used to. I'm getting old, and all of that isn't good for my health and well-being. But, sometimes I get invited to play here and there, and sometimes people come and visit me," Mr. Mean Old-Man Jones said.

"But why you want to live in that little tiny house? How come you don't live in a mansion, if you're famous?" Kade asked.

"What am I gonna do in a mansion all by myself? You know how big those things are? Too many bedrooms for me. I'm fine with what I have. It may not be a mansion, but it's home," Mr. Mean Old-Man Jones said as he removed a handkerchief from the inside of his jacket and wiped his forehead. "How about another song?" Mr. Mean Old-Man Jones scanned the room and landed on Mayfair and Xembi. "Why don't the two of you come on up."

Mayfair and Xembi got up and stood beside him. Mayfair could smell the aroma of a cigar mixed with a hint of men's cologne that hovered around him, and she liked his sense of style that was stately and classic. She looked at his beautifully polished vintage guitar and noticed his manicured hands that gently strummed it.

"What are your names?"

"I'm Mayfair."

"Mayfair, what?"

"Mayfair Tootle."

"And what's your name?"

"Xembi Bower."

"Xembi and Mayfair...y'all best friends?"

"Yes," they chimed together.

Mr. Mean Old-Man Jones took a moment, then strummed out a tune.

"Two peas in a pod.
Just as pretty as can be.
One sweet, like a peach.
And the other, lovely as a plum.
Two little beauties.
Summer like fun.
Bumblebees.
Nectarines.

> Honey-scented pears.
> Sticky sweet
> Drip juice glistens
> Down your chin.
> Not quite like an orange or maybe an apple.
> But the peach and a plum
> Are the prettiest of friends."

The children applauded, and Mr. Mean Old-Man Jones wiped his brow again. "I think I'll call that 'Peach and Plum,' and if I can remember what I just sang on the spot, I'll record it and send you a copy of the song," he said.

Jeorgie's hand shot up.

"Don't worry, young Jeorgie. If I can remember the song I did about you, I'll record that too."

Then, of course, the other children started clamoring about wanting a song about them.

"Now that you've gotten to know a little bit about me, I'd like to introduce you to someone else that you might have heard of," Mr. Mean Old-Man Jones said as Mr. Freelander went to the door and opened it, and Ms. Mothped entered the room with Monster.

The children gasped, all happy to see a dog in their classroom.

"Most of you know my dog, and she isn't a monster. Her name is Maxine, and she's a gentle old soul. If you rile her up, she'll get crazy on you, but for the most part, she's a sweetie."

Jeorgie, Green Eyed Mike, and Nestor sat frozen again. This was not what they were expecting on their last day with Mr. Freelander, who was getting a kick out of their startled reactions.

"Would anyone like to come up and pet Maxine?" Mr. Mean Old-Man Jones asked.

When nobody got up or raised their hand, Leah Olomua finally got up in a huff. "You act all tough when she's behind the fence! I ain't scared," Leah said, loud enough for the boys to hear as she cautiously approached Monster, who started wagging her tail. Leah put her hand on Monster's head and rubbed her ears, when Monster suddenly jumped up for a hug.

"She won't hurt you," Mr. Mean Old-Man Jones said as Monster tried to lick Leah's face.

Then everybody wanted to pet Monster as she slowly evolved into Maxine. Green Eyed Mike and Nestor went up, but Jeorgie still had beef with the dog.

Despite the fact that he blamed her for always starting the morning fights, somehow it gave Jeorgie a sense of purpose, a sense of power, like he could handle anything that was thrown at him. It made him fearless, like a fearless leader who took on challenges and handled conflict with a strong resolve. Fighting with Monster gave Jeorgie the courage to be everything he wished he were in his daydreams, and not the goofy-looking child with a side of silly.

The whole class was staring at him.

"Now that you've thought it through, I think it's high time that you formally introduce yourself to Maxine," Mr. Mean Old-Man Jones said.

Jeorgie let out a big sigh, got up, went to the front of the classroom, and stood before his arch nemesis. He held his breath when she sniffed him over, from chest to toe. Then Jeorgie slowly reached his hand out and smoothed it over her head. She lifted a paw for more and the children all breathed a sigh of relief. Jeorgie petted her again and gave her a heartfelt hug, and Monster licked the side of his face.

It was the beginning of a new friendship. The boys never bothered Monster again, even brought doggie biscuits for her in the morning, and looked forward to seeing Mr. Mean Old-Man Jones from time to time, who would complain about Monster getting fat off of the doggie biscuits. He never talked down to the boys, and always talked shop with them like they were men, sitting around the big-screen TV, down in the man cave with cold drinks and good barbeque. But, in a few years, Mr. Mean Old-Man Jones wouldn't be able to live by himself anymore. His son would pack up his things and move Mr. Mean Old-Man Jones in with him. The children would miss him, especially seeing Monster every day, but for now, things were good, and eventually, Jeorgie would come to realize that he had always been a fearless leader, and it would take him to places he never dreamed he could go—like bungee jumping off of the world's tallest structure, and competing as a snowboarder in the *X-Games* trials, where he broke his leg in three places.

# Chapter Fifteen

*A-List Platinum HBD Party*
*Just for Xembi*
*Maverick Elem Cafeteria*
*This Friday @ 4:30 p.m.*

It was almost 4:30 p.m., and hardly anyone was there yet, except for Mayfair, Jonathan Chang, his little brother Timothy, Little Laura, and Peppertina. The cafeteria shimmered in balloons and streamers of bright pink, silver, and gold, with matching tablecloths and fancy gift bags that Mrs. DeMauvé-Pflume arranged, with the help of Xembi's mother, Binda. Jonathan's grandfather neatly folded and arranged the napkins, forks, and spoons, while Xembi's father and Mr. Dalewood helped her cousins Bryce and Brandeis set up Brandeis's DJ equipment. Mrs. Stone hovered over the buffet table of nacho platters, and arranged the sides of tomato-chunked salsa, guacamole, sour cream, and shredded cheese.

As soon as Brandeis set up the speakers, he started with his mix of Cutie Boy Band's latest single "White Sneaker," and then their hit single "Fan-O-Matic." He even brought his expensive turntables that he only used for high-profile events, because his mother, Xembi's Auntie Banata, informed him that Xembi's party was no different. Brandeis, who was a semi-famous local

DJ, better known as Loco Hero, cleared his schedule just to DJ Xembi's party.

And as she watched Timothy, Little Laura, and Peppertina cut up on the dance floor, Xembi's pit of dread turned into utter sadness, and she began to deeply hurt for her parents. Binda and Ted had spent money, time, and effort on the party, and when Xembi noticed her other cousin Bryce and his stank attitude—it came across that an eight-year-old's birthday party was totally beneath him—Xembi tried not to cry.

"The cake's here! Xembi, your cake is here!" Timothy yelled as Xembi's Uncle Bender carefully walked in carrying a large pink box that held her birthday cake.

"Yo, Bryce. Do me a solid and go get the rest of the stuff out of the car," Uncle Bender said, but Bryce acted like he didn't hear him. Uncle Bender set the cake down and poked Bryce on the shoulder. "What's the problem? I can see your attitude from a hundred yards back."

"I don't have a problem, Uncle Bender. I'm good," Bryce said, and tried to conceal his attitude.

"Well, I'm glad you're good, but make sure when you come back in here with the rest of the stuff, your good turns to great. Just because this little shindig ain't the VIP room down at the little hip-hop joint y'all hang out at don't mean you have to act all saditty up in here. Rearrange it, player. Ree-aah-rrrrange it."

Bryce fought to keep from rolling his eyes, and walked out of the cafeteria.

"This cat is acting like *he's* the DJ up in this joint," Uncle Bender said to himself.

Once Mr. Marci and Xembi's other cousin, Brownie, carried in the boxes of large, gooey chocolate cupcakes, everything was in place. The scene was set. The music was pumping, and it looked like no one was going to show up. Xembi couldn't keep the tears in her eyes from gushing down her face when she looked over at her father and thought about how he had taken her shopping for the new dress she was wearing and the new pair of patent-leather shoes she wore. She covered her eyes and started to sob uncontrollably.

"Oh no!" Peppertina gasped and ran over to her sister.

Mayfair returned from the restroom and rushed over to her friend.

Uncle Bender signaled for Brandeis to turn the music down, and everyone watched Xembi fall apart. Her mother and father started to see what was wrong, but Uncle Bender stopped them. "I got this."

Uncle Bender sat down next to Xembi and put his arm around her. She buried herself against him and wept. As soon as Bryce came back, Uncle Bender yelled, "Bryce, come here!"

Bryce reluctantly moped his way over, still looking sour as ever.

"You see this, Bryce? You did this."

Bryce kept quiet, knowing dang-gone well he had nothing to do with why Xembi was in tears.

"You don't think you had anything to do with this? You got the nerve to come up in here and act like you bigger and better than an eight-year-old birthday party, just 'cuz you a chump and think you all that and hang with a DJ? But hey, if you got something better to do, if Baby Girl's party is beneath you, then guess what? You can leave!"

"But I don't think this party is beneath me," Bryce flatly said.

"Understand this, bruh—if you don't change or rearrange your attitude, I'll put you out this joint myself!" Uncle Bender said while Peppertina, Little Laura, and Timothy all glared up at Bryce.

"It's just...."

"It's just what?" Uncle Bender said.

Ted and Binda walked up behind him, and Bryce started to say something but chose not to, with everybody staring at him. "Never mind. I'll just go wait in the car."

"Whoa, partner. I ain't gonna let you off the hook that easy. What's the problem? No need to be embarrassed. We all family here. What's got you all uptight?"

Everyone waited. Bryce looked like he could've shed a few tears himself, and Binda gently put her arm around him.

"Well?" Uncle Bender impatiently said.

"My girlfriend broke up with me this morning." He felt like an idiot just for saying it out loud.

"That's what got you all out of shape? Sorry to hear that, but guess what? There are other fish in the sea, other fields to graze upon, and a lot more stars in the sky. We gon' talk about you and your situation later, but you apologize to Baby Girl."

"Sorry, Xembi."

"Well, that was lackluster. Maybe you *should* go and sit in the car for a minute, 'cuz you bringing us all down, bruh. And we can't have no party poopers up in here. Ain't that right?" Uncle Bender said as Bryce slowly walked away.

"Come on back when you think you can handle it."
Uncle Bender then turned his attention to Xembi. "Listen to me, Baby Girl. If nobody shows up, ain't no thang. Nothin' but a dang chicken wang. You feel me? We have enough people right here, right now, to party with you." He noticed Jonathan's grandfather patiently sitting across the cafeteria with his arms folded and legs crossed. "Well, I don't know about him over there, but I bet he's down for something to pop off. I wouldn't be surprised if he ended up pop-locking it down the Soul Train Line."

She looked over at Jonathan's grandfather and it made her smile.

"Wipe those tears away, girl. It's your birthday and you should be happy. You got your cute little outfit on, looking all pretty." He looked over at Mayfair. "And look at sister-friend over here. Got her hair all nicely coiffed and styled."

"Look at me! Look at what I got on," Timothy said as Uncle Bender checked him out.

"Oooh weee! Young man here is all spiffed up. Gotta say, I like the way you're wearing your shirt. That's pretty cool, bruh. Right on!"

Timothy beamed with fashion pride.

"What about me? Do you like my hair?" Little Laura asked.

"Yes, indeed. Your hair reminds me of some soft, silky sunshine, and that pretty little flower you got tucked to the side is just high fashion all the way around. You go, girl!"

Little Laura blushed.

"And Tina, my girl. Peppertina! You always know how to rock the house with your glitter and glam."

Peppertina looked down at her feet. She was wearing a pair of open-toed dress sandals.

"Look at that! Even got the glitter on your little toes. That's how you rock the house, baby!"

Uncle Bender stood up and slapped Timothy a high-five. "Let's get this joint rockin'. Brandeis, pump that music up, baby. Pump it!" But Brandeis was nowhere to be found. "Where'd he go?" Uncle Bender asked.

"Well, I think he had to take a call and went outside," Ms. DeMauvé-Pflume said.

Uncle Bender looked at her as if he were just noticing her for the very first time. "Well, aren't you lovely on the eyes. If you were a little bit older and I was a little bit younger, we could meet somewhere smack-dab in the middle...."

Ms. DeMauvé-Pflume was taken aback but flattered that he implied that she was a young woman, even though she was probably twenty years older than him.

"Uncle Bender, that's really rude," Brownie said, who had overheard his flirty pick-up line.

"Baby, black don't crack, and when you see a bejeweled treasure such as this lovely cup of café au lait, how you *not* gonna say nuthin' and pass that up?" Uncle Bender's cell phone chimed in a text alert. "Oh, Lawd. It's Bryce. Let me go check on the boy and see if he needs my shoulder to cry on. Po' thang," Uncle Bender said as he left the cafeteria.

"Sorry about that. My uncle is just, all over the place," Brownie said to Ms. DeMauvé-Pflume.

"Oh, no need to apologize, my dear. Your uncle is quite the charmer. Very charismatic. I found no offense in his flattery," Ms. DeMauvé-Pflume said, suddenly appearing a bit more regal and stately.

"Xembi, why were you crying?" her mother asked.

"I just, I dunno...I guess I'm just afraid that no one will show up. And you and Daddy did all of this for nothing," Xembi said, and tried not to cry again.

"Well, we'll just have to wait and see. Do you want to open your presents?"

"Um, sure."

"Here, Xembi! Open mine," Timothy said, and grabbed his present off of the gift table and handed it to her.

"Jonathan! We're opening presents now!" Timothy yelled.

To Xembi's surprise, and everyone else's, Timothy's small, rectangular gift turned out to be a pack of the elusive Digital flavored NowLaters.

"Wow, Timothy. Thank you," Xembi said.

Timothy's hyper-activity kicked into gear, and he excitedly hopped around on one foot. "You're welcome. I got it from my sister, out of her purse, when she wasn't looking."

"You did WHAT?!" Jonathan said.

It was the first time it dawned on Timothy that snooping around inside of his sister's purse was going to get him in trouble. "Well, it was just sitting there, and I thought Tina didn't want it, so I gave it to Xembi."

Jonathan let it slide. He knew at some point Timothy would eventually get caught doing something stupid again, so...

Xembi had never tried the Digital flavored NowLaters, and she shared them with the group.

"The flavor is intense," Jonathan said.

Everyone agreed.

Then, one of the cafeteria doors quietly opened.

Rachel Ward peered in, and Timothy jumped for joy. Xembi and Mayfair were glad to see her, too. She had a gift bag and handed it to Xembi.

"Guess what we're eating? A Digital NowLater," Timothy said.

Xembi gave her one, and they all watched for Rachel's reaction, which was mildly ecstatic.

The cafeteria doors quietly opened again, and Lydia Jackson, Sandra Jang, and Trendy Brown came through, all nicely dressed in their best Tatum Nicole outfits, bearing gifts. The doors opened again, as Erica Ross and LaDera Levitt came in, looking extra fabulous, each with a gift for Xembi.

Everyone just kind of stood around, not sure what say or do. After a few minutes, the doors quietly opened again, and everyone was surprised to see that it was Leah Olomua, and she looked absolutely amazing! But she seemed awkward and very uncomfortable with her girly make-over. All she had on was a pair of really cool jeans and a girly T-shirt, but OMG! Her hair! It had soft curls in it, and she looked like the beautiful Samoan princess that her family always knew she was. She still had the tomboyish gait in her walk, but overall, she looked rather sassy.

No one dared to give Leah a compliment, unsure of how she would take it. She looked around the cafeteria and noticed that it was just the girls in their class. "We don't need the boys, anyways. They'd mess it all up. Jonathan, you can go now," Leah jokingly said, and everyone started laughing.

By now, Uncle Bender and Brandeis returned, minus a brokenhearted Bryce. "That's what I'm talking about. Now this party can get into gear," Uncle Bender said.

Just as Brandeis pumped out Penelope's "Lip Gloss Wish," the cafeteria doors opened again. This time it was Jeorgie, Green Eyed Mike, and Nestor who came in. As usual, the three of them were in a deep in conversation, each holding a gift, oblivious to everyone. They wandered over to Xembi and handed their gifts to whomever took them, then sat down at an empty table and carried on with their discussion.

The doors opened again, and Demetrius Applethorn appeared with a large gift and gave it to Xembi. "Happy birthday, Xembi," Demetrius said, and sat down with Jeorgie and the others.

The doors opened again, and Kade Bondshea, Deshawn Sanders, James Yoro, and Ryan Keefe walked in.

"Thanks for inviting me to your party, Xembi," Kade said as he and the others went over to Jeorgie's table.

The doors opened again, and Derrick Bay wandered in. "Hey, Xembi. Birthday wishes and Earth day blessings to you," Derrick Bay said, with an ancient warrior bow. Then he headed over to Jeorgie's table.

"Wow! Everybody's here. Well, everybody in our class, not counting Derrick Bay. What do you think of that?" Mayfair asked.

She noticed that the girls were on one side of the cafeteria, while the boys were clustered together at Jeorgie's table. Uncle Bender noticed it, too, and just as he was about to mix things up, the cafeteria doors slowly opened, again.

All heads turned to see who it could possibly be, as Sneaks and Q-Tech entered. Mayfair was so happy to see them, and Rachel was just over the moon. Sneaks and Q-Tech just kind of stood there, not sure what to do or where to go.

"You guys actually came!" Mayfair said, almost wanting to hug them.

Sneaks tried not to lose any cool points, and kept his googlie-eyed crush on low, while Q-Tech and Rachel grinned at each other. Mayfair pointed the way over to Jeorgie's table, and Sneaks was relieved to see boys at the party.

Mayfair was so excited about how the party was suddenly turning out, and said, "Oh my God, Rachel, this is going to be the best party ever! Xembi didn't think anybody was going to come, but..."

The doors opened again, as heads turned to see who it was, and the girls were shocked. LaRae Davis, Shandelina Smith, Naomi Braithwaite, Starmesha Collins, and Skyy Jones walked in the cafeteria like they owned the place, dressed to the hilt, hair styled to the gods, attitude galore, and happy to see Mayfair at the door.

"Hey girl, is it turnt up yet?" Skyy said as she and her girls scanned the cafeteria, quite impressed with what they saw.

"Oh! It's about to be lit up in here!" Starmesha said.

They all made a beeline to Xembi, with their gifts and a hug.

"Oh my God! Who is that?" LaRae said, pointing at Brandeis.

"That's my cousin," Xembi said.

"Girl, he cute! And who is that?!" LaRae said when she saw Bryce enter through the back of the cafeteria.

"Oh, that's my other cousin."

Xembi couldn't believe it. Maverick Elem's five most notoriously popular girls were at her party, and yet Xembi couldn't recall giving them an invitation. Must've been Mayfair.

"Dang, girl, you got some cuties up in your family," LaRae said.

"But why are all of the boys over there and the girls over here?" Naomi noticed.

"Oh my God! Leah! Is that you?!" Shandelina squealed.

Leah wanted to hide and die.

"Look at you! See, I knew you could look cute. You should dress like this all the time and stop wearing all of that baggy stuff," Shandelina said.

"And look, she even got a butt and everything! Dang, girl, I'm jealous," Starmesha said.

The girls oooh'd and aaah'd over Leah's hair. Leah was surprised that The Snootish Girls even knew her name.

The cafeteria doors opened again, and Mr. Akrahm from the S&K walked in, carrying a large gift bag. Everyone was surprised to see him, and the boys started chanting, "RAHM-RAHM-RAHM-RAHM!" Mr. Akrahm waved hello, made his way over to Xembi, and handed her the bag. The boys gave fist-bumps and handshake-hugs to Mr. Akrahm, and asked a bunch of questions:

"You invited Mr. Akrahm? Wow!" Someone said to Xembi.

"What's up, Mr. Akrahm?"

"Where's Mr. Fariq?"

"Did you give Xembi candy for her birthday?"

Xembi's mother introduced herself.

"I was so happy to get an invitation to Xembi's party. My business partner and dear brother, Fariq, really wanted to come, but you know, he has to mind the store. I am so glad that I've gotten to know Xembi, and all of the kids, really. Thank you for inviting me," Mr. Akrahm said.

After that, Brandeis pumped the music up and hit the jackpot with Patholo-G's "Don't Know," and every child in the cafeteria went nuts over it as Timothy led the way to the dance floor. With all the dancing going on, no one noticed that the cafeteria doors had slowly opened. . .again.

The boys in Mr. Marci's class would argue about this for the rest of their grade-school lives, but Jeorgie would claim the honor of spotting Damarcus first, who poked his head around the doors. Actually, it was Little Laura who first saw him and said, "Look who's here!" Being that she was Jeorgie's sister, it only made sense that she had said it to him when, in actuality, she had said it to nobody in particular. So when Jeorgie let out a guttural yelp, everyone followed his finger that was pointed across the cafeteria at the doors, and that's when pure mayhem ensued. Damarcus, Keem, Terrell, TyRhaj, Golden Arms Chance, Phron Thompson, Big Julius, and Thad came through those doors like the larger-than-life sports stars that they were.

Jeorgie couldn't believe it. He was hyperventilating. "I can't believe what I'm seeing. This is...this is...I don't even have words to say what I'm seeing!" Jeorgie said.

Xembi couldn't believe it, either.

Leah Olomua was glad her mother made her dress up for the party because, finally, the boys could see that she really was just a girl who liked to play ball, and not some weird tomboy.

"I knew you weren't going to let me down," Mrs. Stone said. She had told the crew that if they didn't go to Xembi's party, they wouldn't be able to play One Fly Up for a week. She was happy to see them and dabbed away proud-mama tears from her eyes.

But it wasn't over yet. The doors opened again, and this time it was Tayla Reynolds and her girls Sekoya, Channen, Penelle, Kenda, K'Lixia, Rezen, Nosha, Taronka, Simonay, and Tandra who came in, and were just as fly and fierce as The Snootish Girls. As soon as they heard the music, they all got into formation and strutted their stuff across the cafeteria, lip syncing to the song, with choreography, as if they were all in a music video, and slaaaayed! YASSSSS!

The party was on and poppin', and just when they thought it couldn't get any better, the doors opened...again! The adults should've braced themselves for what was about to happen, as chaos erupted when a high-end, haute-couture gift bag, followed by a hand with a sophisticated manicure that held a sleek cell phone, followed by a pair of icy-cold aquamarine eyes, peered around the door. The cafeteria exploded when the most popular girl at Maverick Elem, a title unknowingly bestowed upon her, who was simply known as Pop Star Girl to those who didn't know her name, came through the doors, and every child in the cafeteria completely lost it.

"What in the world is going on?" Uncle Bender asked in bewilderment. He kept his eyes on the cafeteria doors, not wanting to miss a thing.

The children were having an explosive meltdown over the presence of this one child, who seemed unfazed by the high-voltage reaction she was getting, when she spotted Xembi and gave her a heartfelt hug.

Gushy tears streamed down Xembi's face while Mayfair and some of the other girls cried and held onto each other.

The boys were blown away and instantly knew that whoever missed Xembi's party, those who weren't invited, or even those who were invited but chose not to attend, were all going to feel left out that they were not there for this momentous event.

But wait a minute....

Pop Star Girl didn't come alone. Three of her best girlfriends trailed in behind her, and if the student body on the Upper Yard at Maverick Elem thought Pop Star Girl had it going on, her friends took "it" and them to the next level, looking like they all went to one of those Manhattan private schools in NYC that cost ten thousand dollars a month!

"I don't know how Mayfair did it, but she said she was going to invite Pop Star Girl, and she's here. She's actually here!" Lydia Jackson said as she grabbed hands with Sandra Jang and Trendy Brown, and the three of them ecstatically jumped up and down in total bliss.

Mayfair found her in Ms. Plan's class, reading a book, and remembered that the last time she spied on Pop Star Girl, she waved hello to Mayfair. So Mayfair hoped she was still friendly and went in and said, "Hey, um, my friend Xembi is having a birthday party next week, and we wanted to invite you, and a plus-one. So, here's your invitation," Mayfair said, and quickly turned to leave. Those icy-cold aquamarine eyes were too much to handle.

"What's your name?" Pop Star Girl asked.

"It's Mayfair."

"Oh, okay. Thank you."

When the children thought things couldn't get any more unexpected, things were about to get cray-cray-CRAZY!

No one saw him since everyone was recovering from Pop Star Girl and her entourage, but when the One Fly Up Crew noticed him standing there, they were so overwhelmed that they couldn't hold back the tears. There he was, in the flesh, Flint Swinns, the star quarterback at Local High! When Jeorgie saw him, he collapsed to the floor. Every boy in the Ranunculus District who had a thing for sports, knew of Flint Swinns's trajectory path to becoming a legend.

His brother came in with him, and Mayfair blurted out, "That's the paper boy!"

Golden Arms Chance totally geeked out, and Uncle Bender looked around at the adults, completely bewildered, and went over to the mic that was set up near the DJ table.

"What in the world is going on up in here? Everybody's crying and carrying on. Can somebody please tell me why y'all crying?"

The cafeteria quieted down, and Big Julius stepped up to the mic.

"What you got to say, bruh? Lay it on me," Uncle Bender said, and handed the mic to Big Julius.

"I'm just so happy to be here. At first, I wasn't going to come, not because of Xembi or anything, but I just wasn't going to come. And then Mrs. Stone told us that we had to, and now I am so glad I did, or else I would've missed all of this," Big Julius said.

"But why is everybody crying?" Uncle Bender asked.

"Man, I'm just, I dunno..." Big Julius said.

Derrick Bay ran up and took the mic. "See that guy over there? He's a legend and he's at this party."

Uncle Bender examined Flint Swinns and finally said, "Young bruh, could you come up here for a sec?"

Flint Swinns was used to the constant adulation at Local High but was a little surprised he was getting the superstar treatment at an elementary school.

"So let me get this straight. This young man here, is what got all the boys choked up, and I'm to assume that young lady over there is the one who has all the girls in a hissy? Well, now I guess I done seen everything," he said, and just shook his head. "You have anything you'd like to say?"

"Um, no, not really. Just hope it's all right that I crashed the party. I heard DJ Loco Hero was going to be here, and me and my brother wanted to come and check him out, so I asked my little sister Brenna if we could come with her. And uh...so, yeah... go Natives!"

The children wildly cheered like they were at the Super Bowl.

So Pop Star Girl had a name, and it was Brenna. The paper boy was her brother, and so was the legendary football star at Local High? Mayfair didn't see it at first, but they all had the same aquamarine-colored eyes, except that they weren't as cold-looking on the brothers.

"Does anyone else have anything they want to say?" Uncle Bender said with a slight sarcastic tone.

Jeorgie marched up and took the mic. "I'd just like to say that this is probably one of the greatest days in my life. Like, you have no idea how geeked I am to be here. First, the One Fly Up Crew shows up, and guys, it's just an honor to have you here..."

All the boys in Jeorgie's class applauded.

"...And then, I'm even more honored to be in the same room with Flint Swinns! This day will go down in Maverick Elementary School history."

Starmesha Collins grabbed the mic. This was starting to turn into an awards ceremony. "I'm Starmesha Collins, and me and my girls, LaRae, Skyy, Shandelina, and Naomi just wanted to give a big shout-out to Xembi and her BFF Mayfair for inviting us. Thank you!"

And then the doors had the nerve to slowly open AGAIN! Who could it possibly be now? Everyone was there. A high murmur flooded the cafeteria, with high-pitched shrieks and low-toned yelps in anticipation, as the children craned their necks to see who would step through.

"Oh, Lawd, here we go again," Uncle Bender flatly said.

It was Green Eyed Mike's older sister Davina, with Jonathan and Timothy's older sister Tina, along with Nestor's older brother Raymundo and their cousin Camilo, followed by Demetrius Applethorn's Uncle Ced. Demetrius smuggled in his cell phone and called Uncle Ced, who was parked outside, and told him he could come in. The children wildly applauded.

Tina and Davina came dressed to impress, like they were hitting up an underage club, and The Snootish Girls spied on them, thoroughly impressed.

"What is she doing here?!" Green Eyed Mike asked, and went right up to his sister and asked her what was she doing there.

"Because of DJ Loco Hero, duh!" Davina said, all annoyed.

"Tina's here! Tina's here!" Timothy said, and ran up to his big sister and gave her a tight hug.

"Will you get off of me!" Tina said and pried Timothy off.

Jonathan discreetly hid behind Derrick Bay while Tina scanned the cafeteria for him, and saw their grandfather waving hello at her.

Tina rolled her eyes and said to herself, "Really?"

"Can you take Timothy away and leave us alone?" Davina said.

Green Eyed Mike was mad at her. Maverick Elem was his spot. You never saw him going up to Local High, getting all up in Davina's face.

But Nestor, on the other hand, was happy to see his older brother Raymundo and their cousin Camilo.

"'Sup? Where's DJ Loco?" Raymundo said, and spotted Flint Swinns. "Oh, daaanggg! Flint is here? Whaaat?"

"Yup! This is the best party ever!" Nestor said, which Tina and Davina overheard, and they adjusted their attitudes.

Flint Swinns was single, handsome, and a catch, but they also put calculating eyes on Bryce and Brandeis.

"Hopefully nobody else is coming, 'cuz we can't feed *every*body," Uncle Bender said. "But before we get this party started, let's get the birthday girl over here. Come on, Baby Girl. Come on up. Don't be shy."

The cafeteria erupted into a rousing applause, and Xembi burst into tears again. Mayfair and Peppertina both took her by the hand and led her over to the mic, and everyone started chanting, "XEMBI-XEMBI-XEMBI!"

"I want to thank everyone for coming to my birthday party. I want to thank my mother and father..." Xembi couldn't go on. Too many emotions.

"Yeah, let's get Binda and brother-in-law up here," Uncle Bender said.

All Binda could say was, "Thank you all for coming," while wiping away a few of her own tears, overwhelmed by the children's gratitude and appreciation, especially after everything that Xembi went through with her week of dealing with Kiara Campbell.

Xembi's birthday was turning out to be no ordinary party, almost like one of those sweet-sixteen shows, and every child in there, including the Local High Natives, felt lucky to be there. Brandeis saw it too, so he pumped up the music and switched things up with Triality's "Snap It Back," and the place went wild! But when he flipped it and brought in some heavy bass that went into Twesta's "Double Up," it was total pandemonium that brought the house D-OW-NNNN! The moment was so electric that Flint Swinns, the paper boy, Tina and Davina, Raymundo and Camilo couldn't believe it. They were seeing DJ Loco Hero doing what he did best, and it was OFF THE CHAIN! His mixes were dope, the song choices on point, orbital, bombastic! The boys almost lost their minds over Dirty Cash's "Low Beat," and the girls formed a sister circle and sang their little hearts out along with LaAngel's "Light of Times."

Aside from finding out what Pop Star Girl's name really was, Mayfair also found out that she lived across the street from Sneaks, and that Q-Tech lived next door to Sneaks. It reminded her of her two Aunt Raquels, who both lived in the same apartment building. Q-Tech, by the way, spent some time with Rachel at the party, and she did her best to talk a little more, but he didn't mind it so much that she was super shy. Sneaks hung with the fellas, but whenever Mayfair was on the dance floor, he made sure he was her only dance partner.

Golden Arms Chance mustered up the courage to talk soccer shop with the paper boy and told him how the world-famous soccer player Brenton Bruger was Xembi's cousin.

"What? No way!" the paper boy said.

"There's his sister, over there," Chance said.

The paper boy was just as star struck at seeing Xembi's cousin Brownie as if he were looking at Brenton Bruger himself.

"Yeah, he's playing a few games in Côte d'Ivoire right now, in Africa, but whenever he gets back and has a game, I can get you tickets," Brownie said. She got Chance and the paper boy's numbers, and they tried not to lose their minds over getting tickets to a Brenton Bruger game.

The Snootish Girls managed to take glam selfies with Tina and Davina, while Derrick Bay and the One Fly Up Crew decided to call a truce and forget about whatever the old beefs were and let go of the stubborn grudges. Derrick Bay still saw them as a team of self-glorified ballers, but he kept that to himself.

When Flint Swinns wasn't trying to be part of DJ Loco Hero's crew, the boys hovered around him and talked about sports and Flint's future plans with football. "Well, my dad really wants me to go to his alma mater and play ball there, but I'm hoping I can convince him that I can play at State University."

Flint would bring his dad around to State University, eventually. He'd start as quarterback in his junior year, but by the time he was picked up by the NFL, his heart wasn't in it anymore. Flint lived out his father's dream and kept it alive until he walked away from football after his second season. He went back to college and got a degree in Sports Theory Mindset and became an instructor at State University. He eventually crossed paths with Xembi's father. After all those years ago, at Xembi's eighth birthday party, it took a minute for Ted to remember Flint.

"Hey, I know her! I went to her birthday party," Flint said, when he noticed Xembi's school picture on Ted's desk.

"You did?"

"Yeah, I don't remember her name, but she was turning eight, and the only reason I was there was because her cousin was the DJ."

Ted racked his brain, since it was so many years ago that Xembi had that crazy birthday party, and then the dots connected. "That was you? I remember now. The kids were going crazy over Flint Swinns. Oh my God! I never even put the two together. Wow...who knew back then that we would be working together? Wait 'til I tell Binda about this."

As one of the biggest birthday bashes of the year wound down, Uncle Bender had Brandeis play some old-school funk and got a Soul Train Line going, and there was Jonathan's grandfather, going down the line as he smiled, nodded, and waved at everyone, just like Uncle Bender said he would.

Xembi's birthday was a party for the ages, an event that the children would never forget.

Ever.

# Chapter Sixteen

*You're invited!*
*Nestor's Birthday Party*
*Saturday, May 12$^{th}$ at 3 p.m.*
*420 Moon Roof Circle*
*No RSVP*
*Just show up*
*See You Then*

<u>Nestor's Family Tree</u>

Nestor Reyes
|
Eva and Mateo
(parents)
|
Ingrid – Michella – Raymundo
(siblings)

Auntie Lu (Luana)
|
Nestor's aunt (his mom's sister)
Uncle Esteban (Auntie Lu's husband)
|
Auntie Lu and Uncle Esteban's children:
(Nestor's first cousins)
Malena – Bianca – Osias
|

Uncle Esteban's nephews (on his side of the family):
Juan Pablo – Elias – Luca – Abran
Nestor's uncles (his father's brothers):
Uncle Joaquin and Uncle Josue
(their children – Nestor's first cousins)
Camilo – Maribel – Diana – Jake – Alex – Savanah

Cousins of Nestor's on his late grandfather's side:
|
Hugo – Luna – Abigail – Silviana
(all of their children)
Priscilla – Caesar – Hector – Felix – Dexter – Lunita
Anaya – Jacinto – Ramiro – Nosario

Cousins on his grandmother's side:
|
Lobo – Achai – Putty – Agustina – Knucks – Big Chub
(all of their children)
Leo – Eladio – Caius –Gabriel – Thiago – Fabi – Socorro

Family friends:
|
Eduardo – Romina – Matias – Calixto – Amancio – Lucero
Eusebio – Cutie – Amora – Hombre – Juan Carlos – Emiliano
Paciano – Victor – Teresa - Jesus (Hay-soos)

Plus:
wives – husbands – girlfriends – boyfriends – and all of their children

Since Nestor lived the furthest away from Maverick Elem, everyone in his class made carpool arrangements to get to his birthday party. He could've gone to Perk Elementary, which was two blocks away from his house, but he wanted to go to Maverick Elem, which was where Raymundo and his older sisters went when they were in elementary school. Keeping family traditions was a big deal to Nestor.

The first carpool to arrive was Demetrius Applethorn's group. Kade Bondshea, Ryan Keefe, and James Yoro all hitched a ride with Demetrius and his Uncle Ced. There was enough room in the back seat for all of the boys, and they were so excited to ride in Uncle Ced's remodeled 1986 Oldsmobile Cutlass Supreme. It didn't matter to them that the body of his car was still in that matted gray primer color, awaiting its glossy make-over paint job. It was the twenty-two-inch rims, the massive sound system that was heavy on bass, and the newly upholstered seats that the boys were excited about, and when Uncle Ced turned up the volume on Ace Boom's song "Bottle Top," the boys knew every inch and inflection of the song and performed it as if they were Ace Boom himself.

Nestor's birthday party was on a lazy Saturday afternoon, with warm weather that was so perfect—it was like the day was handing out free samples of sunshine. When the boys pulled up to Nestor's house, Nestor's cousin Big Chub was in the driveway, manning a large barbeque grill loaded down with all kinds of meat, as the smoke from the charcoal woodchips floated around, and Chicano rap music quietly boomed from Big Chub's car, a red Dodge Magnum he called Miss Lola, that was written in fancy lettering on the driver's side. When Uncle Ced slowly rolled up and stopped in front of the house, Nestor's other cousins Gabriel and Thiago, who were out there with Big Chub, stood up in defense mode and got in position, ready for some weird confrontation, until Uncle Ced rolled down the window and Big Chub went over.

"Man, I thought it was about to be a situation, but when I saw all of those little heads in the back, man, I forgot it was Nestor's birthday. You can park right over here, behind me," Big Chub said, and Uncle Ced parked behind Miss Lola.

When everyone got out, Big Chub and Gabriel admired the rims on Uncle Ced's car.

"Go through there," Thiago said, and the boys followed the loud musica urbana that led them through the garage and to a door that opened to the backyard.

The boys just stood there and gawked at the size of Nestor's family. There was some dancing, lots of eating, a dominoes table, and a card game, with the DJ in the corner of the backyard.

"What's up, Nestor. Happy birthday," Demetrius said, and handed Nestor a gift.

"Dang, man, you got a big family!" Kade said.

Nestor's party looked more like a family reunion, with close to a hundred people there. When Mayfair and her carpool group arrived, Rachel Ward, Jonathan Chang, his little brother Timothy, and their grandfather were equally amazed at the size of Nestor's family.

"Mayfair, how come your dad's not staying? He can stay, you know," Nestor said.

"Oh, he's coming back. He had to go back home and get my little sisters, since there wasn't enough room for their car seats."

Everyone else in class arrived on time, including Mr. Marci, who was already there, feasting on one of Big Chub's grilled hot dogs.

Nestor's cousin Osias got things rolling. "I am DJ Osias..." Some of Nestor's relatives made low toned O sounds and raised their drinks. "Giving a shout-out to Nestor. Happy birthday, lil' homie. We're about to get things loud. Loud enough for the neighbors to call the cops..."

Nestor's mother wagged her finger at Osias and yelled, "Oh, no we won't! We won't be getting it that loud, Osias!"

"All right, Auntie Eva. We'll get it loud enough for the neighbors to come over and party."

Nestor's mother cut her eyes at Osias and gave him a stern warning expression.

When Somina's "Adivina Quien?" blasted from the speakers, all of Nestor's relatives jumped up and hit the center of the backyard and started dancing. And then, when Mayfair's father returned with her little sisters, the children were playing a game called Pass the Present, where a present gets passed around while the music is played, and when it stops, the child holding the present gets to unwrap the first layer of gift wrap. The gift gets passed around until it's down to the last layer of gift wrap. Since there were so many children at Nestor's party, there were at least ten gifts going around. Sandra Jang and James Yoro were two of the lucky ones who got to unwrap the last layer of gift wrap, and they each got a T-shirt with DJ Osias's logo on it.

Nestor's birthday party was festive, fun, and loud, and about twenty minutes into it, a very familiar face appeared, the last person on Earth Nestor expected to see. It was Flint Swinns.

"Nestor! What's he doing here? You invited him too?" Jeorgie asked.

Before Nestor could even respond, the entire One Fly Up Crew came through, as did The Snootish Girls, and Tayla Reynolds and her girls, Sekoya, Channen, Penelle, Kenda, K'Lixia, Rezen, Nosha, Taronka, Simonay, and Tandra.

"Nestor! What is going on?!" Jeorgie said as Tina and Davina tried to sneak in.

"What is she doing here?!" Green Eyed Mike asked.

"Tina's here? She didn't tell me she was coming," Jonathan said out loud, to no one in particular.

Even his grandfather was surprised to see her, as he kind of pointed in her direction from across the yard.

Green Eyed Mike walked right up to Davina, and boy, was he mad! "Dude! Why are you here?" Green Eyed Mike demanded to know.

"Raymundo invited us, duh!" Davina said.

Apparently, Raymundo invited just about everyone from Xembi's party, and soon Derrick Bay, Pop Star Girl and her same back-up BFF girls arrived. Raymundo became so inspired by Xembi's and Nestor's birthday parties that he ended up becoming an underground club promoter, especially after both of his sisters, Ingrid and Michella, encouraged him to take a few marketing classes at City Community College.

When Xembi's cousins Bryce and Brandeis came through, Osias lost his cool. He didn't believe it when Raymundo told him that DJ Loco Hero would be there, and yet there he was, in his little cousin's backyard, listening to his mixes.

"Xembi, did you know your DJ cousin was coming to my party?" Nestor asked.

"Well, yeah. But Brandeis told me not to say anything because your brother wanted it to be a surprise."

When Mr. Fariq arrived with his niece Mulesha and his nephew Yohannis, they were welcomed with cheers. "Akrahm really wanted to come, but I told him it was my turn since I missed Xembi's party, and oh boy, what a party I missed!" Mr. Fariq said to Nestor's mother.

Nestor's birthday party went on for hours, and people didn't start leaving until close to 9 p.m. Mayfair's father danced the Mucara Walk line-dance, once he got the hang of it, and ended up having a dance-off with Nestor's father.

Jonathan's grandfather played a round of Simon Says and actually won, and got one of DJ Osias's T-shirts and wore it for the rest of the evening.

Demetrius's Uncle Ced got a part-time job at Big Chub's automotive-restoration shop as an apprentice car-stereo installer and rims expert. Flint Swinns invited the One Fly Up Crew for a game of flag football, with some of his teammates up at Depot Park, which inspired Flint to start a mentoring summer program at Local High.

Thad hung out with Pop Star Girl and her BFFs, who all thought he was drop-dead gorgeous, and the two of them developed a nice little friendship that lasted until Thad went to Glick Mid for sixth grade and Brenna went to some exclusive middle school with her BFFs.

Sneaks struck up a conversation with Mayfair's father, who was rather impressed with the little boy, and Sneaks asked if he could take Mayfair out on a date, which ended up being a chaperoned double date with Rachel and Q-Tech, on a Saturday night, with everyone's parents just a few tables over.

Nestor's cousin Dexter, who was a fourth grader at Perk Elementary, had gotten the lovesick googlie eyes for Leah Olomua. He took one look at her and fell hard. He didn't mind that she was a little bit taller than him, and that she had tomboyish ways. Dexter was totally smitten, but Leah thought he was ridiculous and didn't have time for his nonsense.

"Nestor, you better come get your cousin. I don't want to be bothered," Leah said.

All of the bombshell surprises and chaos that ensued at Xembi's party didn't happen at Nestor's party, but there was a feeling of belonging, and the dynamics at school were changing. Like, The Snootish Girls all said, "Hey!" to Jonathan Chang whenever they saw him. Probably ninety percent of it had to do with his older sister Tina, who became their fashion goddess, and the other ten percent made up for the parties. Leah Olomua started hanging out more often with Mayfair and her friends, even though she still wasn't feeling a game of High Jump when the girls tried to start back up with it again. Erica Ross and LaDera Levitt started being nicer to Leah, especially whenever they saw The Snootish Girls talking to Leah about her hair. Actually, Erica and LaDera started being a lot nicer to all the girls in class, and sometimes they'd all eat lunch together in the cafeteria. Other times, there'd be group lunch dates with Sneaks, Q-Tech, Golden Arms Chance, and Jonathan Chang.

Jeorgie hoped that with all of this bonding going on, he'd get the chance to play with the One Fly Up Crew, but it was still a no-go. He was always trying to figure them out, devising a plan to someday play with them, and he was also working on another project that involved his birthday.

* * *

Just days after Nestor's party, the pressure was on, and Jeorgie was stumped as to how his birthday party could ever equal or top the other two parties. His mother suggested some ideas, but they were just lame.

"We could have your party at Kino's Parlor. That would be fun, wouldn't it?" Jeorgie's mother said.

Kino's Parlor was a kiddie ice cream parlor for tons of good, wholesome family fun, and it wasn't exactly the theme Jeorgie was going for.

"Okay. What about the zoo? The zoo's a good place for a birthday party," his mother said.

Jeorgie just gave her a blank look with sarcastic eyes that said *Nope, try again*.

"Well, do you have any better ideas? I'm starting to run out of them. We might as well just have some cake and ice cream here at the house," Jeorgie's mother said, getting a little agitated with her indecisive middle child.

One thing Jeorgie was clear about was that he didn't want anyone to know that he had a birthday coming up, and the first thing he had to do was find out if his older brother Arnie knew anything. Because if he did, he could slip and off-handedly say something to either Raymundo, Tina, or Davina.

"Arnie, did Mom say something was happening next month?" Jeorgie nonchalantly asked while Arnie was in the middle of texting someone at the breakfast table one morning.

"Uh, not sure. Ask mom," Arnie said, and got up and left the kitchen. The brief conversation would disappear in the recesses of Arnie's brain, never to be recalled again.

Next thing Jeorgie had to do was see what Little Laura knew, because she did pay attention and overhear things. "So Laura, uh, do you know what's happening next month?" He found her in her room, quietly playing with her Cutie Face dolls.

"Um, no. I dunno," Laura said, not really paying attention.

"Oh, okay," Jeorgie said.

When he turned to leave, Little Laura let out a squeaky gasp. "It's your birthday, isn't it? Oh! Can Peppertina and Timothy come? Please?"

Jeorgie let out a big sigh and had to decide whether or not he should tell her. "Okay, here's the deal. Yes, my birthday is next month, but nobody knows about it yet," Jeorgie said, and sat down next to her on the floor.

"Not even Green Eyed Mike and Nestor? Because those are your best friends."

"Nope. They don't know anything. . .yet."

"Does Arnie know?"

"No. He probably can't remember his own birthday. So can you keep it a secret? I'll do anything you want me to do, if you promise not to tell anyone."

Little Laura thought it over for a moment. "Okay, but can Peppertina and Timothy come?"

"Of course they can. Mom will probably invite Riley and Tess, so that'll be good for you too, right?"

Little Laura's face brightened, but then she frowned as a thought suddenly crossed her mind. "You'll do anything?" she asked.

Jeorgie let out another big sigh and said, "Yup. Whatever you want." As he waited to hear what she was going to say, he picked up one of her Cutie Face dolls and started brushing its hair.

"Well, I just want you to do one thing. Could you hold my hand when we walk to school in the morning? Not just one time but every morning? I don't like walking behind you and Nestor and Green Eyed Mike," Little Laura sadly said.

"That's it? That's all you want me to do is hold your hand in the mornings?" Jeorgie was surprised by this and suddenly felt bad that he had been neglecting his little sister. He put his arm around her and squeezed. "Okay. I can do that."

"Okay."

Their seventy-year-old grandfather walked by and stood in the doorway. "Can I play?" he finally said, and Little Laura got up and sat him down on her bed.

"Here, Grandpa." She gave him a doll and handed him a tiny hairbrush.

"Thank you," Grandpa politely said, and brushed the doll's hair. "You know, I don't smoke cigars anymore, but this hair brushing works just as well for the relaxation. But oh, what I would give for an old stogie right now. Say, Jeorgie, you wouldn't happen to have a Madridian on you?"

"No, not on me. But I can try to get you one, Grandpa," Jeorgie said as he tried to put the doll's hair in a ponytail.

"Just you saying that you'll look into getting me one is good enough. They're bad for my health, and if your mother caught me smoking again, well, I don't know what kinds of terror she'd throw at me. I'll just have to survive off of the memories, I guess."

For the rest of the afternoon, Jeorgie spent some quality time with his little sister, with their grandpa in tow. He took his two youngest grandchildren out for a late lunch down at the deli-café across town.

"So Jeorgie, you have a birthday coming up. Tell me what you want, and I'll get it for you," Grandpa said as he bit into a salami and roast beef sandwich.

"I don't really know what I want right now. Just trying to figure out how I can have an awesome party, better than the ones that I just went to. Grandpa you have no idea...those two parties were amazingly awesome, especially Xembi's birthday party, and I just don't want anything lame and stupid. Maybe I shouldn't have a party at all," Jeorgie said as he ate a plate of French fries smothered in chili sauce and cheese.

"You could have a surprise birthday party," Grandpa said.

Jeorgie looked at him with concern. "How will it be a surprise if I already know about it?"

"No, not that kind of surprise. That's not what I'm talking about. What you need is the element of surprise. The art of a good mystery. Let your guests be surprised."

Jeorgie became transfixed, while Little Laura took a chili-cheese fry off of his plate.

"Make your guests work for their invitations. Give them clues and hints they have to figure out, that will lead them to your big event, and not until the very last second will they realize it's all been leading up to your birthday," Grandpa said, and covered up a very loud belch and fanned it away.

Jeorgie sat in awe of his grandpa, as the brainstorming wheels in his mind began to turn, and suddenly Jeorgie had an epiphany, as a little light bulb switched on, over his head. His orchestration would take strategy and innovation, with a dedicated team that would require loyalty and sworn secrecy. Jeorgie's vision was taking hold, and it was time for him to either go big or just have cake and ice cream at home.

# Chapter Seventeen

Congratulations!
YOU have been cordially invited.
Invited to what?
Just wait and see.
<u>PLEASE</u>
Send this invite back to the address below,
in the accompanying
SASE
(self-addressed stamped envelope)
in order to receive your second
set of instructions
(and no, this is not a joke)

When Jeorgie told his mother what he wanted to do, she got really excited about it and took Jeorgie to the stationery store across town and helped him pick out the perfect invitation. He managed to write out his guest list. He knew the last names of most of the invitees, and some he did not. His grandpa even went as far as getting a P.O. box at the post office for Jeorgie, just to ward off anyone from looking up the return address. Mr. Marci was in on it, with strict instructions on how to hand out the invites when Jeorgie brought them to school, stashed away in his backpack. After lunch, it was game on!

"Everyone, I have an announcement to make," Mr. Marci said, with the stack of envelopes in his hand.

"Is somebody having a birthday party?" Kade asked.

"I don't know. We'll find out. If I call your name, come up and get your envelope. And do not open them until you get home. Understood?"

Excitement ran through the children, as everyone anxiously waited to see if their name would be called.

Mr. Marci looked at the first envelope. "Ahhhh. Speak of the devil. Kade Bondshea."

Kade got up and grinned from ear to ear and kissed his invite. "It's about to get lit! WOOp-WOOp!" Kade said.

"Lydia Jackson."

There was a pleasant applause from the girls as Lydia got up.

"Demetrius Applethorn."

The boys caught on quick and went wild with applause for Demetrius.

"Rachel Ward."

The girls tried to outdo the boys with their applause, but the boys came back even stronger when Ryan Keefe's name was called. When Xembi's name was called, the whole class went wild and gave her a standing ovation. But why did she get a bigger envelope than everyone else? As a matter of fact, why did Nestor, Green Eyed Mike, Mayfair, and Jonathan Chang get bigger envelopes than everyone else? The only person who didn't get an envelope was Jeorgie. He had to bite down hard to hide his excitement, yet he managed to look devastated.

"Mr. Marci, where's my envelope? Did you lose it? Maybe it fell on the floor?" Jeorgie said.

"Maybe you could tell the person that they forgot about Jeorgie, and then they'll give him one tomorrow," Nestor said.

Mr. Marci looked on his desk, through his papers, under his desk, he went to the back of the class and retraced his steps, and Jeorgie acted like he was trying not to cry.

"Don't worry, Jeorgie. We got you! You coming with us. And we gon' walk up in there and be like, 'Now what?! You thought you forgot, but we didn't!'" Kade said.

"And they better not say nuthin' about it, either!" Deshawn Sanders chimed in.

"That is so messed up. How are they gonna forget Jeorgie? That's messed up for real," Leah Olomua said.

Suddenly the invitation jubilation quickly turned into outrage.

"Mr. Marci, you got to do something!" Nestor said.

Jeorgie put his head down on his desk.

"Okay, everyone. Calm down. We're going to figure this out," Mr. Marci said with thirty-six pairs of eyes staring at him as he slowly went over to the door and opened it. He went out into the hall for what seemed like an eternity. Mr. Marci finally came back, and gravely looked over his students.

"Well..." Mr. Marci said.

"Well, what?" Kade asked.

Mr. Marci let out a big sigh and slowly held up Jeorgie's invitation. The class went wild.

"Now remember, you are not to open these until you get home. If they are opened before you get home, you may have your invitation rescinded. Understood? Is everyone clear?"

"Rescinded? What does that mean?" Jonathan Chang asked.

"The word *rescind* means that you will have to give your envelope back."

Well, of course, nobody wanted that, so the children made extra sure that their envelopes were safe and secured inside of their book sacks.

As for those who weren't in Mr. Marci's class, Ms. Mothped and Dr. Nickeldime were also given a strict set of instructions on how to distribute the envelopes, as anxious and worried children who had been called to the principal's office, not sure of what they had done or why they were called in, were relieved when they received their envelopes.

"Man, I didn't know what was going on. I was like, 'What did I do?'" Big Julius said when he walked home with Damarcus and Keem, who also had their invitations.

"We are the bomb! I bet this is another party, and we're getting invited to all of them. I got to figure out what I'm going to wear," Shandelina Smith said to Naomi Braithwaite on the school-bus ride home.

When Nestor got home, he immediately opened his envelope and found three more envelopes that were addressed to Raymundo, Ingrid, and Michella.

Jonathan Chang got home and had envelopes for Timothy, his sister Tina, and their grandfather.

Xembi had envelopes for Peppertina, her cousins Bryce and Brandeis, her cousin Brownie, and her Uncle Bender. Mayfair was surprised that Myla and Makayla had envelopes to open, along with their father.

And, of course, Green Eyed Mike had an extra envelope for his sister Davina, which he didn't like.

She immediately got on the phone with Tina. "OMG! Did you get one?" Davina frantically asked.

"Yeah, I got one. But so did my little brothers and my grandfather. It must be another party. What do you think?" Tina said.

"Wait a minute. Let me find out from Michael."

But the only thing Green Eyed Mike could explain was what had happened in class when Mr. Marci passed them out. "Are you going to mail yours in?" Davina asked.

"Sure, why not? Let's see what happens."

When Raymundo got his envelope, he got so excited that he ran down to the mailbox that was right down the street from his house and dropped it in.

Ingrid and Michella seemed less enthused and set their envelopes down somewhere, never to be thought of again.

When Raymundo got to school the next morning, he went looking for Flint Swinns and found him at his locker. "Yo, you get your invitation?" Raymundo asked.

"What invitation?" Flint asked.

Raymundo looked at him, shocked. "Man, you didn't get an invitation? Your little sister didn't have an extra one for you?"

"No," Flint said, perplexed. "An invitation? An invitation to what?" Flint asked.

"Well, it didn't really say. It just gave some instructions."

"Do you think it's another Maverick Elem party?"

"Not a hundred percent sure, but it probably is."

"But don't you think it's kind of weird or strange for us to even go to some kid's birthday party, some kid that we don't even know, and we're getting invited? To a kiddie party?"

"I know, but it's like we're all connected to something bigger than just the party. It's like we're family all of a sudden."

"Maybe I didn't get one."

"Oh, I'm pretty sure you're gonna get one. If I got an invite, I *know* you're gonna get one," Raymundo said as the bell rang and he headed to class.

And sure enough, Flint was called down to the main office and picked up his mysterious invite later that day.

✲ ✲ ✲

Everyone was on edge for some sign about the mystery envelopes they all mailed in. Days had gone by without a hint, trace, or word of anything, and Jeorgie sat back and watched the children spin their theories out of control as to who could've sent the invites and what in the world could be coming next.

"Mr. Marci, we haven't heard back anything on those weird invitations yet. Do you know when they're going to send us something else about it?" Sandra Jang asked in the middle of Mr. Marci's math lesson.

"Oh, uh, I'm not sure," Mr. Marci said.

"Well, can you tell us who handed them out?" Sandra asked.

"I've been sworn to secrecy. Sorry," Mr. Marci said, and everyone groaned.

It felt like they had been waiting for weeks, months even, but it was just a few days after everyone mailed in their invites. The children were beginning to forget about the whole thing, when they each received a new envelope in the mail. Sounds of envelopes being ripped opened trickled through the Ranunculus District as everyone frantically read their new invites. All it said was:

*Shhhh .*
*Take this to*
*S&K Groceries*
*Give it to*
*Mr. Akrahm or Mr. Fariq*
*Ask no questions*

Taped to the bottom of the invite was a penny with an arrow pointed at it. The children did as they were told, and kept their second invites a secret, for fear of any sort of rescinding or whatever. They even went so far as to not speak of it among each other and just gave knowing glances and side looks to each other.

Raymundo made sure he was on time when he picked up Nestor and his two best buds after school so that they could hurry down to the S&K, and the children who took the school bus home, like Deshawn Sanders, Erica Ross, LaDera Levitt, Shandelina Smith, and Naomi Braithwaite, along with those whose parents picked them up, like Mayfair and Xembi, all made sure they made arrangements on how to get home once they left the store.

So when they trickled down to the S&K after school, they were relieved to see that Mr. Akrahm and Mr. Fariq seemed normal as usual, upbeat and social. Demetrius Applethorn's Uncle Ced's bass system could be heard booming just outside the store when Demetrius went in, surprised to see almost everybody in his class already there. Lydia Jackson was first in line.

"What'll it be, princess?" Mr. Akrahm said.

Lydia quietly slid her penny across the counter. Mr. Akrahm grabbed it, pulled out a small brown paper bag from behind the counter, dropped a NowLater in the bag, and handed it to her. Everyone was curious to see what was inside the bag, including Jonathan Chang's grandfather, who was also in line, but Lydia kept it moving and left.

When Ingrid and Michella entered the store, Nestor couldn't believe it, and said to Raymundo, "But I thought they forgot all about it."

The One Fly Up Crew was in line, along with The Snootish Girls, Tayla and her girls, Sekoya, Channen, Pennelle, Kenda, K'Lixia, Rezen, Nosha, Taronka, Simonay, and Tandra, and when Flint Swinns wandered in, there was a big sigh of relief. Seeing him go to the end of the line broke the tension. When Raymundo finally got his little brown bag and looked inside, all eyes were on him as he pulled out another envelope, ripped it open right there in front of everybody, read the little note, and started grinning.

"What does it say?" Timothy asked.

"It's nothing bad, lil homie. Man, everybody acting all scared," Raymundo said.

When it was Timothy's turn, he ripped open the envelope and screamed, "It's party time, everybody!"

**You are cordially invited to
Cosmic Star Lanes
On Saturday, June 6th
7 p.m. to 9 p.m.
Come and find out whose birthday it is!**

# Chapter Eighteen

After following all the instructions for Jeorgie's surprise birthday party, the day had finally arrived, and the children were beyond excited. The party started at 7 p.m., and it made the children giddy and hyper because it was a party at night. Everyone arrived on time because they didn't want to miss a thing, and showed up with parents, siblings, relatives, and friends outside of school. Mr. Marci was there with Mr. Freelander; Ms. DeMauvé-Pflume and her niece Iantha were there; Mrs. Stone and her husband were there; Mr. Akrahm and Mr. Fariq were both able to be there since they closed their store early on Saturdays, and they brought Mulesha and Yohannis, and their wives (who knew Mr. Akrahm and Mr. Fariq were married? WOW!). Mayfair's mother was able to come with Richard and the twins, and Richard was glad to see Rachel's father since they were becoming really good friends. When Sneaks and Q-Tech showed up with Sneaks's father, who was Q-Tech's uncle, Richard and Rachel's father were glad to see him too, almost like they were The Three Musketeers among the fathers. When Xembi arrived with both of her parents, class fan-favorite Uncle Bender, and Xembi's cousin Brownie, Richard and the other fathers invited Ted and Uncle Bender to join their man-cave circle. And of course, Nestor brought a lot of people with him, including his parents, a few of his cousins—Big Chub, and of course, Dexter, who had a mad crush on Leah Olomua and went looking for her as soon as he got there—while Raymundo brought a few of his buddies that he hung with at Local High. And Nestor's older sisters, Ingrid and Michella, brought their boyfriends.

Most of the One Fly Up Crew were dropped off, except for Golden Arms Chance, who came with his mother. He wanted to introduce his mother to Xembi. For Chance, it would always be Xembi. The Snootish Girls were there and kept their watchful eyes on Tina and Davina, who were there with their Local High clique. Tayla and her girls, Sekoya, Channen, Pennelle, Kenda, K'Lixia, Rezen, Nosha, Taronka, Simonay, and Tandra were all there. The last one to arrive was Flint Swinns, who came with a couple of his teammates, along with Pop Star Girl and her usual BFFs. Her other brother, the paper boy, couldn't make it since he had a soccer game that weekend. Leah Olomua's older brother Lisati hung with Flint Swinns since he used to play for Local High and was now on the football team at State University. Leah's other brother Loto was there, and so was her older sister Leilee, who was an eighth grader at Glick Mid.

Now that everyone was there, they stood around, wondering and waiting to see what was going to happen next.

"But where's Jeorgie?" Green Eyed Mike asked Nestor, and they both looked at each other as if they were wondering the same thing: *Could it be Jeorgie's birthday?*

The lights suddenly cut out, and loud gasps and a few shrieks floated around until a familiar voice boomed through the darkness, over the stereo system. "Ladies and gentlemen, welcome to the Cosmic Star Bowling Alley..."

Uncle Bender said, "I know that voice. I'd know that voice anywhere."

Brownie loudly shushed him.

"This is DJ Loco Hero..."

"See, I told you I knew that voice!" Uncle Bender yelled back at Brownie.

"...And let's find whose birthday it is," DJ Loco Hero said.

The children cheered as the lights suddenly came back on in a whirl of bright neon colors in strobe and spotlights flashing about, while a sports anthem blasted through the bowling alley.

The doors to the main entrance swung open, and a group of boys all dressed alike, wearing sunglasses, entered and descended the flight of steps that led to the main floor.

"Hey! I know them!" Green Eyed Mike said to Nestor.

"Yeah, they go to the skate park!" Nestor said.

The Skate Park Boys positioned themselves on either side of the stairway, when Little Laura entered with her friends Tess and Riley. The three of them held hands and danced to the beat when they hit the main floor.

"Oh my GOD! It's Little Laura! Look everybody! It's Little Laura!" Timothy screamed.

"And now, ladies and gentlemen, here it is, what you've all been waiting for. Let's give it up for ya birthday boy: the one, the only, James Jeorge Sterrrrrrrrrrliiiiiiinnng!"

The place went nuts with catcalls, whistles, and applause when Jeorgie entered wearing a golden crown, sunglasses, and a very cool T-shirt that said: HBD to ME.

As the strobe lights fluttered about and the spotlights zoomed around, Jeorgie and his skate-park buddies huddled together to the beat of the music, like NBA players right before a game. Little Laura handed Jeorgie a wireless mic, and Jeorgie went into a spot-on lip-sync performance of Tyler Blanc's "Yo, Dude," which caused the children to go absolutely spastic in a frenzy of adrenaline. It was what they had been hoping for, and Jeorgie was giving it to them. Little Laura and her friends were his back-up singers, and The Skate Park Boys were his back-up dancers.

"It was Jeorgie's birthday this whole time? Why didn't he tell us?" Nestor said, kind of ticked off about it.

"He didn't need them. We could've been his back-up dancers," Green Eyed Mike said.

Then Jeorgie's grandpa appeared and eased himself down the staircase, dressed identical to Jeorgie—golden crown and all—and lip-synced the part in the song where Tyler Blanc says, "Yo, dude, I *know* you got schooled!" which, of course, brought the house D-OW-NNNNN! Then Jeorgie and his birthday crew, including Grandpa, went into a very cool choreographed dance performance, like they were dancing live at a music-awards show. Kade Bondshea couldn't resist the urge and jumped in with them and tried to keep up with the dance moves, which sparked Deshawn Sanders and James Yoro to jump in, too. When it was over, the cheers and adulation satisfied his worries, and he succeeded well beyond his dreams, flying high on exhilaration.

"Hey, everybody. Thanks for making it out to my party. Sorry I had to keep it a secret, especially to my two best buds, Green Eyed Mike and Nestor. I want to give a shout out to my mom—thanks, Mom, love you. I wanna thank my grandpa for helping me plan all of this...."

Grandpa was out of breath after that dance routine, but he managed to give a most gracious bow when everybody applauded him.

"...And a shout-out to my little sister, Little Laura, for keeping everything a secret, and to Mr. Marci, and Ms. DeMauvé-Pflume, too. And to Ms. Mothped and Dr. Nickeldime, who couldn't come. And my brother Arnie, who also couldn't come 'cause he had to work. And thanks to DJ Loco Hero, my skate-park dudes, everybody in my class, and everybody else for coming..."

Jeorgie's mother appeared and took the mic. "Hello, everyone. We've got a smorgasbord of pizza over in the game room, courtesy of Cosmic Star Lanes, on the other side of the bowling alley. And just letting you know that the first game is free, but after that, you gotta pay to play."

Jeorgie had also invited fourth-grade teacher, Ms. McQueen, who was there with her husband. When she kept overhearing the children talk about the other parties, she complained about how she never got invited. "Well, how come nobody gave me an invitation? Maybe I wanted to go to one of y'all's little parties and kick it."

She was so thrilled to be there that she went up and took the mic. "Now I see what y'all been talkin' 'bout. And that little dance y'all did, that right there, was off the chain! Thank you, Mr. Jeorgie! I really enjoyed that. And if y'all have any more parties, don't forget to invite me, 'cause I'll be there!"

The children who were in her class all shook their heads as if to say, *"That Ms. McQueen is something else!"* After that, Brandeis went into Oswald's "Drain," and the bowling games began.

✢ ✢ ✢

Mrs. Stone's grandson, A.J., finally showed up and caused quite a stir among The Snootish Girls, who bowled with Mrs. Stone and her husband.

LaRae Davis spotted him first. "Oh-my-God. That boy is fine!" LaRae said as A.J. walked up.

He took one look at the girls and wanted to turn right back around and leave. He didn't want to bowl with a bunch of girls.

"Hey, you finally made it. Look, I want all of you to meet my grandson, A.J.," Mrs. Stone said with grandmotherly pride.

In spite of his twelve-year-old, moody self, A.J. had wholesome good-boy good looks. He gave a lackluster, "Hello."

Skyy Jones wanted to make it clear she was the leader of the group, and smartly asked, "Do you go to Glick Mid?"

"Yeah," A.J. said, just as dour as ever.

But when his friend Loto walked up, who was in most of the same classes with A.J. at Glick Mid, A.J. was so happy to see him that when he flashed a stunning smile, it leveled the girls. And suddenly, they became their authentic, normal nine-year-old selves, without all of the snooty little attitudes.

"Granny, can I go bowl with my friend?" A.J. asked.

"Can you just bowl one game with us first?" Mrs. Stone asked.

The semi-scowl on A.J.'s face said *Fine!*

The girls didn't mind that he was moody. It was his good looks that started to pit the girls against each other, each hoping that they would be the one to break him out of his bad mood. Things kind of got way out of hand with all of the foolish eye-rolling, twisted stank looks, and extremely mean-girl sarcastic sighs as the girls ridiculously flirted with A.J., which showed just how immature they really were. Naomi Braithwaite couldn't take it anymore and ran off in tears to the restroom, and bumped right into Sandra Jang as she was coming out.

"Did Naomi come in here?" Skyy said.

"Yeah, she ran right into me. Almost knocked me down," Sandra said.

"Where is she?" Skyy demanded to know.

Sandra pointed to the very last stall at the end of the restroom.

The girls crowded around the stall as Skyy peered in through the slit of the door. "Why are you crying?"

"Naomi, he's too old for you. But shoot, I'll take him. He was looking at me anyway," Shandelina said.

Starmesha glared at her. "Why would he look at you for? You ain't nuthin to look at."

Skyy and LaRae looked at Shandelina for her reaction, which was swift and quick.

"For one thing, I AM sumptin' to look at! With a Tatum Nicole designer bag. All you got is a fake Branded Box you got from the swap meet, and probably paid a dollar for it!"

It was true. Starmesha did carry a fake Branded Box, but it was one of the higher quality fake designer bags. It was all in the stitching and the trademark electric-purple lining.

"Well, at least I don't go around pretending I'm Christine Chatel. Whoever told you you look like her, they lied. You just a broke-down version of her, with ya stank attitude and ugly pigeon toes," Starmesha said, with a heavy neck-roll swerve, followed by a severe eye roll.

Yes, it was true that Shandelina thought very highly of herself in that she actually did, kind of, look like the pop icon superstar, Christine Chatel, but she wasn't exactly pigeon toed, just a little bit.

"Before you start calling somebody stank, you better look in the mirror. With your hair looking like rats been sucking on it!" Shandelina said.

Well, that wasn't true because Starmesha had just gotten her hair braided, and it looked really pretty.

"With those ugly French tips you be trying to wear. Like, how you gonna have French tips when you only in the fourth grade?" Shandelina said, and tried to match Starmesha's sarcastic neck roll.

Well, yeah. Starmesha's French tips did look a bit mature for her nine-year-old fingernails, but in her mind, she was rocking it. Sometimes it was hard to remember that The Snootish Girls, in all of their designer wear and wanna-be grown attitudes, were just a group of nine- and ten-year-old girls.

"And your name. Like, what is up with that? It is soooo ghetto. It ain't even ghetto fabulous! Ain't nobody gonna hire you with a name like Starmesha! Except for flipping French fries with your stupid French tips."

But Shandelina was wrong about Starmesha's name not being ghetto fabulous, because, actually, it was totally BLINGED ALL THE WAY OUT ghetto fab! How could it not be with a name like Starmesha Collins? However, when it came to her name, Starmesha didn't play. Anybody who cracked on her name meant they were talking about her mother, since it was her mother who named her.

"Don't talk about my name. You better check yourself," Starmesha calmly said as her expression went cold.

"I ain't gotta check nuthin'. You better take your fake nails and your fake handbag and get outta my face! Looking like a nasty cockroach!" Shandelina said.

"Yo' mama's a cockroach! Ya mama, ya daddy, ya whole generation!" Starmesha said, and got all up in Shandelina's face.

By now, Naomi had stopped crying and was watching through the door slits of the stall, while Skyy and LaRae watched the quick exchange in disbelief. The girls never fought each other, ever. The very second Starmesha called Shanelina's mother a cockroach, Shandelina lunged at her, and Skyy and LaRae tried to pull them apart. Ms. DeMauvé-Pflume's niece, Iantha, came in the restroom and quickly diffused the fight.

"Don't you ever put your hands on me!" Starmesha screamed. "You ain't nothing but a two-faced, lying—"

Sandra Jang, who was still in her spot by the entrance, let out a dramatic gasp that was so loaded with shock and terror that it sounded like she took a long, exaggerated gasp for air. She just stood there, completely open-mouthed, when Starmesha called Shandelina out of her name. It was the most degrading and vile thing a little girl could ever say to another little girl, and Starmesha spoke the vicious word with such nastiness that it was like she spit it in Shandelina's face.

And if calling Shandelina out of her name was bad, Starmesha went even lower. "Shandelina, you ain't foolin' nobody. You be acting all stank and stuck up, like you better than everybody, but we know where you really come from, and it ain't from no Lilac neighborhood, 'cuz we know your daddy's a crackhead!"

Quiet and loud gasps could be heard from Skyy, LaRae, and Naomi, and Sandra Jang's mouth hit the floor. But Starmesha was right. Shandelina lived in the wealthy neighborhood on Lilac Lane, but before her mother divorced Shandelina's father, they were living in the Tangerine Court area, which wasn't all that bad, but it was true that her father had some problems. What they were, only Shandelina knew.

"We drove by him last week, on Third Street, and I said, 'Mama, look! There goes Shandelina's daddy, all strung out, begging for money,'" Starmesha said.

That's when Shandelina's face went cold. "You don't know me! But you 'bout to find out!" Shandelina said, and snatched away from Iantha's grip and tried to claw at Starmesha's face.

The girls were entangled in a nasty hair-pull, and when Iantha finally managed to separate them, Shandelina snatched away from her, pushed past Sandra Jang, and stormed out. Skyy, LaRae, and Starmesha were on her heels, running after her, and Naomi came out of the stall and went after them.

"Oh my God! What was going on? Why were they fighting?" Iantha asked Sandra Jang.

Sandra replied, "Over who looked better."

After that, Shandelina was pretty much done with the girls and kept to herself during the last week and a half of school. It was Starmesha's scathing dig about Shandelina's father being a crackhead that did it, and she was done with Maverick Elem. Nobody would really notice that she would transfer to Secondary Academy for fifth grade, except for The Snootish Girls and Kiara Campbell. It was a private school that was closer to her mother's job, where Shandelina would make new friends, still be her snooty self, and never think of her old clique again. The most important thing was that the rumors of how her father abandoned the family wouldn't follow her. All anyone would know at Secondary Academy was that Shandelina's stepfather was her real father.

* * *

That night, back at the bowling alley, the news quickly spread about the ugly bathroom brawl, by way of Sandra Jang, who couldn't believe how lucky she was to have been in there to see the whole thing go down. When Jeorgie finally found out that there was a girl fight at his party, that nobody saw, except for Sandra Jang, he was bummed about it. "Man, that sucks. Could've been another birthday present."

Jeorgie's party was the last one in the season of birthday gatherings that had become something of an unexpected occurrence. If anyone else wanted in this new, irregular Maverick Elem/Glick Mid/Local High clan, it was going to be tough.

# Chapter Nineteen

Envy was what he felt when he watched the One Fly Up Crew. They had a kind of swagger that reminded you of the bond that pro-athletes had after a game, after an afternoon of practice, a fraternity of sorts, where everyone looked out for each other, protected one another, which strengthened their bond, and Jeorgie wanted it bad.

He started having that look in his eye again, and this time he wasn't taking no for an answer. So the plan he finally decided on was to assemble his own kickball team. Nestor and Green Eyed Mike were his co-captains, and the first person Jeorgie recruited was Leah Olomua. Of course, when he approached her, she wasn't in the mood. But was she really ever in the "mood" for anything?

"Yeah, right, Jeorgie. Why would I want to be on your team when I can play with the best?" Leah said in a flat tone as she sat across from Jeorgie in the cafeteria.

"Well, that's fine. I just want to play them, and I think I have a good team, with you on it," Jeorgie said.

But Leah was hardly impressed. "I'll think about it and let you know," she said as she got up and left.

When Mr. Marci's class shared the yard with Ms. Deckey's third-grade class during P.E., Jeorgie rounded up his team. Kade Bondshea, Deshawn Sanders, Ryan Keefe, and James Yoro were in, but Jeorgie wanted at least three more players and scoped out Sneaks and Q-Tech.

"Hey, Q-Tech. I'm putting together a team to go up against the One Fly Up Crew. Are you in?"

Q-Tech was surprised by Jeorgie's request. "Um, are you sure you want *me* on your team?" Q-Tech asked.

"Uh, yeah!" Jeorgie said.

"Oh, well, uh, it's not that I don't want to be on your team, but I'm probably the worst kickball player, so..."

Jeorgie wasn't expecting Q-Tech to turn him down since he played pretty well in the football games they had on the basketball court.

"But I could record the game and edit it for you. Like a movie."

"Really?"

"Oh, yeah. I can put music on it and everything."

"Oh, okay. That sounds good. What about Sneaks? Would he want to be on the team?"

"Yeah, probably so."

With Sneaks on the team, Jeorgie needed just one more player and thought about asking Demetrius Applethorn, but he knew Demetrius wasn't the athletic type. Since none of the other girls in class had Leah Olomua's skills, that only left Jonathan Chang, and Jeorgie found him sitting with Demetrius.

"Hey, Jonathan, can I talk to you for a second?" Jeorgie said, and pulled Jonathan out of earshot from Demetrius. "Okay, so

I'm putting together a kickball team to play against the One Fly Up Crew. Are you in?"

Jonathan frowned at Jeorgie, totally unsure of what he was being asked. "Am I in? In what? What do you mean? I don't understand."

"I mean do you want to be on the team?"

Jonathan's confusion slowly turned into elation, and he finally said, "Oh yeah, sure." Jonathan was ready to play.

"Okay, good. So we're going to meet up tomorrow during recess, and maybe at lunchtime, too," Jeorgie said as Leah Olomua walked up and poked him on the shoulder.

"Okay, I'll do it," Leah said, and promptly walked away.

So now that he had Jonathan and Leah on the team, things were squared away, until Demetrius said, "Can I be on the team, too?"

Jeorgie looked at Demetrius and wanted to say, "*Well, I think I have enough players already, but if somebody drops out, I'll let you know.*" But Jeorgie caved. "Okay, but now that you're in, you can't back out."

Can't back out? Well, in that case, maybe Demetrius didn't really want to be on the team if he didn't have the option to change his mind.

The next day, Jeorgie and his teammates met over in a corner of the school yard, by the monkey bars, huddled together.

"All I want to do is play one game. They hog the kickball court. They never let any new players play with them. I mean, they're a bunch of cool guys, and great athletes, but I just want to play them, for once in my life, before school is over, because all of them, except for Chance, are graduating, and then we won't get to play them," Jeorgie said.

"But what is your plan? It's more than kicking a ball. What's the strategy?" Derrick Bay asked.

Jeorgie glared up at him. This was his show, not Derrick Bay's. He was always appearing out of nowhere. Then Jeorgie remembered that Derrick Bay used to be part of the One Fly Up Crew, so he thought maybe he should listen instead of getting all annoyed at him. Everyone looked to Derrick Bay, and for once, he had nothing else to say.

Finally, Jeorgie said, "You want to be our coach?"

For the rest of that day, Jeorgie's team trained and strategized, and the more they plotted and planned, the more Demetrius Applethorn wanted to back out.

"But we need you, Demetrius. You're like our secret weapon because everybody knows that you aren't a strong player, but I've seen your fake-outs, and it totally confuses the pitcher, who hates being a field catcher, because all he's thinking about is pitching the ball."

"Yeah, but..."

"It's not like you're gonna get tackled or anything. It doesn't matter if you suck at kickball. You can still use your fake-outs in a One Fly Up game, right Derrick?"

"You are correct."

Jeorgie knew he wasn't going to use Demetrius; he just needed him for intimidation—strength in numbers. Now all he had to do was get the One Fly Up Crew to agree to a game, and he knew just who to ask.

Like a disjointed band of misfits, you could almost hear the official music as Jeorgie and his teammates walked with purpose and honor across the yard, over to Mrs. Stone.

"Oh, my! What's all of this about? What's going on?" Mrs. Stone said, surprised to see Jeorgie's team looking so serious.

"Mrs. Stone, we wanted to ask you if you could ask the guys if they'd be willing to play a game of One Fly Up with me and my team," Jeorgie said.

Mrs. Stone was delighted! "I think I can do that. That's a great idea. Let's see if we can round up the guys."

They were in the middle of an intense game, with Big Julius on his fourth kick, with no catches, and he got mad when Mrs. Stone interrupted them.

"But Mrs. Stone, you don't understand!" Damarcus said as he threw his arms up in frustration.

"Why did we stop? What happened?" Golden Arms Chance asked as he ran up from the other side of the yard.

"Okay, okay. Calm down. You'll get back to your game in a moment. Jeorgie and his team would like to challenge all of you to a game," Mrs. Stone said.

The One Fly Up Crew responded with absurd looks.

"Well? What do you say?" Mrs. Stone asked.

"Against these guys?" Keem asked.

"Sure, why not? I think it'll be fun," Mrs. Stone said.

"Who's the team captain?" Phron Thompson asked.

Jeorgie raised his hand. "I'm the team captain, and Nestor and Green Eyed Mike are my team co-captains."

"Jeorgie, you sure you want to play us? 'Cause we're really good at what we do, and I don't wanna have to hurt you out there on the court," Phron Thompson said, and put his arm around Jeorgie.

"Yeah, Jeorgie. I mean, you're cool and everything, but if you play us, you better come with your A-game, 'cause we will destroy you," Keem said.

At this point, Demetrius definitely wanted to back out. Sneaks was up for the challenge, Q-Tech was secretly taping the whole thing, and Jonathan Chang was loving every minute of it.

"We're not scared. We just want to play," Jeorgie said.

"But how good are your skills? Your pitcher, your outfielders? Even your best kickers? We're out here every day, and we know the game, but what about you and your crew? How good are they? I mean, like, I don't want to beat you guys where it's like, fifty to zero, but I'm just sayin'…it could go down like that," Terrell said.

"But don't you ever want to play somebody else other than yourselves? We just want to play, and we kinda care if we score, but we just want to play. That's all," Jeorgie said.

He was starting to see what Derrick Bay had said all along. Their entitlement to the court was nauseating, and the way they were so stuck on themselves, at how great they were, was just downright repulsive. Fine, if that's how they were going to act, then maybe Jeorgie and his team didn't want to play with them after all.

Just when they were about to give up, Big Julius cleared his throat, stepped to the front of the group, and placed his hand on Jeorgie's shoulder. "Jeorgie says he wants to play, so let him play. What's the big deal? Yeah, we're great, so what? Nobody goes up against us. Let's get a game."

The boys let that sink in for a moment. Big Julius was right. They never played with anybody else, so how would they even know how great they were when it was just them?

And so it was agreed that Jeorgie's team would play against Maverick Elem's undefeatable One Fly Up Crew, at the end of the week, during lunchtime.

✳ ✳ ✳

During their week of training, Jeorgie was the team captain among captains and trained like he had a demo reel. Nestor and Green Eyed Mike envisioned themselves as star-studded number-one draft picks, and Jonathan Chang saw himself kicking the ball so far that he daydreamed of walking home from school all by himself. What did that mean? Well, it meant that being asked to play on a kickball team to go up against Maverick Elem's best ball players, took all of the embarrassment that Jonathan had with his hovering grandfather, and gave him something to be confident about. And that's when he started leading the way home after school, instead of always following behind. Sneaks played in some of his best sneakers, and tried to find the right shoes to play in on the big day. Q-Tech filmed their training sessions and did personal interviews. Leah would do her signature kick for the day and leave. Demetrius kept quiet as the team's secret weapon. And the other guys, Kade Bondshea, Deshawn Sanders, James Yoro, and Ryan Keefe trained hard but kept it silly with their jokes and foolishness. Lastly, Derrick Bay would give his words of ancient wisdom as the head coach. On the day of the game, instead of getting in one last session of intense training, Derrick Bay made the team do some mindful meditation at recess, and had them pretend that they were the One Fly Up Crew.

"You want us to pretend that we're them?" Jeorgie asked.

"Yes," Derrick Bay replied.

"Why?"

"Pretend you're a baller."

Just when Jonathan was about to ask, "What's a baller?" Derrick Bay cut him off.

"—Like you think you're better than everyone else, better than your own teammate, and nobody can beat you."

Everyone noticed the slight shift in Derrick Bay's calm demeanor. And then he went into a gradual attack. "Like you got a big head and can't nobody tell you nuthin' cuz you won't listen. But that's okay. Go ahead and be all stuck on yourself and think you all that, cuz you ain't! I know what's up! What's good?!" Derrick Bay said, and walked off in a huff, leaving everybody looking at him like he was out of his mind.

Totally perplexed, Jeorgie said, "Well that was weird."

"Uh-oh. He's coming back," Demetrius said.

Derrick Bay walked up with his hands in his pants pockets, full of remorse. "I flipped out. Shouldn'a done that."

"Okay. It's cool," Jeorgie said.

"Forget trying to be ballers. Just be yourself," Derrick Bay said.

"Is that why you don't play with them anymore, because they wouldn't listen to you?" Deshawn Sanders asked.

"Yeah, something like that, but you don't have to pretend to be them. You want respect from the One Fly Up Crew? Just be yourselves. You already have the confidence you need to play against them," Derrick Bay replied.

"Man, I been had confidence! I don't care what they think! Shoot, they better be afraid of me! I'm comin' for 'em!" Kade boldly said.

* * *

None of Derrick Bay's coaching did anything to ease Demetrius's fear. He liked being on the team, but he didn't like everybody looking at him if he had to kick, and he discovered very quickly that he liked watching sports instead of playing them.

"I dunno if I can be a secret weapon," Demetrius said.

Everyone was tired of him being all nervous and scared.

"Can you say something to him?" Jeorgie asked Derrick Bay.

"Nope. I've done all I can do. It's up to you now, Captain."

Jeorgie took a moment to gather his thoughts, and after a long, dramatic pause, he let out an exaggerated sigh and said, "Okay fine, Demetrius. We know you're the worst player on the team. If you don't want to play, then don't."

Well, that was harsh. But what else could Jeorgie say?

"I really want to tell you what I really think, but I don't want to hurt your feelings. And I'll probably make you cry. So all I can say is, let us know when you figure it out," Leah said. After that, she headed for the kickball court, and everyone else followed, leaving Demetrius behind.

They made a pit stop at the restrooms for a urinal deposit, got some water at the fountain, wiped their mouths, and faced their opponents, who were waiting for them at the sideline, near home plate, as they all quietly chanted, "I am my brother's keeper."

"All right, y'all, I've got the quarter. Where are my team captains?" Mrs. Stone said as Damarcus and Jeorgie stepped forward. Mrs. Stone flipped the coin and it came up tails. The One Fly Up Crew would play first. "Now shake hands," Mrs. Stone said.

Jeorgie looked up at Damarcus and saw no trace of his usual demeanor. Damarcus had his game face on, and it was terrifying and deadly serious. Jeorgie noticed the other players' game faces, and it sent chills through him, and he suddenly lost his nerve. The One Fly Up Crew was set to destroy them.

"Have a good game, and have fun," Mrs. Stone said.

All eyes were on Jeorgie, waiting, and Nestor knew something was wrong.

"Jeorgie? You still want to play, right?" Nestor asked.

Jeorgie looked up at the sky for a cloud to focus on, but there wasn't a cloud in sight. It seemed like the glowing-spiritual Father Sun made special arrangements for a clear day, just for the game. He took a deep breath, exhaled, looked over at Demetrius, across the yard, looking back at him from the basketball court, and started to rethink the whole thing. Maybe playing against the One Fly Up Crew was just a bad idea, after all. He never expected them to be so serious about it because, in his daydreams, it was all fun and games. Lots of laughing and politeness, with some slick special effects like kicking the ball around the world and catching it with all kinds of cool sound effects and stuff. The more Jeorgie thought about his silly daydreams, the longer he stayed zoned out.

Derrick Bay became concerned and put his hand on Jeorgie's shoulder. That's when Jeorgie accidentally let out a very loud, long-winded fart!

**fwop-op-op-puh-puhh-tuhzzz-fwop-op-op-op!!!!!**

"Now that's real talk. Stay woke. One love," Derrick Bay said, and everybody got in a good laugh about it.

"Ready to kick some butt?" Jeorgie finally asked.

"We ready. Just waiting on you, Chief," Kade said.

Jeorgie picked up his confidence and tucked it in his pants pocket. "Let's do this!" Jeorgie said, and everyone went to their positions.

But instead of a regular game of One Fly Up, Mrs. Stone had them play an old-fashioned game of kickball.

Let the games begin.

※ ※ ※

*Welcome to Maverick Elem's Upper Yard kickball court for today's game between Jeorgie's team and the One Fly Up Crew.*

*Here's the starting line-up for the visiting team:*

*Sneaks – Kade Bondshea – Leah Olomua – Jeorgie Sterling – Jonathan Chang – James Yoro – Ryan Keefe – Nestor Reyes – Green Eyed Mike Morrison – and Deshawn Sanders.*

*The reserve players: Demetrius Applethorn, but only if he decides to be a team player and leaves the basketball court.*

*Head Coach Derrick Bay, Team Captain Jeorgie Sterling, and Co-Captains Nestor Reyes and Green Eyed Mike Morrison.*

*Now, the starting line-up for the One Fly Up Crew:*

*Keem – Thad – Big Julius – Damarcus – Terrell – TyRhaj – Phron Thompson – Golden Arms Chance.*

*The head coach is Big Julius, and the team captain is Damarcus. There are no reserve players for this team.*

*Let's play ball!*

*First up to kick is Keem. James Yoro pitches a glider, and Keem murders the ball as it shoots across the court and Keem almost makes it to first base, but the ball is caught by Ryan Keefe. Next up is Thad. Another glider from Yoro, and Thad slams it up high, and the ball is caught by Jonathan Chang. Uh-oh. Is the One Fly Up Crew in trouble? Not with Big Julius, who's up next. A "slow your roll" pitch from Yoro, and Big Julius sends the ball flying! And caught by, who's that? It looks like, Demetrius Applethorn? Where did he come from?*

"Dude! This is like, in a movie! Not only did you come to play, you caught the ball, too!" Jeorgie said as he slapped Demetrius on the back.

The One Fly Up Crew wasn't looking so big-headed right about now, and didn't like that they were being taken down by a bunch of second graders. The teams switched places, and Jeorgie scanned the yard for Golden Arms Chance, who was positioned way on the other side, in the corner, by the monkey bars. You could barely see him. Sneaks was up.

*This should be an interesting play since Sneaks is wearing the latest pair of Spitfires of the Five-Point-0 Collection. Let's see what the shoes do. TyRhaj pitches a flawless high-speed roll! And Sneaks kicks it good enough to send him to first base.*

*Kade Bondshea is up. TyRhaj in for the pitch. Sneaks on first.*

*TyRhaj pitches the ball and shoots a bounce-roll as the ball skids towards home plate. Kade Bondshea slams it, and it's a foul ball.*

*First-baseman Damarcus gets the ball and tosses it back to TyRhaj. Kade Bondshea gets into position at home plate for a second pitch.*

*Oh, boy! TyRhaj is showing off all of his pitching skills today! He goes in with a classic finger-roll spin, and Kade Bondshea slams it straight at TyRhaj! TyRhaj grabs the ball and throws it to first base, and*
*Uh-oh!*

What was supposed to be a tag-out when TyRhaj threw the ball to Damarcus at first base turned into TyRhaj throwing it dodgeball style and hitting Kade in the head. On the side of his face. Like a hard slap with a thudded SMACK that made him stumble. Actually, that smack was Kade's ego getting hit upside the head, and Kade went from zero to sixty in the blink of an eye.

"You don't want none of this! I ain't no punk! Do sumptin!" Kade said as he got all up in TyRhaj's face.

As of that moment, TyRhaj, who had a record of two hundred and seventy-five days of zero conflict, was going to break it when Kade shoved him. TyRhaj came back with a sucker-punch swing. Both teams flooded the court. Big Julius picked Kade up and carried him off while Derrick Bay got in TyRhaj's face and tried to push him away.

"Man, he did that on purpose!" Kade said.

Big Julius held him against the fence behind home plate. TyRhaj kept a steely death stare on Kade while Derrick Bay held him back.

"You ain't about that life! You don't know ME! I'm tick-tick BOOM, baby!" Kade yelled. And then he leveled the BOOM when he went into a tirade of expletives that was so shocking that Big Julius slapped his hand across Kade's mouth. The kickball court faded into silence, and everyone cringed.

Everyone waited for Mrs. Stone to step in and march little Kade with the big mouth, off the court and down to the principal's office. Everyone looked around, looked at each other, waited some more, and wondered where she was. Mrs. Stone wasn't there. They didn't know she had trotted off, down to the faculty/staff restroom right after Kade's first foul ball. Derrick Bay saw an opening for an immediate truce. He and Big Julius had a private discussion with Jeorgie and Damarcus.

"If Kade has to be ejected from the game, then I want TyRhaj benched for five minutes, for unnecessary roughness," Derrick Bay said.

Big Julius quickly thought it over and said, "Okay."

The teams were quickly informed of the calls, Phron Thompson stepped in as relief pitcher, and Kade was ejected from the game.

By the time Mrs. Stone got back, everything was as if nothing had happened in the few minutes she was gone.

*After that minor hiccup, Phron Thompson will be pitching in for TyRhaj. Leah Olomua is up, and boy, does she ever look bored.*

Phron Thompson pitched a corkscrew to intimidate her, but Leah put a hurtin' on the ball, kicking it with such force that she sent the ball sailing over the yard into No Man's Land. Terrell caught it just in time, and tossed it to Thad, who almost threw the ball to Big Julius, to keep Sneaks from going to home plate.

With Sneaks on third and Leah on first, it was Jeorgie's turn. He positioned himself in a semi-squat, eyes focused, foot ready. This was his moment, the moment he had been dreaming about for the entire school year, and now it was happening. He looked for Golden Arms Chance again. Jeorgie respected the One Fly Up Crew, but it was Chance who he thought was the best player on the team. Instead of Golden Arms, he should've been called Young Eagle Eye, because Chance never fumbled a ball, ever. Jeorgie spotted him in his usual place, near the monkey bars, and quickly calculated how he'd kick the ball as he took a deep breath, let some silent gas out (he was gassy that day), and gave a nod to Phron Thompson.

Phron Thompson nodded back, and everything quieted down. Jeorgie kept his eye on the ball, slammed his foot into the smooth pitch that glided across the court, and the ball shot up into the sky like a speeding rocket as it swooped by the glowing-spiritual Father Sun.

Every eye was on that ball, watching it like a shooting star, as the ball soared straight into the heavens, just above the Earth's atmosphere, and then suddenly did a pivot and plummeted back to Earth, as necks and eyes strained to see where the ball would land. There was no way Chance was gonna catch it. Jeorgie didn't even run to first base; he was on his tip toes, looking to see what Chance would do. Kade and the other boys stood on the bench, while Demetrius had both hands on his head like he had a headache, and Leah was hardly impressed. The One Fly Up Crew held their breath.

Chance backed up with little room to spare, his hands stretched out, and fell to the ground as the ball dropped out of the sky. No one could see him tucked away in the corner by the monkey bars, and the suspense was mind-boggling.

"Did he catch it?" Terrell asked.

"Should we go over there?" Sneaks asked.

"Is he all right?" Mrs. Stone asked, getting concerned as she got up.

Just when Jeorgie thought he had beat the best ball player at Maverick Elem, Chance raised his arms in victory, with the ball.

It was a magnificent, thrilling catch that would become mythical for the ages and epochs. Tears of astonishment and pure joy were shed; manly side-hugs and affectionate headlock noogies were exchanged. When Chance showed up with the ball, he was greeted with a hero's welcome, and a celebration was in order. He had lived up to his name, Chance—The Boy With The

Golden Arms, golden indeed. How could they continue the game when *that* just happened?

And as the boys would run into each other as they got older, even when they would reach their sixties and seventies, they would always talk about that day on the kickball court at Maverick Elem as if it were something magical, making sure it wasn't just a figment of their imagination lodged somewhere in their memories.

It was a rare sighting that needed to be kept alive, until the very last story of it was told.

# Chapter Twenty

As the school year began its annual path to the last day of school, Mr. Marci took his students on a much-needed field trip to the aquarium-planetarium. By now, Jonathan's grandfather had become an honorary member of the class, and tagged along on the trip, as did Mr. Freelander. The sights of the ancient skeletal T-Rex that stood like a skyscraper in the lobby of the museum, the dioramas of the African savanna plains where the life-like zebras, giraffes, lions, and herds of gazelles stared back, and the prickled starfishes and the other squishy sea creatures the children were allowed to touch, was such a welcomed breath of fresh air. The children looked at the motionless alligators down in the alligator pit, and nodded off into early-afternoon naps in chairs that slanted back in the dimly lit planetarium. They ate lunch in the park, across the street from the aquarium-planetarium, and the children played like they had been cooped up in some sort of strict boarding school that had harsh restrictions on playing.

Some of the boys tossed around a football with Mr. Marci and Mr. Freelander. The girls climbed all over the concourse band shell and pretended to put on a show with Ms. DeMauvé-Pflume. The children played tag; they did tai chi with Jonathan's grandfather; they created new worlds and scenarios that could only be done on a field trip, at the park, with lots of grass and tons of sunshine that didn't reflect off of a gray pavement on a school yard, and it allowed the children to be wild and free.

Wild and free.

Apparently, there was a little too much of that wild and free stuff, because the children no longer had the attention span to do classwork during the last week of school. The last few days were such an exciting time. Mr. Marci allowed the children to do arts and crafts, clean out their desks, watch educational programming about nature, and bring their favorite books back to school again and share them with the class, which was how Mayfair ended up losing one of her books. She brought one book called *Kitty Cat Whack*, and the other book called *Monty: A Little Dog Who Wanted to Be Taller (Not Too Tall, Just Taller)*. She had set them down for a hot second, when Tayla and her girls, Sekoya, Channen, Penelle, Kenda, K'Lixia, Rezen, Nosha, Taronka, Simonay, and Tandra invited Mayfair and her friends for a sister-circle song that also included The Snootish Girls and a bunch of other girls on the yard.

It wasn't until after lunch, when Mr. Marci asked if anyone brought a book to share with the class, that Mayfair suddenly realized she had lost one of her books.

"What's wrong?" Rachel Ward asked as she watched Mayfair frantically dig through her book bag.

"I thought I...I could've sworn I had my *Monty* book. I know I brought it to school, or I thought I did."

For the rest of the day, Mayfair racked her brain about her *Monty* book, and when she couldn't find it at home, she knew she had lost it. "I really liked that book," Mayfair quietly said to herself, totally bummed.

The next day, when her father dropped her off, Mayfair found her *Monty* book! It was clutched under the armpit of Kiara Campbell as she was getting out of her mother's car. Mayfair couldn't believe it. Did she have the chutzpah to go over there and get it back? Mayfair was about to find out. She already had one confrontation with Kiara and didn't want to do it again, but she knew what she had to do.

"That's my book," Mayfair said, as Kiara, caught red-handed, sized her up. "If you open it, you'll see that my name is written on the first page because my mother wrote it in there," Mayfair said.

Kiara had already seen the inscription but pretended she didn't know what Mayfair was talking about. She actually liked the story of Monty, thought it was cute, but she wasn't going to hand it over so easily. She wanted to see how far Mayfair would go to get it back. Really Kiara? All she had to do was say something like, "I couldn't find you yesterday, so I was going to take it to the lost and found." Or "I was going to find you today and give it back." But Kiara being Kiara, with her little devious and foul ways, had to go the extra mile just to swirl up some unnecessary drama, so she totally snubbed Mayfair and tried to walk away.

Mayfair grabbed her by the arm. "That's my book, and you need to give it back!" Mayfair said, and tried to snatch the book away, but Kiara held on to it, and the girls were in a tug of war. "Kiara, you better let go or I'm going to hit you over the head with it!" Mayfair said as she pulled even harder.

That's when Kiara let go, and Mayfair stumbled backwards to the ground. When Mayfair looked up and saw that ridiculously smug smirk on Kiara's face, Mayfair became flushed with anger.

She had never been so angry in her life! She made good on her word when she jumped up and clunked Kiara over the head with the book. That smirk on Kiara's face turned into an ugly sneer as she went for Mayfair's face, windmill style, and then, it became official. Mayfair and Kiara Campbell were fighting in front of Maverick Elem, on the morning of the last day of school.

Not a lot of hair-pulling, just a lot of arms flailing as the girls fell to the ground. And just when Kiara managed to sit on Mayfair, someone grabbed her and pulled her up in a mid-swing that was about go upside Mayfair's head. At first, Mayfair couldn't see who it was because the sun was in her eyes, but when she sat up, she was so surprised to see Pop Star Girl standing there. She had a grip on Kiara by the front of her shirt. Kiara didn't scare easily, but when she looked up into those cold aquamarine eyes that glared back at her, try as she might, with thoughts of, *"I ain't afraid of no Pop Star Girl!"* and *"I know she ain't tryna handle me!"* her nerve failed her, and she tried to pull Pop Star Girl's hand away.

"The book belongs to Mayfair. You're going to pick it up, hand it to her, tell Mayfair you're sorry, and then you're going to leave her alone," Pop Star Girl said in a calm tone, and released her grip on Kiara's shirt, which stayed wrinkled for the rest of the day, no matter how much she tried to smooth it out. Pop Star Girl's calm was so threatening that Kiara did exactly what she was told to do.

"Sorry for taking your book," Kiara said, and ran inside the school.

A hand reached down and helped Mayfair up.

"Are you all right?" Pop Star Girl asked.

"Yeah..." Mayfair looked a mess. Her hair was jacked up, her clothes were in disarray, she had a concrete scrape on the palm of her hand that stung a little bit, and a few minor scratches on her face.

"Okay. Good," Pop Star Girl said, and went inside the school. Oddly, after that, Mayfair hardly ever saw her again.

After Maverick Elem, Pop Star Girl went to an upscale middle school where all of her friends were going, that was on the other side of the city. So what happened to Thad? Well, he had to let her go. When he didn't see her anywhere at Glick Mid, that's when he knew he'd probably never see her again. She wasn't at Local High, either, when he got to ninth grade, and by the time he was a freshman at State University, Thad forgot all about the girl with the beautiful light-green eyes, and got on with life.

Some thirty years or so later, Pop Star Girl saw Thad at the airport. She was going to her gate and thought she saw a familiar face she hadn't seen since childhood. Thad was in line, about to board his plane, when she walked up and placed her hand on his arm. When he turned around and saw those aquamarine eyes that he hadn't seen since fifth grade, it knocked the wind out of him. "Brenna?" Thad said, and she nodded with a smile. She was still every bit of the earthy fifth-grade goddess that he remembered her to be, and Thad still had his athletic good looks that were fused in her memoires of him on the kickball court on the Upper Yard at Maverick Elem. Wow, Maverick Elem.

Thad missed his flight that day, and Brenna missed her flight. It would take thirty years, but Pop Star Girl would finally let her guard down, and spend the rest of her life with Thad.

\* \* \*

"You hit Kiara Campbell on the head with your book?" Lydia Jackson asked, shocked.

"And Pop Star Girl told her to leave you alone?" Trendy Brown asked.

"Yep."

Lydia, Trendy, Rachel Ward, Sandra Jang, Xembi, and Leah Olomua all stared at the little scratches on Mayfair's face. They were huddled around her in the girls' restroom while Mayfair tried to fix herself up.

Xembi was shocked, seeing Mayfair all disheveled. Yet she was intrigued by Mayfair's account of what had just gone down, and was secretly relieved that it wasn't her. But she was glad Mayfair took Kiara on, something Xembi could never do.

Mayfair herself couldn't believe it! She had just gotten into a fight with Kiara Campbell, on the last day of school, and no one was there to see it. But what really blew her mind was how Pop Star Girl came out of nowhere and handled Kiara like she was Mayfair's big sister! And Mayfair was glad for it.

"Wow, that's pretty cool," Trendy said.

"But why? You don't even know her like that," Sandra said.

Maybe it had to do with Pop Star Girl seeing Mayfair and her father drive by on her way to school every morning, or seeing Mayfair at the mall with Rachel and her little sisters. Maybe it was that tribal-clan bonding thing they all had from the birthday parties.

"Maybe she just doesn't like Kiara," Leah said.

It was times like this where it felt good to have your friends around you, and it seemed like Mayfair and her girls, Xembi, Rachel, Trendy, Lydia, Sandra, and Leah, would be just like Tayla and all of her girls, Sekoya, Channen, Penelle, Kenda, K'Lixia, Rezen, Nosha, Taronka, Simonay, and Tandra, who would stay friends and be in each other's lives forever.

But sometimes, good friendships don't always last.

# Chapter Twenty-One

From second grade to fourth grade, Monday through Friday, Mayfair and Xembi had spent almost every day of their lives together. Before school, all day at school, and after school. But when they got to the fifth grade, everything changed.

It seemed as if they weren't friends anymore. Well, in actuality, they hadn't stopped *being* friends, but if either of them had just talked to each other when they started to drift apart, maybe things wouldn't have gotten all weird and awkward.

Mayfair thought Xembi wasn't her friend anymore, while Xembi thought the same thing of Mayfair, both unsure if they should talk about it.

They were split up between the two fifth-grade classes, with Mayfair in Ms. Plan's class (along with Rachel Ward, Sandra Jang, Leah Olomua, and Lydia Jackson), while Xembi wound up in Ms. Mack's class (with Trendy Brown, Erica Ross, and LaDera Levitt).

Eventually, Trendy would start up a friendship with classmate Tashar Phillips, who had come to Maverick Elem back in third grade, and Xembi gradually became better friends with Larinda

Hines and Judy Knight, who were both new to Maverick Elem, also in Ms. Mack's class.

Then when Xembi's mother started a new job, her sister started picking Xembi and Peppertina up after school, and Auntie Banata was always on time, which usually left Xembi little time to spend with Mayfair after school, like they used to do. And sometimes when Uncle Bender picked them up, he always arrived before school let out, and on those days, Xembi didn't see Mayfair at all.

The girls had gone from being BFFs every day of their lives to hardly at all. They tried to play with each other at recess and lunch, but with newbies like Larinda and Judy hanging around, as nice as they were, it just wasn't the same. That's when things became weird and awkward.

For Thanksgiving, Mayfair's grandmother came to visit (Roxanne's mother), and Mayfair opened up about everything that was going on in her fifth-grade life when her grandmother asked how she was doing in school.

"School is okay, but my best friend isn't my best friend anymore. I mean, we're still friends, I guess, but it's not the same anymore," Mayfair explained.

"Was she the plum in the song that blues singer wrote about when you were in second grade?" her grandmother asked, as she knitted a scarf she was working on.

Mayfair sadly nodded her head yes and tried not to cry.

"What happened?" her grandmother asked.

"Nothing really happened. I just hardly ever see Xembi anymore. And we used to have so much fun, and now we don't."

"Well, I am so sorry to hear that," her grandmother said, and gave Mayfair one of those grandmother hugs that tried to make everything better. "I had a best friend growing up. Her name was Darlene, and she and I were just like the song, a peach and a plum. Except, maybe we were more like, a strawberry and a pineapple. And we thought we'd be best friends until we reached a hundred years old."

"But she's not your friend now?" Mayfair asked with the most pitiful eyes.

"Well, I hope she is."

Mayfair's pitiful eyes widened with surprise. "What happened?" she asked.

"Darlene moved away. She promised she'd call me as soon as she could, since she already knew my phone number by heart. Back in those days, you know, we didn't have cell phones, and we had to memorize the phone numbers. But I never heard from her again."

Mayfair searched her grandmother's refined face and saw just a hint of sadness in it. "Was she mad at you, Grandmommy?" Mayfair asked.

"Darlene and I cried our eyes out when she had to leave. And when I didn't hear from her, I thought she couldn't call because it would've been a long-distance call. They don't really have that sort of thing anymore. And depending how far away it was, a long-distance call was expensive."

"Were you mad at her because she didn't call you back?"

"Well, I probably missed her more than I was disappointed. And over time you move on. But, I hope that I'm a part of her childhood memories, and I hope Darlene still thinks of me as a friend."

"Maybe Xembi will do the same thing with me?" Mayfair asked.

"I'm sure she will. You know, things happen in our lives that we have no control over. And as *your* life changes, so will your circle of friends."

Her grandmother's words of wisdom helped a little. And when Kade Bondshea started calling her, "Yo, Peach!" back in third grade, never calling Mayfair by her first name again, which meant that whenever he saw Xembi, he'd say to her, "What up, Plum?" Mayfair didn't have the heart to tell him that the song really didn't mean anything anymore, since she and Xembi weren't friends like they used to be.

After she left Maverick Elem and went on to Glick Mid, Mayfair eventually stopped being sad about everything like her grandmother said she would, especially when Rachel Ward was the one who would turn out to be the friend of a lifetime. They'd be friends when they'd turn into grandmothers.

But what about Xembi? She had her own story of how her friendship drifted away from Mayfair. It began when she started feeling left out of everything and hated when the inside jokes that happened in Ms. Plan's class had to be explained. Then when her Auntie Banata started picking her up after school, she hardly ever saw Mayfair all that much.

How did things go from having the best BFF ever, to being unsure if she still thought of you as a friend?

Like, how did all of the boys, who were also split up between the two fifth-grade classes, manage to stay friends? It was really too bad that she wasn't able to blend Larinda and Judy into the group. But it had more to do with Xembi's feelings of not being a part of her old clique than it did with Larinda and Judy not fitting in.

The other thing that really started to bother her was that darn "Peach and Plum" song. She wished the song never existed, and hated it whenever someone would mention it. When her cousin Brandeis did a remix of the song, Xembi burst into tears when he tried to give her a copy of it.

"I don't want it," Xembi said.

"Oh, okay," Brandies said, confused. "But what's wrong? I made this especially for you."

Xembi took a deep breath to keep from crying even harder, and finally said, "Me and Mayfair aren't really friends like we used to be. The song just reminds me of everything, and I just want to forget about it."

"So, y'all not friends anymore? Y'all get into a fight or something?" Brandeis asked.

"I don't know what happened. But we're not in the same class anymore. I don't see her after school anymore. And when we try to play with each other, like at recess or lunchtime, it's just weird now."

Brandeis didn't know what to say exactly, so he put his arm around his little cousin. The only thing he could say was, "Sometimes it be like that."

Xembi took the CD of Brandeis's remix, and she decided not to listen to it. She purposefully packed it away, along with the copy of the original song, so that she'd forget where they were, never to be seen or heard of for many, many years, until she came across them when she herself was a grandmother. The very second she found them, a flood of childhood memories came back, even the brief conversation she had with Brandeis. It all seemed so far away, the things she had forgotten about. All the things she made herself forget about. And the more she remembered, the more she appreciated her memories of Mayfair. The pain of losing her friendship was gone, but a new ache settled in. Why didn't she just go and talk to Mayfair instead of walking away from her? But she had to remind herself that she wasn't as confident at ten years old, before many of her life experiences would rub some of her shyness and apprehension away.

So Xembi planned a Sunday family dinner, and she told them the story of a little girl named Mayfair, who had a light complexion with a smattering of freckles, with a head full of thick, rich auburn-colored hair, and how she was Xembi's best friend at Maverick Elem. Before she played each version of the song, Xembi told the story of how the cranky old man across the street from her elementary school was actually the world-renowned blues singer John Arrow Ever. She held her family captive with the story of how he composed the song off the top of his head, right there in class, about her friendship with Mayfair, and called it "Peach and Plum."

Maybe she'd look Mayfair up on social media. What if Mayfair excitedly replied back? Maybe they'd plan a reunion with the other girls? Maybe Mayfair and Xembi would pick back up where they had left off, as if fifty some-odd years hadn't passed by.

Only time would tell. . .

# Chapter Twenty-Two

The children treated the last day of school like it was a regular school day, like they would return on Monday, after the weekend. Most of the children in Mr. Marci's class would be in Ms. Deckey's third-grade class next year, with a few new faces, and The Snootish Girls would move on to Ms. Plan's or Ms. Mack's fifth-grade classes. Tayla and all of her girls, Sekoya, Channen, Penelle, Kenda, K'Lixia, Rezen, Nosha, Taronka, Semonay, and Tandra, would move on to Glick Mid for sixth grade, and still be tight as ever. Actually, they'd all stay friends for life, be in each other's weddings, and be godparents to each other's children, who would all grow up together.

Pretty soon, all of the summer and sports camps would start, along with summer school, and maybe there'd be a vacation or a family reunion to go to. The new season of *My Name Is Cool* would premiere after the Fourth of July, and Lydia Jackson had a viewing party over at her house. Her father let the girls watch the show down in his ultra-cool game room, on his sixty-four-inch flat-screen TV. *My Name Is Cool* would have a short lifespan when Kamen Wright, the kid who played the character of Dennis Dean, would officially drop out after season two, for a normal life, and leave the world of television forever.

Ms. DeMauvé-Pflume got all misty eyed when the final bell rang for the day. She gave out her aromatic hugs and farewell greeting cards, personalized to each child. When she got to Kade Bondshea, her tears splashed all over the top of his head while she hugged him, like she didn't want to let go.

"Now you mind your manners, think before you speak, no cursing, stay out of trouble, and respect your father," Ms. DeMauvé-Pflume said.

Kade tried to look up at her while his head was lodged in her bosom. "Yes, ma'am," Kade said, and the tears started rolling down his cheeks. He sure was going to miss hearing her say, "Up in this here."

She gave him one last squeeze and wanted to kiss him goodbye, but school policy did not allow such things; plus, she knew it would leave a gooey lipstick mark on his forehead.

"What am I going to do without my little ones?" Ms. DeMauvé-Pflume quietly said as she and Mr. Marci watched the children leave the classroom for the very last time.

When the children exited Maverick Elem, they came upon the One Fly Up Crew, who were gathered in front of the school, and Jeorgie and his teammates were pulled into the circle.

"Can I get in, too?" Timothy asked, and Big Julius pulled him in and motioned for Jonathan's grandfather to step in.

The crew had tears in their eyes. What should've been a day of utter joy and sheer happiness was the opposite for them. Most of the One Fly Up Crew had been at Maverick Elem since kindergarten, and now they were about to embark on a new journey at Glick Mid. They'd still see each other, but Maverick Elem was their home, and they hated to leave it. They hated to leave their kickball court. They would desperately miss Mrs.

Stone. They'd miss being the stars of the Upper Yard. They'd miss their game of One Fly Up.

"Family isn't always blood," Derrick Bay said as he stood in the center of the gathering. "The fam are the ones who accept you. Love you like a brother."

That was followed by, "I am my brother's keeper," which everyone said in unison.

"Maverick Elem is our fam. Where we found it, and where it will always be. But it is time for our tribe to move on. It is now our time to grow, our purpose to learn. Let's gather strength from this pain, for it is only temporary. We are one. Real talk. Stay woke. One love." Deep.

The boys held on to each other as they cried. Somehow they must've forgot that they'd see each other later on, around 7 p.m. that evening, at Tayla's White Party, but they were all caught up in their feelings at the moment.

Soon the loud, muffled, thudding bass could be heard in the distance. As it got louder and came closer, Demetrius Applethorn's Uncle Ced finally rolled up, and his car was no longer in that dull matte gray primer. It was painted in a slick electric blue, with two white stripes that went from the hood to the trunk. Demetrius wiped his tears and hugged the boys in his class before he got in the car. Jeorgie couldn't take it, as he wiped his eyes and gave Derrick Bay a quick hug, then took off across the street with Nestor and Green Eyed Mike. Kade Bondshea and Deshawn Sanders gave a couple of fist-bump hugs, and then Deshawn took off before his school bus left without him. James Yoro and Ryan Keefe left with Kade.

Jonathan Chang's grandfather found the whole emotional gathering amusing and said, in Mandarin, "Too much crying. You'll see each other in a few months." And off he went with Jonathan and Timothy, as they raced each other down the block.

Golden Arms Chance hugged his best friend Terrell and tried not to cry. He and Terrell had become close since they became a part of the One Fly Up Crew, when Chance was in third grade and Terrell was in fourth grade. They would miss each other, and hopefully by the time Chance would make it over to Glick Mid, they would still have the bond.

Before he left, Chance went over to Xembi and said, "So I'll see you at Tayla's party tonight?" He melted when Xembi gave him a pretty smile and nodded yes. Chance didn't want to leave, but he took off and caught up with Ryan, James, and Kade.

When Mayfair's mother pulled up, earlier than her usual daily pick-up time, Mayfair hugged Xembi goodbye, even though she knew they'd see each other later on at the party. When she got in the car, Mayfair looked back at the One Fly Up Crew and got all teary eyed, because after Tayla's party, she'd probably never see any of them again.

Then it finally hit her.

It was indeed the last day of school.

The end of the school year seemed like the end of an era. As the transitions were made, The Snootish Girls would hold things down on the Upper Yard. The boys of Mr. Marci's second-grade class no longer played football on the basketball court and thought it was time to use it for basketball games. They even started a league, with jerseys and everything. Leah Olomua, with the help of Golden Arms Chance, would form a girls' One Fly Up Crew, or rather, The Girls Kickball team, that would include Mayfair and her BFFs, all of them out there on the court, trying to play ball.

* * *

The rich blue sky in the late afternoon had clouds in it, shaped like race-car skid marks, and the glowing-spiritual Father Sun finally took his evening dip, down beneath the earth, as the reflective orange light set those skid-mark clouds ablaze. Pretty soon the sky would turn into a beautiful dusky lavender color with a hint of pink that was the perfect setting for Tayla's party. It was like a movie premiere, with a red carpet and a Maverick Elem photo backdrop that the children posed for pictures in front of. DJ Loco Hero picked up a lot of business after Xembi's birthday, and there he was, pumping the music at Tayla's party. There was a digital photo booth, strobe lights galore, mocktails, VIP sections, and there was even a stretch limo parked outside in case anyone wanted to take a spin around the block with friends. Everyone was there: the One Fly Up Crew, The Snootish Girls, Derrick Bay, everybody in Mr. Marci's class, Timothy, Little Laura, Peppertina, Jonathan's grandfather, Sneaks, Q-Tech, Pop Star Girl and her BFFs, the rest of the fifth grade from Ms. Plan and Ms. Mack's classes, and of course Tayla's girls. A sea of children all dressed in their best white outfits.

   The oven-baked Brother Moon slowly rose into the glamorous sky, against the stars that were blinged-out to the heavens. "Yes, it's a fine night. A pretty one, indeed. Even the stars are glittering. Do you see? Tell Tayla I said hello. The night is young. Enjoy yourselves. Stay up late, as long as you want, because I'll be here when it's time to go."

The End

*Author's Notes:*

How did I come up with the story of Peach and Plum?

I had just turned 17 (many, many, many, so many moons ago). My friend Kenya (not her real name) and I were on the 15 - Third Bus (a really great bus route that took you from one side of the city near City College, to the other side of the city near the Fisherman's Wharf area), which had just finished the route through the Sunnydale Projects, and made a stop at the corner liquor store, across the street from the community pool.

As people were getting on and off the bus, an older, petite Black man got on the bus, who happened to be a bit tipsy, pretty much drunk. He stood right above where Kenya and I were sitting, and I started to wonder if I should've gotten up and gave him my seat, since he was probably somewhere in his mid-60s and, drunk. And just as I was about to ask Kenya if she thought we should get up and move, this man had the nerve to flirt with us! He looked at me and said in a slurred voice, "Lookatchu, girl, lookin' like a nice, ripe peach, where the juice drips and glistens down your chin!" Then he looked at Kenya and said, "And I bet you just like a nice, ripe, sweet, mouthwatering plum!" I think Kenya rolled her eyes, and I ignored him. After that, my stop finally came up, I got off and walked the rest of the way home.

But the tipsy, flirtatious man's slurred words stayed with me. There was some poetry in the way he had described the differences in our complexions as a peach and a plum, instead of using the usual metaphors of coffee or chocolate. And that's when the story of Mayfair and Xembi started to form. But I began to realize that there was much more to it other than the differences in their complexions. And as I started writing, Peach and Plum almost took on a mind of its own, as new characters came to life and the story wrote itself. Weird, I know.

So I'd like thank that man, wherever he is. My assumption is that he has since passed away, God rest his soul, but who knows? He could still be alive and doing well. I'd also like to dedicate this book in honor of my second grade teacher, Mr. Sinton; the elementary school I went to from 2nd grade to 5th grade, El Dorado Elementary; and the district that I grew up in, Visitacion Valley in San Francisco, all of which, had such a positive impact on me as a child.

And no, Mr. Sinton did not resemble anything like Mr. Marci. Quite the opposite. He was more in line with the glowing-spiritual, Father Sun, "...looking down onto everything with a strict glare of authority...."

One more thing I'd like to clarify, is in regards to the Natives at Local High in the story. I should've stated it in the beginning of the book, but the word Natives just refers to the students who were all native to the Ranunculus District.

## *Acknowledgements*

I'd like to thank my editor, Charlene "HustleDiva" Green, for stepping in and telling me, "Girl, you know you need to have your book edited, right???" After many months of our arm wrestling matches over what I wanted vs. what Charlene said wasn't in the proper format, things that were grammatically incorrect, and the weird sentence structures that only made sense to me, Charlene and I always arrived at a happy medium. It was a humbling editing experience, that edited away all of my big-headed opinions about my finished manuscript. I just knew we'd be done in a month. Ha! Yeah, right...

And a shout-out to my son, Cannen, for his insightful input by suggesting that I keep the book blurb simple.

And to everyone else in my life who has heard me talk about this book forever, and wondering when I was ever going to finish it.

## *About the Author*

M Johnson was a graduate film student at Howard University when she started writing Peach and Plum as a screenplay, which led to her write the story as a book. Along with her debut picture book, When Wug turned into Doug, the story of Peach and Plum is M Johnson's debut novel in children's literature. She currently lives in Zachary, Louisiana.